I0762346

LET ME GO

(An Ashley Hope Suspense Thriller—Book 1)

Kate Bold

Kate Bold

Debut author Kate Bold is author of the ALEXA CHASE SUSPENSE THRILLER series, comprising three books (and counting); and the ASHLEY HOPE SUSPENSE THRILLER, comprising three books (and counting).

An avid reader and lifelong fan of the mystery and thriller genres, Kate loves to hear from you, so please feel free to visit www.kateboldauthor.com to learn more and stay in touch.

ISBN: 978-1-0943-9290-5

BOOKS BY KATE BOLD

ALEXA CHASE SUSPENSE THRILLER
THE KILLING GAME (Book #1)
THE KILLING TIDE (Book #2)
THE KILLING HOUR (Book #3)

ASHLEY HOPE SUSPENSE THRILLER
LET ME GO (Book #1)
LET ME OUT (Book #2)
LET ME LIVE (Book #3)

PROLOGUE

Ethan Barrett picked up the book and shook out the remnants of the photograph. He'd stared at her face every day for the past eight years, had counted every hour she'd stolen from his life. Trapped in the six-by-nine concrete tomb – his new home at the Middle Tennessee State Pen – he'd had a lot of time to think. He'd packed on an additional fifteen pounds of solid muscle and traded in his dark mop of curls for a buzz cut.

He'd waited. And he'd planned.

Word was that after the trial – after her testimony had put him away – she'd moved. Created a whole new life, while he rotted in this hell hole.

Sensing movement behind him, he palmed the shank and stood, careful not to rise too fast. Only a book remained on the desk, nothing more.

It was his cellmate coming through the open door to the block. The lifer with the cobra tattooed on his face, known around the pen for beheading a rival gang leader.

Ethan stretched to his full height and took a step forward, his muscular frame filling the tight space. The lifer stopped short, glanced toward the toilet.

"Use a bottle," Ethan ordered, making it clear the room was currently off limits, not caring if the cellmate pissed himself.

The lifer wavered beneath Ethan's steel gaze as if calculating his odds – probably wondering whether the rumors that Ethan had strangled the biker in the laundry room were true – then nodded and backed out of the cell.

Ethan turned back to the picture. He raised the shank, plunged it into her throat first. He sliced from the top of her pretty blonde hair, across her forehead to her cheek and then back to her chin. Smiling at his handiwork, he pushed the blade between her breasts and cut the photograph in half.

Wherever she'd gone, he'd find her.

The time had finally come to set his plan into motion.

It was time to make Ashley pay.

CHAPTER ONE

Please don't let him die, Ashley Hope thought, her eyes squeezed tight to help fight back the tears.

Her older brother, Kyle, was on the other end of the phone, calling with an update on their father's condition. "The doctor said it was a heart attack," he told her. "But they think he's alright for now. They're gonna let me take him home from the hospital in about an hour."

Ashley sighed in relief. She shared a special bond with her father. As long as she could remember, he'd always been her biggest supporter, encouraging her to follow her dreams but also warning her when he felt she was headed in the wrong direction. She couldn't bear the thought of losing him.

"We'll be there around lunchtime tomorrow," she said into the phone, hoping the doctor was right, that her father really would be okay.

When her brother clicked off, she slid her cellphone onto the breakfast-room table in the midst of her schoolbooks, laptop, and documents from the case file. She knew she needed to get back to work writing her thesis – the final step in obtaining her master's in criminal justice – but concentrating on the psychological profile of a serial killer proved to be a rough task with her father's health on her mind.

She jumped as the unarmed security system chimed, a signal someone had opened the door leading to the garage. Knowing her fiancé, Brett Holbrook, was due home at any moment, she resisted the urge to grab a knife from the block on the kitchen counter. The events of the day had definitely set her nerves on edge.

"Ash?" Brett called out.

"In here."

He dropped his briefcase onto the tile floor, concern evident on his face, and pulled Ashley into his arms. "Any word?" he asked.

Although Brett's relationship with her family had been rocky up to this point, his actions since receiving the news that morning proved that he cared about her father. A fact that made Ashley love her husband-to-be even more. Still, she wished he would agree to let her make the trip alone.

"It's too soon to say," she replied. "The doctor says he's okay for now. Depends if he takes care of himself. Which he won't."

Her father had always put his children first in his life. The business he shared with her Uncle Russ came in a close second. Working long hours to pay the bills, he tended to push his own needs aside.

"Is there anything else I can do?" her fiancé asked. "You know, to make things easier?"

"If you're talking about money, there's no way he'd ever accept it. It's a pride thing."

Brett nodded. "Yeah, I get that. But there are ways for me to pay for his medical treatment without him ever knowing."

Ashley appreciated the offer, but like her father, she wanted to earn the money to help her family herself rather than take it from someone else. Even if that someone was her future husband. At the same time, she didn't want her father to be denied the medical care he needed. She felt it would be best to play it by ear.

"It means a lot to me that you want to help Daddy, but let's find out how much the insurance will pay first."

Brett nodded and then glanced at the table. His nose wrinkled in disgust at the sight of the crime-scene photos – nine young women murdered and left handcuffed in their own beds. "When does your thesis have to be turned in?"

"Not until Wednesday." She had hoped to complete it over the weekend, but now that they were going out of town, she realized that might not happen.

He hugged her tighter. "You've worked so hard. I'm really proud of you," he said, his brown eyes shining. "I know your mom would be too."

Ovarian cancer had claimed the life of her mother when Ashley was only twelve. She still remembered their last conversation. "Keep your grades up," her mama had insisted. "Go to college and get a fancy degree." A feat neither of her parents had been able to accomplish. Left to raise her younger brother, Shane, and to cook, clean, and care for her father and Kyle, there were years she'd worried it was a promise she wouldn't be able to keep.

Brett pushed back a lock of honey blonde hair from Ashley's face and planted a quick kiss on her lips. "How did I get so lucky? Beauty and brains all in one package."

She felt her face grow warm from the compliment.

"Stop, you're making me blush," she said. "And you know – good and well – that I'm the lucky one."

And she meant it. Meeting Brett was the best thing that had ever happened to her. He could have married anyone he wanted. It still amazed her that she'd been the one he'd asked.

"I saw Travis outside," he told her. "Amanda made lasagna. They want us to join them for dinner. I thought it might help take your mind off of things. Would be a nice kickoff to Memorial Day."

Ashley managed a smile. "With everything going on, it would be really nice to relax and not have to cook."

Brett pulled a bottle of merlot from the wine rack, grabbed Ashley's hand and led her out their back door to the patio and then across the lawn. They'd purchased the home just five months prior when they'd moved from Chattanooga to Briarwood, an affluent suburb of Nashville, Tennessee.

Awestruck would best describe her feelings when she first crossed the threshold into the four-bedroom house on Marigold Court. A two-story foyer boasting a winding staircase greeted her, flanked by a formal dining room on the left and a study for Brett on the right. She floated across the gleaming hardwood floor past a powder room into a vaulted family room adjacent to an open kitchen area. *Can we really afford this?* she thought as she ran her hand along the cool granite countertop. Although she already knew the answer (Brett wouldn't have insisted she see the house otherwise), none of it seemed real.

A personal financial advisor with Parker Stone Investment Management, Brett held a steady rein on their finances. But Ashley would never forget what life had been like before she became engaged. In those days, she'd been drowning in student-loan debt while living off of ramen noodles and begging for extra shifts at the department store. Throughout the time they were dating, Brett had repeatedly offered to help her with her expenses, but she'd refused. When he learned his transfer to Parker Stone's Briarwood office had finally been approved – after almost two years of waiting – he'd asked Ashley to marry him and make the move to the suburb which was near Belle Haven, his parents' home.

Although they'd purchased their new home together and were now living as a family, she'd insisted on repaying her loans with money she'd earned rather than use Brett's. Student debt aside, the bulk of her financial worries had been left in the past.

Travis Robinson met them on the steps to his screened porch, pushing the door open and allowing Ashley to enter first. As a CPA with one of the largest accounting firms in Nashville, Travis shared Brett's fascination with the financial markets as well as his love for golf. The two had forged a swift friendship, resulting in several evenings spent at their neighbors' home.

Leaving the men chatting near the doorway, Ashley hugged Amanda, careful not to press too close. Although it had only been a week since she'd last seen her neighbor, Ashley could swear the swell of Amanda's belly had grown by at least an inch. The floral sundress she wore further accentuated the roundness of her midsection in stark contrast to her otherwise petite frame.

"What can I help you with?" Ashley asked her, noticing the wicker table already set, a salad next to each of the four dinner plates, and the lasagna occupying center stage.

"Everything's done; just take a seat and I'll go get Zander."

Ashley spied the toddler playing in the family room on the other side of the French doors. "Let me get him."

Zander giggled as she scooped him from the sea of toys scattered across the floor. "You're getting heavy, little man." His soft, caramel hair brushed against her cheek, and she caught the distinct aromas of animal crackers and apple juice. She wondered what it would feel like to hold her own child one day. With both her studies and the planning of her upcoming October wedding consuming so much of her thoughts and time, she hadn't yet asked Brett how long he wanted to wait before starting a family. Seeing all the other women in the cul-de-sac with children on their hips, Ashley hoped her future husband would be receptive to the idea of trying for a baby within a few months after they were married.

When she returned to the screened porch, the wine had been poured and everyone was seated; their conversation focused on the new family moving in across the street. She placed Zander in the highchair at the end of the table, took her position next to Brett, and prepared to dig into her salad.

Travis fixed his gaze on Ashley. "Brett mentioned that you're going out of town for the holiday," he said, half statement and half question.

A pang of guilt hit Ashley when asked about the trip. It had been so long since she'd last visited her father – over seven months – and now he was sick. She wished she'd made the time to see him more often.

"My father had a heart attack. We're going to visit my family."

"I'm sorry to hear that," Travis said, a note of concern in his voice. "Where does your dad live?"

"Not far, just a couple hours east of here," Ashley answered, intending to be vague.

"What town?" Travis pressed.

Ashley hesitated. "Mettler Ridge."

She caught the glances exchanged between Travis and Amanda and felt her stomach tighten. She was well aware of the stereotypical view many people held regarding those living on the Cumberland Plateau, and in rural Appalachia in general. The fact that Mettler Ridge was located in Laurel County, the poorest county in the state, didn't help.

Amanda wiped a smudge of tomato sauce from Zander's chin and then turned toward Ashley. "I thought you grew up in Chattanooga," she stated, sounding shocked to learn her neighbor came from the backwoods.

"I earned my bachelor's from the university in Chattanooga, but I was born and raised in Laurel County."

Ashley felt the climate in the room change, as though the temperature had dropped twenty degrees. Like Brett, Travis and Amanda both came from prominent families in the Nashville area, and they must have assumed that Ashley's family was wealthy as well.

"There's no hospital in Laurel County, is there?" Travis asked.

"No. My brother took him to the one in Cedar View. It's the closest. About thirty minutes from my father's house."

She realized the lack of a medical facility would further reinforce the notion that the area was completely uncivilized.

Amanda was quick to fire off the next set of questions, leaving Ashley feeling as though she was being interrogated.

"What kind of work does your father do?" Amanda asked, her tone implying that she suspected it would be a job that required little to no education.

"Automotive repair. He and my uncle have their own shop."

The smirk that crossed her neighbor's face cut Ashley to the bone. It obviously wasn't enough that her father was co-owner of a business; he was still a blue-collar worker, and thus in Amanda's world, likely not up to par.

Ashley admired her father for the hardships he'd overcome, building the business with her Uncle Russ from the ground up. But her father's grit likely wouldn't matter to her neighbors.

"And what about your brother? What does he do?" Amanda asked. "Did he graduate from UT Chattanooga too?"

"No," Ashley admitted, her voice low. Like her father, Kyle had dropped out of school in order to take a full-time job. Her younger brother, Shane, had graduated from high school, but he'd never gone to college. Ashley wasn't about to volunteer the information; it was none of her neighbors' business. "He and my younger brother both work at the auto shop."

Amanda nodded, the superior gleam in her eyes revealing that she had suspected as much.

Ashley had already been excluded from Amanda's monthly Sunday brunch, a gathering for the neighborhood women with young children, a group which included the majority of the females in the subdivision. She felt certain that as soon as the news of her background spread (and she knew it would happen fast) she'd be left off the guest list of many other functions as well.

There'd been a few times over the course of the last five months when she'd felt like an outsider in the community, but she'd had hope those feelings would change. Now she doubted she would ever fit in. Wasn't sure she belonged in Briarwood at all.

"I guess there aren't that many employment opportunities in Laurel County," Amanda continued, the smug look still planted on her face.

Brett cut into the conversation. "There may not be any industry in the area, but you should see the mountains – the wildlife – it's really a beautiful place," he said, as though needing to come to Ashley's rescue. "And any place that produces Ashley has to be pretty amazing."

She felt her heart warm in the icy room as Brett came to her aid. She could always count on him for support. They shared a love stronger than she'd ever thought possible.

And he was right; the mountains *were* beautiful – thick hardwood forests, jagged moss-covered bluffs, and towering waterfalls that crashed into emerald pools.

But as much as she longed to see her family, wanted to make sure her father was truly okay, the thought of returning also filled her with a sense of dread.

The last time Brett had seen her father was at their engagement party. What had begun as one of the happiest days in her life had soon ended in total disaster. After drinking too much champagne, a few of her cousins had made crude comments to some of Brett's female relatives, resulting in an actual fistfight between the families. Brett became so upset that Ashley feared he'd cancel the wedding before the day was over.

After dealing with the fallout from the brawl, she realized the only way to ensure the success of her future marriage would be to keep her fiancé and her family apart.

But now, wanting to be there at Ashley's side while her father might be dying, Brett had insisted on accompanying her to Mettler Ridge – and no amount of pleading would change his mind. It was her worst nightmare come true.

Brett grabbed her hand beneath the table and met her gaze with a look that said, *who cares what they think?* She smiled and squeezed his hand in return, as though it was the two of them against the world. Together, they made the perfect team. He was everything she'd ever wanted in a husband. And more.

Ashley knew she didn't deserve to be engaged to such an amazing man, and not only because of her lack of wealth.

The feud between her fiancé and her father and brothers wasn't the only reason Ashley wanted to keep Brett out of Laurel County. Once he was there, she feared what he might find out. There were things in her past that she hadn't yet told him about. Things that were too dark for words.

Would Brett still love her if he learned the truth?

CHAPTER TWO

Ashley couldn't help feeling as though she was making the biggest mistake of her life as the silhouette of the mountains materialized on the horizon on the other side of the windshield. Allowing Brett to visit Mettler Ridge was a huge risk. She hadn't slept well – waking several times during the night – worried both about her father's medical condition and how to keep the peace between her fiancé and her family. The resulting fatigue made matters that much worse.

She stared out the passenger window of Brett's SUV as they drove east on interstate twenty-four, counting the signs that proclaimed, "See Rock City" and "Visit Ruby Falls," ending with a total of seven each before the roadside billboards were replaced by walls of limestone. It was a silly game but helped to take her mind off of the impending visit.

She looked at Brett and wondered whether he felt as anxious about the trip as she did. As if sensing her unease, he glanced toward her – his rich chocolate hair peeking out from beneath his Ralph Lauren ball cap – winked and rested his hand on her knee. His touch still had the power to command her heart to stand still.

Smiling back at Brett, she hoped she'd be able to run interference between him and her relatives. Her plan was to limit his contact to only the members of her immediate family. She'd keep the visit short – two hours at the most. And after they'd been there around thirty minutes, she'd make an excuse to send him into town on an errand. That way, once he returned, there would only be around fifteen minutes or so left before it was time to say their goodbyes.

She hated cutting the time spent with her father so short, but she could think of no better alternative. After Brett's visit was over – once he felt he'd given her the support she needed – she'd be able to return to Mettler Ridge on her own. And from now on, for her father's sake, she promised herself she would make the trip at least once every month.

Ashley's ears popped with the altitude change as they began the climb up Mettler Mountain. She pulled two sticks of gum from her purse and handed one to Brett.

"This will help with the pressure," she said, thinking that the steady chewing rhythm might also help to calm her nerves. If that didn't work, she'd have to find something else to count.

Brett chuckled and pointed to the fifteen-foot-tall standee of Bigfoot lurking next to the highway as they exited interstate twenty-four on their final trek into Mettler Ridge. The black paint had peeled, exposing rust spots on the metal beneath, making it look as though the creature was suffering from mange.

"Was that statue there the last time we were here?" he asked.

"Yeah. I'm surprised you didn't notice it." Having been erected when Ashley was no more than five years old, the metal monster had essentially become Mettler Ridge's mascot. Now the sign had been left to rot in the hazy mountain air.

Just like the town, she thought.

Brett tilted his head and smiled. "Well the last time we visited, the only thing I had eyes for was my beautiful fiancée."

Ashley knew his playful banter was most likely an attempt to lighten her mood – and she loved him for it – but it would take more than sweet words to lift her tension.

As they rolled into town, a row of coke ovens greeted them. The cave-like brick structures built into the side of the hill had been used during the town's mining days to cook the bituminous coal, turning it into industrial coke. Now they lay abandoned, covered in kudzu vines. Ashley's father had often told stories about her ancestors who had worked in the coal mines for very little wages in the late eighteen-hundreds. Although she'd also grown up poor – the majority of her clothing coming from the donation box at the church in town – she felt sorry for her ancestors whose lives had been short and rough.

Before turning onto Main Street, they drove past a white shotgun style house with a sagging roof, its fenced yard dotted with at least a dozen baby goats. Brett smiled and pointed again as the kids chased each other around the yard, their bleating loud enough to penetrate the SUV's closed window.

"I can't believe they allow goats right in the middle of town," he said.

Although the animals were cute, instead of bringing a smile to Ashley's face, the sight made her heart ache.

"When I was around ten years old, Daddy bought two kids to raise for their milk. I went crazy over those little babies, playing with them every chance I got. Then one evening a bobcat broke into their pen. It killed them both and dragged one of them off into the forest."

Brett squeezed her hand. "I'm sorry. I guess that kind of thing must happen a lot around here."

Ashley nodded. The incident had left her devastated and, from then on, she never wanted any more pets.

The shortest route to her father's home would take them past Hope Auto Repair, the shop co-owned by her father and Uncle Russ. Since it was Saturday, she knew her cousins – responsible for starting the engagement party brawl – would be there. To avoid the shop, she directed Brett south down Barfield Street. Because he'd only been to her father's house once, right after they became engaged, she hoped he wouldn't notice the detour. To her relief, he made the turn without question, never mentioning the shop.

Ashley turned away from the window when they reached the trailer park on the north side of town, right at the edge of the city limits. She didn't want to see the place where she had lived right after graduating high school. Preferred not to think about that time in her life. Pushing away the images that threatened her mind, she focused on the road ahead.

As they turned onto Fenton Hill, a stand of oaks flanked both sides of the roadway creating a canopy so thick it blocked the sun's rays like a treed tunnel.

"I used to hate this part of the road when I was growing up," she told Brett. "I would never ride my bicycle through here. I was always afraid something would reach out of the darkness and grab me."

Back then, she'd been teased by her older brother for being scared, but now she realized it was normal behavior for a little girl raised on stories about Bigfoot. Even though she no longer believed in monsters – at least the nonhuman kind – the chill from the sudden absence of sunlight still made her uncomfortable.

Just as they exited the canopy, her father's mailbox popped into view. The SUV wobbled as they drove up the hard-packed dirt driveway. Ashley hoped Brett wouldn't be upset by the fine grains of dust now pummeling his new black car. When they reached the wooden bridge that stretched across the creek on the one-hundred-and-fifty-acre property – passed down in the Hope family for generations – he slowed the SUV to a crawl. Although the weathered structure appeared ready to fall, she knew Kyle and Shane kept the piers underneath in good condition.

"Don't worry about the bridge," she told Brett. "It will hold."

They continued through the tangle of hardwoods and thick underbrush past the fork that led to Kyle's trailer. The drive then snaked left into the clearing. As she caught sight of the house her great-grandfather had built, a wave of dread hit Ashley, making her want to run in the opposite direction.

Trees cleared from the home site had been milled into the lumber for the house, the labor bartered, and the rock used to build the foundation and fireplace gathered from the land. The small Appalachian farmhouse had gone through many changes since her great-grandfather's time – electricity had been added and water from the well piped in – but the long narrow front porch remained the same.

As Ashley hopped from the door of the SUV, she heard a sharp baying split the air. Her father's Bluetick hound dog, Ace, ran to greet her, his tail flopping from side to side. She kneeled down to scratch his head and noticed her father walking toward her from the back yard.

Spencer Hope appeared years older than the last time she'd seen him just seven months prior, his gait slow and uneven. More gray ran through his auburn hair than what she had remembered, his once healthy complexion had turned sallow, and his blue eyes seemed dull and sunken in their sockets. His appearance tugged at her heart. She worried the doctor had discharged him from the hospital way too soon.

Ashley wrapped her arms around her father's neck, breathing in the minty scent of dipping tobacco.

"Daddy, what are you doing out here?" she asked, her voice stern. "You just had a heart attack; you should be inside the house. Resting."

Knowing how stubborn her father was, she hadn't really expected to find him in bed, but she wasn't sure it was a good idea for him to be out walking around so soon.

"I reckon I'll rest once I'm dead," he told her.

"Don't say that, Daddy."

Although she wasn't really superstitious, Ashley didn't want her father to tempt fate with his words.

Brett appeared at Ashley's side.

"Hello, Spencer," he said, offering his hand as a gesture of peace. "I hope you're feeling a lot better today."

Ashley could tell by her future husband's eyes that the sentiment was genuine. She held her breath, waiting for her father's response, fearing the worst.

Spencer stared at Brett's outstretched hand, hesitated a moment, and then gave it a quick shake. Ashley let go of her breath in relief. She longed for her father and Brett to become friends, not just in-laws. But she realized that due to her past mistakes, Spencer would have trouble trusting any man she chose. At least until after they'd known each other for a while.

"I'm a mite better," her father replied, his eyes hard and voice rigid. "I was fixing dinner when y'all pulled up."

Her father always referred to the mid-day meal as dinner and the evening meal as supper.

"Let me do that for you, Daddy. I don't think you need to be cooking right now," she said, concerned that her father was pushing himself too hard. As he always did.

Brett and Ashley followed Spencer behind the house to the old stone grill located in a shady area bordering the forest. The edges of the charcoal were already white from the heat. Spencer pulled a few strips of bark off of a nearby shagbark hickory tree and handed them to Ashley before relaxing in a lawn chair next to the grill. Using a tire iron, she lifted the grate and tossed the strips onto the fire. The wood added a savory flavor to meat and anything else cooked over the flame.

Ashley heard rustling in the woods. Her brothers emerged from the trees wearing camouflage shirts and hunting caps. Kyle carried two shotguns, each open with the muzzles pointed toward the ground. Shane followed close behind, a white-tailed buck arched across his shoulders. Although Shane was younger, at six foot three, he stood a head taller than Kyle and was clean shaven, whereas his brother sported a goatee. Both Ashley and Kyle were blonde like their mother, but Shane had inherited his father's auburn hair.

"About time we seen you again," Kyle said as he accepted a hug from his sister, his shaggy hair tickling her forehead.

Ashley loved her brothers, but their bond was not as strong as it had once been. The older she became, the less connected she felt to her family and their way of life.

Shane stared at Brett, his jaw rigid.

"Best not keep her away for so long," he said as he carried the buck toward a maple tree a few yards from the grill.

"She's free to come here for a visit any time she wants," Brett replied. "I haven't tried to keep her away."

Her fiancé was telling the truth. Ashley could have made the trip alone, but she'd been too focused on earning her master's degree and making wedding plans, something she now felt guilty about. But she also understood the reason for her family's assumption that Brett was responsible for her absence.

"Don't blame Brett; it's my fault," she told her brothers. "I know I haven't been back here as often as I should, but I'm planning to change that." And with her father in bad health, she would.

Shane gave her an unconvinced look as he hoisted the buck onto the meat pole hanging from the maple. He secured its hind legs in the air with the head pointed toward the ground as Kyle spread a tarp underneath. Ace sat close by, as though waiting for a treat.

Pulling a knife from his pocket, Kyle split the deer open, starting from the anus, cutting down to the neck. He reached inside the body cavity and began pulling out the internal organs, laying them aside on the tarp.

Ashley glanced at Brett. His face, tanned from the golf course, had turned pale. She followed his gaze back to the half-butchered buck dangling from the maple tree with the discarded entrails below and remembered he'd never been hunting.

"Are you okay?" she asked him, wishing she had known her brothers were planning on bagging a deer today so that she could have prepared Brett ahead of time.

"Yeah. Fine," he said, his voice clipped.

Kyle and Shane exchanged glances as if noticing Brett's discomfort. It was clear they wanted the opportunity to taunt the city boy dressed in the Polo shirt and freshly pressed khaki shorts.

"You like deer?" Kyle asked him, his arms covered in blood up to his elbows.

"I'm not sure," he answered. "I've never eaten venison before."

"Ain't nothing better than fresh deer back straps on the fire," Kyle told him.

Brett glanced at the grill, seeming to realize for the first time that Kyle and Shane were preparing their lunch. Even more color drained from his face, making him appear nauseous.

Ashley put her hand on Brett's arm.

"Why don't you run into town and pick up some sandwiches from the grocery store?" she asked him, feeling horrible that her family had ambushed him this way and also wanting to stick to her plan of limiting her fiancé's time with her father and brothers.

"I can eat the venison, it's fine," he said.

Ashley knew Brett was trying to save face, not wanting to appear weak in front of her family.

Shane smiled. "Stick around till dark. We're frog gigging down at the creek. We can cook you up a mess of frog legs," he teased.

"Stop it," Ashley said, not amused by her brothers' behavior.

Shane continued, "Ace is getting some age on him. But he can still tree a possum. You like possum? Or how 'bout some rattlesnake?"

"Polecat," Kyle suggested.

"That's enough," Ashley warned her brothers, anger rising in her chest.

She turned to Brett. "We don't have to eat the deer."

"I know that," he said. "But if nobody minds, I'd like to use the restroom."

Good idea, Ashley thought. "Go through the kitchen and down the hall. It's the first door on the left."

She waited until her fiancé had disappeared inside the house before turning on her brothers.

"What's wrong with the two of you?" she asked. "Can't you just try to be civil for five minutes? Brett has made every effort to be nice to you and all you want to do is embarrass him."

"He ain't no man if he can't take some ribbing," Kyle said, preparing to skin the buck.

Ashley heard her father cough. She turned around and looked at him, wondering if he wanted to add his opinion to the argument.

"Y'all quit your squabbling," Spencer chided.

Still infuriated, Ashley continued her rant.

"If you all really loved me," she stated, "you'd try to get along with Brett for my sake. With the way you're acting, he might just decide that he doesn't want to marry me."

Her father looked at her, worry etching his haggard face.

"You done got yourself a heaping bigger problem," he told her.

The apprehension in Spencer's eyes sent a chill down Ashley's spine.

She flashed back in her memory to the day her father had told Ashley and her brothers that their mother was sick. That she was dying of cancer. The expression he wore now was hauntingly similar.

But she knew the news couldn't be about her father's health. He had said that the problem was specifically Ashley's. That it was much worse than the conflict between Brett and her family.

What could be more important to her than marrying Brett?

“She ain’t got no problems,” Shane said, walking over to their father. “Ain’t had none since she hooked up with Fat Cat.”

Ashley wished that her family could understand that although money helped a lot, it didn’t make all your troubles magically disappear.

“What is it, Daddy?” she asked. “What’s happened?”

Spencer nodded toward the lawn chair next to him.

“Better sit,” he told her.

Hearing that she couldn’t take the news while standing caused her stomach to twist. Doing as she was told, Ashley perched on the edge of the battered metal chair, bracing herself in anticipation of her father’s next words.

He met Ashley’s gaze.

“Looks like husband number one’s getting out of the pen,” he said.

CHAPTER THREE

Upon hearing her father's words – that her ex-husband was getting out of prison – a bolt of panic shot through Ashley. How could the report be true? Ethan had been sentenced to fifteen years and had only served eight so far. A criminal of his caliber would never be released early. Would he?

"That's not possible," she said. "He's got seven years left on his sentence."

Ashley heard the screened door creak open and looked up to see Brett emerging from the rear of the house.

A fresh wave of anxiety hit her. Her fiancé had no idea she'd been married before. She hated herself for keeping the secret from Brett. She'd tried many times to find a way to tell him about Ethan – the first attempt was the day after they became engaged – but she just couldn't get the words out. Her first marriage had left her so scarred, the ordeal so painful, she couldn't force herself to talk about it to anyone, not even the man she loved. By not acknowledging that time in her life, she was able to push the memories into the farthest recesses of her mind and keep them locked there. As if those days had never happened at all.

She couldn't let Brett find out about her ex-husband here and now. Not in front of her family. She'd figure out a way to tell him in her own time. When they were alone. Once she felt she could handle reliving the heartache.

Ashley ran across the back yard to the house, determined to reach Brett before her brothers had the chance to spill the news about Ethan.

"You might be able to eat the venison," she told Brett, her hand on his arm, "but I can't. Not now. So please, for me, would you go to the grocery store and get us a couple of sandwiches?"

Her fiancé glanced across the back yard at her brothers and then nodded in agreement.

She watched Brett climb into the SUV before heading back toward her family. She hoped the news regarding her ex was no more than a false rumor being spread around town. Lies created by Ethan's relatives.

"How could Ethan get out of jail now?" she asked her father.

"He's up for parole," Spencer said.

Parole? She didn't believe it. If it were true, as Ethan's victim, wouldn't she have been notified?

"Where did you get this information?"

"Your cousin, Clarence, done got himself a new job. Correction officer over at the pen," Spencer explained. "Word's from him. Russ told me this morning."

Uncle Russ could always be counted on to keep his facts straight. Clarence had previously worked for the local sheriff's department and out of all of her cousins – out of all of her family members in general – he was the most reliable. If the news had come from him …

She pressed her eyes closed, ordering herself to stay calm, knowing in her heart the information was accurate.

Shane cut in, "Why didn't you tell me and Kyle?"

"Would've been the first thing come out of your mouth as soon as you seen her," Spencer told his son. "Wanted to have a minute with her first."

Ashley returned to the lawn chair, hovered on the edge and looked directly at her father.

"Did Uncle Russ tell you when the parole hearing is scheduled?" she asked him. "Where it's going to take place?"

"Yep. Sometime on Tuesday," Spencer said. "At the prison."

So soon? She had to stop it. She couldn't let them put that monster back onto the streets.

Ashley rose from the chair. She paced back and forth in front of the grill, scrambling to come up with a plan. If they released Ethan, he would search the world in pursuit of her. Even though she'd moved several times during his incarceration, how hard would it be for him to track her down? And once he found her … She couldn't allow herself to imagine what he might do to her.

Should she run? Change her name and leave her fiancé and the life she'd worked so hard to build behind? Ashley loved Brett more than she had ever dreamed possible. A life without him seemed unbearable. But how could she stay knowing that her actions could put Brett in jeopardy as well?

She'd always feared the day her ex-husband's sentence would be completed. But a man as volatile as him, as prone to violent outbursts, usually sealed their own fate once entering prison. She knew jail-house brawls were common, and she knew that Ethan would fight to the death. Up until now, she'd held out hope that he'd be killed by another inmate.

A cold sweat broke out on the back of Ashley's neck.

If Ethan wasn't stopped, Ashley knew it was her own life that might soon come to an end.

There was only one option.

She had to stand and fight.

"I'll go to the hearing and make a victim's statement," she said. "Once they hear what I have to say, there's no way in the world the parole board could ever let him go free."

Ashley knew firsthand the level of evil in Ethan's soul. A man like him could never be rehabilitated.

"We'll all go too," Kyle spoke up.

There were some things Ashley planned to say at the hearing that she'd rather her family didn't hear. Details they were better off not knowing. Especially her father.

"No," she said, her voice firm. "I need to face Ethan alone."

"You sure 'bout that, baby girl?" her father asked. By his tone she could tell he felt she was making a mistake by not allowing her family to go with her.

Her father's intuition had proved to be true in the past. If she'd listened to him all those years ago, she wouldn't be in this predicament now. When she'd first shown an interest in Ethan – the older boy with dark curly hair and eyes so blue she could drown in them – her father, knowing she was headed for trouble, stepped in. He made it clear Ashley would not be allowed to date Ethan. But as a teenaged girl, being told she couldn't have something made Ashley want it even more.

The two had dated in secret, and the day after Ashley turned eighteen, they'd eloped. That's when everything between them began to change. When Ethan's true nature began to surface.

"I'm sure, Daddy. Don't worry about me, I'll be all right," she said.

Although her father had been right in the past, this time Ashley knew his intuition was wrong. There was no way she could recount the horror she'd suffered at Ethan's hands with her father in the room. And she needed her testimony to be as strong as possible in order to convince the parole board to keep Ethan locked away.

"Might let him go anyway. Prison crowding and all," Shane warned.

Ashley had just recently watched a news report on television regarding the problem of overpopulation in the Tennessee prisons. They were currently bursting at the seams. This must be one of the reasons Ethan had been granted a parole hearing. The conditions at the prison would definitely make it harder for her to convince the board not to let him out on parole.

"I'll just have to make sure the people on the board understand that it's not safe for Ethan to be released. I'll make them listen," she stated, determined to present her case so effectively that the board would have no choice but to deny Ethan's parole request.

"He's gunning for Ashley," Kyle said. "He gets anywhere near her, I'll break his neck."

Her gaze snapped toward her older brother as an icy fear flowed through her body. She knew Kyle was telling the truth. If given the chance, he would kill Ethan. Shane would as well. If they followed through on the promise, her brothers would be thrown into prison themselves. Most likely landing on death row.

Ashley heard her fiancé's SUV pulling into the driveway.

"Brett's back from the grocery store. I don't want any of you to say one word about Ethan's parole hearing," she warned them. "Understand?"

Brett strolled into the back yard carrying a plastic grocery sack, a bag of chips peeking out of the top. His face had returned to its normal shade, but his expression made it clear he wasn't happy to be back among her family.

"You get yourself a latte? Some of that tofu stuff?" Shane taunted.

"Be quiet, Shane," Ashley threatened.

"No way Soy Boy can go up against Ethan," he pushed further.

"I said, shut up." Ashley shot her brother a warning look that would freeze the sun.

Brett's eyes narrowed.

"Who's Ethan?" he asked Ashley, obviously surprised and confused.

Why couldn't Shane just keep his big mouth shut for once? Sometimes it felt as though her younger brother enjoyed causing her trouble.

"Shane is just trying to push your buttons. He'll say anything he can think of to get under your skin."

Brett stared at her. For the moment, he seemed to accept her explanation, but she could tell her fiancé was losing his patience with her brothers.

"It's time for us to leave," Ashley told them, hoping that nothing else would be said to raise Brett's suspicions.

She went over to hug her father goodbye. She hoped that his condition would continue to improve. That the next time she saw him – which she promised herself would be soon – he would look more like his old self.

"Promise me that you'll take care of yourself, Daddy. I'll be back to check on you in a few weeks," she said.

"I'll hold you to that. Bye, baby girl." Her father kissed her cheek.

Brett stepped toward the lawn chair. "Goodbye, Spencer," he said, his voice flat.

"You watch over her. You hear?" her father commanded, obviously meaning more than he could say in front of his future son-in-law.

"I will," he promised.

Her fiancé looked toward her brothers, still preparing the buck.

"Guys, I'd like to say it's been fun but ..." He let his voice trail off.

Kyle answered Brett first. "See you around," he said.

"Yeah. Later," Shane replied.

Careful not to step on the tarp, Ashley moved toward her brothers. With blood staining their hands, she decided it would be best not to hug them.

"Please don't let Daddy do too much," she said to Kyle and Shane. "And make sure he takes all of his meds and eats the way he should."

"We'll take care of him," Kyle assured her.

Shane nodded. "Don't worry 'bout us," he said, his eyes letting her know that she should be more concerned about her own predicament.

She walked back to the SUV with Brett close behind. As she climbed into the passenger seat, her fiancé hurled the grocery bag into her lap, startling her, and sending the bag of chips flying into the floorboard.

Brett slammed the SUV's door shut and turned toward Ashley with accusation in his eyes.

"Who," he demanded, "is Ethan?"

CHAPTER FOUR

Ashley was stunned by the anger on Brett's face as he sat in the driver's seat of the SUV and questioned her about Ethan. A pang of guilt filled her chest as she debated whether or not to tell him the truth. She longed to come clean, ached to open her heart to him and share everything that had happened in her life. But she just wasn't ready to face the memories. Wasn't yet strong enough to answer the questions she knew her fiancé would ask.

She thought about the parole hearing. If she could convince the board to keep Ethan in prison – which she was determined to do – wouldn't it be best to leave everything in the past? Finding out about her previous life wouldn't help Brett; it would only cause him pain.

"Ethan is a man I was with for a while," she said, looking directly into Brett's eyes.

"So you mean an ex?"

"Yes."

She watched his face as he processed the information, hoping he wouldn't become even more irate.

Brett nodded. "Okay. So why haven't you ever told me about him?" he asked, indignation clear in his voice.

"Have you told me about every single one of your old girlfriends?" she shot back.

He stared at her, his eyes narrow.

"It was a long time ago when I was really young," she explained. "It was stupid. I was stupid. I just didn't see the point in telling you."

"If it was so long ago, then why did Shane bring him up now?"

Ashley considered her words before she spoke, careful to explain without actually lying.

"Because he may be coming back into town soon," she said.

"So, your brothers want you to get back together with him," Brett stated, "That's what this is all about."

She wondered what Brett would think if he knew the truth – that her family would prefer to see Ethan dead.

"No, they don't," she assured him. "It's just some local gossip. It doesn't matter."

"Okay. Fine. But after today, I don't think I want your brothers at our wedding," Brett announced, his voice firm.

Although Ashley realized her fiancé was livid, she hadn't expected him to banish Kyle and Shane from their wedding. The event would be the most important day in her life. In no way could she condone her brothers' behavior, but they were still her family, and she couldn't really imagine the day without them there.

"Are you serious?" she asked, hoping he would change his mind once he'd calmed down.

"Kyle and Shane planned the whole thing with the deer in advance," he told her. "They gutted it in front of me on purpose. Then they tried to feed it to me. They wanted me to get sick. And then Shane brings up your ex-boyfriend, just itching to start a fight. How do you expect me to feel?"

Ashley knew her fiancé was probably right about the buck. It sounded like the type of stunt her brothers would pull on someone they disliked. They could have field dressed the deer in the forest instead of waiting until they brought it to the house. The sight of a deer having its internal organs removed had the power to make even those used to seeing it a little nauseous, herself included. She'd seen more than one man throw up after watching the heart being pulled out.

And Shane never should have mentioned Ethan. It would take her a long time to forgive him for bringing up her ex-husband, especially since he knew Brett was unaware of her first marriage. And yet …

"But they're still my family," she said.

Her fiancé's nostrils flared as he shook his head. Ashley realized her reluctance to exclude her brothers from the wedding had made her husband-to-be even more incensed.

Brett started the SUV and made a U-turn in Spencer's driveway, kicking up a cyclone of dust. He fixed his focus straight ahead, his jaw rigid, travelling faster than advisable down the bumpy dirt drive. She wondered what he was thinking. If he believed her words regarding Ethan.

As they drove out of Mettler Ridge in silence, Ashley was hit with the ominous feeling that this was the beginning of the end of her life with Brett.

***

Ashley felt a thick wall of tension between herself and Brett as they sat propped in their king-sized bed each staring at their laptops. She tried to concentrate on the screen in front of her, knowing she needed to finish her thesis, but it was no use. She kept stealing glances at her fiancé as he typed away, putting together a portfolio for a potential client.

She wished he would put down his work and talk to her. They'd barely spoken at all during the course of the evening. He hadn't given her the silent treatment; he had been polite, but he was far from his normal attentive self. Since their disagreement about Ethan on the way home from her father's house, it was as though he'd retreated into his own little world, hanging up a "no trespassing" sign, making sure she couldn't enter.

Closing her laptop, she glanced at the clock. Almost half past ten. She inched toward Brett and pressed her cheek against his shoulder.

"How much longer are you going to be?" she asked, hoping they could patch things up.

She was careful to enunciate her words as she spoke. Brett had remarked that her southern drawl had sounded unusually strong during their trip to Mettler Ridge. Now, she made an effort to keep her mountain accent in check.

"Not sure. You should go to sleep," he told her, his body rigid and his voice flat.

His rebuff tore at her heart. He clearly wasn't interested in repairing the void tonight. Wishing she knew the right words to say to coax him out of his icy shell, she scooted back to her side of the bed.

The threat of her ex-husband being released from prison had already shattered Ashley's nerves before Brett heard Ethan's name mentioned. She wondered if her fiancé had picked up on her emotions. Maybe he could feel her anxiety. Not being aware of the source, he might think that she still harbored romantic feelings for her ex.

Brett had never been much of a jealous type in the past. If he'd somehow tapped into her fear – realizing something was wrong, but not knowing what – it could explain his reaction to hearing she had an ex he didn't previously know about.

She worried Ethan might still drive a wedge between herself and Brett even if he remained behind bars.

And there was the whole incident with Kyle, Shane, and the buck. Should she have called her brothers out right there in front of Brett? Demanded they apologize for the stunt? She wondered whether her fiancé was angry that she hadn't taken a firmer stand against their behavior. Or perhaps because he'd become nauseous, he'd felt less of a man in the eyes of her family, which would definitely add to his hostility.

Maybe Brett had decided that he didn't want her family in his life at all.

He'd already stated his desire to keep Kyle and Shane out of the wedding. What if he was reconsidering his proposal? Could he be thinking that marrying someone with her background – with a family so polar opposite from his own – would prove to be a colossal mistake?

Now, with Brett shutting her out, she wasn't sure who the biggest threat to her happiness was. Her family or Ethan.

Ashley opened her laptop again and checked her email. She'd sent a message to the parole board inquiring about the time of her ex-husband's hearing. So far, she hadn't heard anything back. At this point, she feared she wouldn't.

She pulled up the parole board's website. She'd scoured the site earlier searching for the hearing schedule. There was a link for the schedule in the main menu, but each time she'd clicked on it, she had been directed to an error message. She clicked again just to make sure.

404 Page Not Found.

She wondered how long she had left to prepare. Her statement to the parole board had to be perfect. It would be painful recalling the memories, but she had to be strong. She had to tell them everything that happened the day Ethan had tried to kill her.

And the worst part: he would be there, watching her.

The thought of being in the same room with that monster again terrified her. But what choice did she have? She had to make sure that Ethan was never allowed to hurt her again.

Feeling the bed move, she glanced over at Brett. He closed his laptop, slid it onto the nightstand and switched off his bedside lamp.

"Goodnight," he said, pulling the covers up over his shoulder and turning his back toward her.

She stared at him. No goodnight kiss? Except for the few instances when he'd been away travelling for business, it would be the first night since they'd moved in together that he hadn't kissed her before going to sleep.

"Goodnight," she replied, trying to keep her sadness from being reflected in her voice.

A knot formed in her throat. She had to figure out a way to make things right with Brett before it was too late. Before they started growing apart.

Turning out the light on her nightstand, she slid beneath the covers. She lay in the darkness facing the back of her sleeping fiancé, listening to him breathe on the other side of the wide gulf between them.

She had just started to drift off to sleep when she realized she had forgotten to plug her cell into the charger. She reached across the nightstand in the darkness, found her phone and unlocked it. She decided to check her email one last time. She noticed that something had been sent to her spam folder earlier in the day. She clicked it open. It was from the prison board.

Ethan's hearing was scheduled for nine a.m.

CHAPTER FIVE

Grateful she was provided the comfort of sitting at a table in the hearing room at the Middle Tennessee State Penitentiary rather than being required to stand at a lectern, Ashley stared at the members of the parole board. They lined the long table opposite her, their faces stoic.

A red-haired man in an ill-fitting pinstriped suit, who she assumed was the public defender called to represent her ex-husband, sat at another table to her right. To the attorney's right, an empty chair stood, waiting for the monster that would soon fill it.

Almost nine years had passed since the day Ethan had tried to kill her. But now, being in this room with the board resembling the jury who had convicted him of attempted murder, it felt as though it had just happened yesterday. She remembered being on the witness stand that day. Remembered the fury in Ethan's eyes as she testified against him, terrified he would break free of his cuffs and strangle her with his bare hands.

The judge had been far too lenient with his sentence. Fifteen years was not nearly enough time for the agony he had put her through.

It was hard for her to believe that the board had even considered his parole request. A man like Ethan – with such a sick and twisted mind – could never change his ways. She felt he would never regret what he had done to her. In fact, she was certain he was proud of it. Likely bragged about her to his cellmates and no doubt wore his deeds like a badge of honor.

She didn't want to let herself imagine what would happen if his parole request was granted. She knew he would find her and stalk her. She wouldn't be able to stay in Briarwood. Her only option would be to change her name and move to a different state, maybe as far as the west coast. Leaving would be the only way she could ensure her life would be safe. Not only would she lose Brett, but Ethan may even try to harm him as well. She feared for her fiancé's life as much as she feared for her own.

Startled by the creak of the door behind her, Ashley turned and watched as a prison guard led Ethan into the room, his hands cuffed in front of him. Apprehension fluttered in her chest as he marched toward his chair. Dressed in standard prison garb – a light blue V-necked shirt and dark blue pants – he kept his gaze focused on the floor.

He looked different than she remembered. The dark curly mane she had once loved to run her fingers through had been replaced by a military cut which made him seem older than his actual age. Time had altered his appearance not only by adding extra years to his hardened face, but also by packing additional muscle onto his frame. He'd cut a foreboding figure before, all those years earlier, but now the sight of him was even more ominous.

Thankful that his eyes were directed toward the ground, that he had not yet discerned her presence, Ashley held her breath until her ex-husband was seated. She surveyed the room once again, noticing that the only other people in attendance were employees of the prison. To her surprise, Ethan's mother had failed to appear. Ashley surmised that even the woman who gave birth to her ex-husband had realized he was too dangerous to be set free.

When the chairman, a middle-aged man sporting an obvious toupee, called the hearing to order, Ashley felt a chill course through her in the midst of the stuffy room. After explaining the general procedure of the parole hearing, including the impact of risk assessment and mitigating factors, the chairman directed his attention toward Ethan.

"Why do you feel your parole request should be granted?" the chairman asked.

"'Cause I've changed."

The sound of Ethan's voice sliced through Ashley's soul, stirring up a horde of emotions suppressed for years. She gripped the arms of her chair, feeling as though she might faint.

"In what ways have you changed?" the chairman continued.

"I'm not that same man that I was. What I done was wrong. I know that. And I'm deeply sorry for all my sins."

Ethan was using his soft voice, one she knew well, the one that made him sound humble and affable. Not capable of the evil he had perpetrated.

"What led you to commit the crime of attempted murder?"

"I reckon I was confused way back then," Ethan said. "But I got help in here. Counseling. I see things different now."

"What did you learn in the counseling program?"

"That I used to hate myself. That done made me hate everybody else too. But I don't no more. I don't hate nobody."

Ethan had never hated himself. Others – yes. But not himself. He was one of the most narcissistic people she'd ever met.

The chairman nodded before reading off the next question.

"If you could go back in time," he asked Ethan, "what would you do differently?"

"I wouldn't never hurt nobody. I would of got help. Maybe gone to church. Read the good book. Been a better man. Made my mama proud."

After making a note on the paper in front of him, the chairman continued.

"If we grant your parole, how can we be assured you won't commit the same crime again?"

"'Cause it makes me sick, what I done. I'm sore ashamed. I don't never want to be that man I was ever again."

During the testimony, Ashley had focused on the faces of the parole board members. They nodded and glanced at each other as her ex-husband spoke. One by one, she watched as their expressions began to soften. To her horror, she realized Ethan's ruse was working.

He had wielded that same charisma against her many times in the past, making her believe that he was the only person on earth who could ever truly love her. That she needed him to survive. He convinced her that she was the one in the wrong. That she was to blame for his actions, and if she had only been a better wife – the kind he deserved – he never would have resorted to violence. And he had a way of twisting things, making you doubt everything you once thought was true.

"Thank you, Mr. Barrett," the chairman said, a smile on his lips. "From your answers here today, it seems you're well on your way to rehabilitation."

He checked his stack of papers, making a few notations.

"I believe we have one victim's impact statement before we make our decision," he stated and then nodded toward Ashley. "You have the floor."

She felt her ex-husband's eyes light on her for the first time since the hearing commenced. Up until now, he'd seemed so wrapped up in delivering his Oscar-worthy performance that she doubted he'd even realized she was in the room.

Ashley trembled as she met his gaze. Obviously shocked to see her there, his rage was apparent on his face. The hatred in his eyes so intense it felt as though a hot iron was burning into her skin. She knew if he could find a way, he would kill her right here. Right now. Her immediate impulse was to run, to get as far away from him as possible.

But running wasn't an option.

Forcing herself to look away, she concentrated on the face of the parole board chairman, took a deep breath and began her statement.

"My name is Ashley Hope, and I was married to Ethan Barrett. During the course of our marriage, I suffered a tremendous amount of abuse, both mental and physical, at his hands."

She paused for a moment, gathering her thoughts, willing her voice to remain steady.

"As you are aware, Mr. Barrett is serving a fifteen-year sentence for attempted murder. I'm the person he tried to kill."

Ashley could no longer feel the chair in which she sat. The hearing room and all the people around her faded from her vision as the door to her mind's vault, the place she had banished the memories of her marriage to Ethan, inched open. She could smell the earthen walls that surrounded her. Felt the decaying leaves damp beneath her bare legs.

Her mind transported her back to the mountain. She was eighteen again and back inside the pit.

Ashley touched her throbbing forehead and felt the blood crusted on her skin and matted in her hair. Was it the gaudy faux diamond ring he wore that had cut her flesh? Or had he hit her with something else?

She hadn't expected the blow that knocked her out. The last thing she remembered before waking in the dankness of the pit was clearing the dishes from the small card table in the trailer she shared with Ethan. Things had seemed to go well that morning. They'd enjoyed a nice breakfast together. He'd even complimented her on the sawmill gravy she'd prepared – not too runny and not too thick. He'd kissed her cheek, and then ...

Sunlight leaked in between the rough boards covering the mouth of the pit. She looked up and wondered what time it was. How long she'd been unconscious. She tried to stand. A jolt of pain shot through her ankle and ran up her shin. The injury no doubt the result of him dropping her several feet into the hole.

"Ethan?" she called out.

What airheaded mistake had she made to warrant this punishment? Thinking back over the past week, she began compiling a mental list of her shortcomings. There was a stain on one of his shirts she couldn't remove no matter how hard she'd scrubbed. She was a little late with supper on Wednesday because a storm had knocked out the electricity.

And yesterday, she'd been forced to have her grocery items rung up by a male cashier because his was the only register open. Ethan always checked the employee's name on the receipt. Yes, that must be it. It was the cashier. Why had she been so stupid? She should have put the groceries back onto the shelves. Waited until today to do the shopping.

"Ethan?" she called again, wondering how long he planned to make her stay down here.

Scooting to the edge of the pit, she rested her back against the cool earth. She pulled her knees to her chin, covering them with her threadbare cotton nightgown. She wished she'd put on a pair of socks when she'd gotten out of bed that morning.

Hearing a noise above her, Ashley glanced up. She waited, staring at the dust particles dancing in the narrow shafts of sunlight, hoping it was Ethan coming back to check on her and not some wild animal milling about. After a few seconds, one of the boards over the mouth of the pit began to move.

Ethan's face appeared, backlit by the sun.

"You awake?" he called down to her.

"Get me out of here," she shouted back. He had gone too far this time. Ethan had been abusive in the past, had made her live by his strict rules, but he'd never trapped her in a hole before.

"Nope. Can't do that." His lips smacked as he chewed the wad of gum in his mouth.

She wanted to scream at him, curse him out, and tell him their marriage was over, but she knew that would just make matters worse. That he would force her to stay down here that much longer.

"I didn't mean to make you angry," she told him. "Please, just get me out and we can talk about it."

"Nothing to talk about."

She knew she had to calm down, not let him see how upset she felt. Be nice to him. Agree to do whatever he wanted until he let her out. After that, she would leave him. For good this time.

"I'm sorry, Ethan. Give me a chance to explain."

"You done run out of chances." His lips smacked again. "You're just worm food now."

Worm food?

"Once I put this here board back across the top of this hole, won't nobody ever see you again except for the worms. Maybe some spiders."

Fear began to build in her chest.

"Ethan, you can't just leave me here."

"I can and I will. We're married. You're my property. I can do what I want with you."

Tears welled in her eyes.

"My family will come looking for me," she warned, hoping it was true. Hoping that despite what Ethan had told her, that her family still loved her at least a little bit.

"Ain't nobody gonna come looking for you. Already got my story straight. My buddy, Dewayne, done told your brother, Kyle, that he seen you with a man over in Chattanooga."

The tears broke free and streamed down her face. Ethan was serious. He was going to leave her here to die.

"Please, let me out. I promise I won't tell anyone. Just please let me go."

"Say hello to the worms for me."

Ethan pushed the board back across the mouth of the pit.

She clawed at the earth until her fingers bled, trying to find a way to climb out. And when the sun went down, it was so cold in the dank hole she thought she'd freeze to death.

How long would it take for her to die?

The members of the parole board stared at her, their shock at her ordeal apparent on their faces. Just like the alarmed expressions of the hunters who had heard her screams and had pulled her out of the pit.

As she ended her testimony, the hearing room began to come back into focus. Ashley could again feel the arms of her chair beneath her sweating palms. The odor of rotting leaves replaced by the scent of industrial floor wax.

"We'll take a vote now," the chairman stated, his gaze fixed on Ashley.

She felt Ethan's eyes on her again. But instead of shrinking in her chair, she sat rigid, willed herself to be strong. Although the threatening look he shot her still filled her heart with terror, she refused to allow it to show on her face. She returned his gaze with an icy stare of her own.

The vote took only a few seconds, much less time than she'd expected.

"In the matter of parole for Ethan Barrett, inmate number TN92764, the board has voted unanimously," the chairman informed them. "Parole is denied."

Relief flowed through her. She'd done it. She'd convinced the board.

She heard Ethan's chair squeak across the floor as he bolted to his feet.

"You just gonna believe her?" he shouted at the board members. "She done told y'all a pack of lies!"

"Guard, please return Mr. Barrett to his cell," the chairman ordered.

Ethan glared at Ashley, his fists clenched in front of him. The evil in his eyes sent a bolt of fear down her spine.

"This ain't over! Y'all gonna be sorry!" he yelled.

As she watched the guard push Ethan through the door leading out of the room, she realized she was shivering. And she knew the reason why. It was the words her ex-husband had shouted.

Y'all gonna be sorry!

Somehow, deep in her soul, she knew his words would prove to be true.

CHAPTER SIX

Ashley jumped at the sound of her doorbell ringing, grabbing her laptop just before it crashed from the sofa onto the family room floor. Since she'd returned from Ethan's parole hearing that morning, every noise – the landscapers mowing the lawn, the neighbor's dog barking, and even children playing – had chipped away at her nerves. She couldn't get the image of her ex-husband's face out of her mind, couldn't quit hearing his words echoing in her ears, warning her that she'd be sorry for testifying against him.

As anxious as she felt, she was lucky that she'd been able to concentrate long enough to finish her thesis. After working so hard, she'd almost missed the deadline.

She inched into the foyer, her eyes glued to the leaded-glass front door, trying to identify the shadowy figure standing on the other side. With her imagination geared into overdrive, she feared it was a police officer here to inform her that Ethan had somehow managed to get away from the guard at the prison. That he had escaped and was coming after her. At least she knew it wasn't her ex-husband looming at her doorway. He wouldn't ring the bell; he'd just bash the door in.

As the man on her front porch turned, she recognized the familiar brown shirt and shorts he wore. A UPS uniform. She'd forgotten that the sample wedding invitations she'd ordered were scheduled to arrive today. Relieved, she stepped further into the foyer. Since the delivery didn't require a signature, Ashley waited until the driver returned to his truck and backed onto the street before she retrieved the package.

As she closed and locked the door and rearmed the security system, an unsettling thought struck her. Ethan could still harm her even from behind bars. It was anyone's guess what kind of contacts he'd made while in prison. He was sure to have met many hardened criminals, most likely had gotten to know a few murderers. He could send one of them to terrorize her, maybe even persuade one of them to kill her. She inspected the package, double-checked the return address, making sure the box really contained the invitations and not a surprise from her ex. She was convinced Ethan had already thought of a million different ways to fulfill his promise of making her sorry.

Heading back to the family room, she pushed her thoughts of her ex-husband aside and opened the package. As she arranged the sample wedding invitations across the top of the mahogany coffee table, she wondered which one Brett would like. Would he choose the laser cut botanical design, the deep plum monogramed card with the silver ribbon, or the intricate baroque card adorned with seed pearls? What if he didn't like any of the invitations? With the tension between them, she hoped he wasn't reconsidering the wedding.

They'd never fought before. She knew all relationships had their ups and downs. But until now their connection had been so strong, it had felt as though nothing could rock it. Maybe if they had argued in the past, their quarrel wouldn't feel so intense. As it stood now, it seemed as though her fiancé was overreacting. There had to be a reason.

Brett was definitely mulling over something. He'd told her he wanted to skip his normal breakfast of scrambled eggs that morning and had even gone outside on the patio to drink his coffee alone rather than stay inside with her.

Ashley ambled toward the back door, wondering how to repair the rift between herself and her fiancé. She gazed across the patio and noticed Brett's coffee mug still perched on the edge of the round teak outdoor dining table. After turning off the security alarm, she headed out onto the patio. The afternoon sun seared the top of her head, the temperature having climbed into the high eighties. She glanced across the lawn to her right and noticed Amanda sitting on a wicker chair next to an inflatable kiddie pool in the Robinson's back yard. Zander giggled with glee as he splashed his mother's legs. Ashley met her neighbor's gaze for a brief second. She smiled and waved a greeting, but Amanda averted her eyes, focusing instead on her toddler.

Her neighbor could pretend if she wanted, look the other way, but Ashley was certain Amanda had seen her.

Her heart dropped. It was obvious Amanda no longer wished to associate with the backwoods woman living next door. Ashley felt like an outcast in her own community. Would the other women in the cul-de-sac shun her as well?

As though wanting to avoid a confrontation, Amanda pulled Zander from the pool and led him from their back yard onto their screened porch, shutting the door behind them, never acknowledging Ashley's presence.

Dismayed by her neighbor's rejection, Ashley sank into the cushioned patio chair next to the table. She scanned the manicured lawns adjacent to her own. Each home owned by a family similar to the one living beside them. All the other residents from the same social class, all comfortable in their surroundings. She didn't fit in here in Briarwood. And she no longer felt at home in Mettler Ridge – actually hadn't in years – not since she moved to Chattanooga to attend the university.

Where did she belong?

Feeling as though her life was beginning to unravel, she picked up her fiancé's mug and trudged back into the house. On her way into the kitchen, she thought she heard a noise coming from upstairs.

Ashley froze.

She glanced at the clock on the fireplace mantle. Brett wasn't due home for at least another hour. In her heightened state, had she imagined the noise?

The hairs on the back of her neck bristled as she stood rooted between the family room and the open kitchen listening for movement above her.

She heard a thump.

Footsteps.

Someone else was inside the house.

When she'd arrived home from the parole hearing, Ashley had plugged her cell phone into the charging station located upstairs in the master bedroom. There was no landline in the house. No way to call for help. She slid the coffee mug onto the kitchen counter and tiptoed to the foyer closet. Holding her breath, she edged open the closet door. Moving as silently as she could, she pulled a sand wedge from Brett's golf bag.

Ethan had wasted no time sending someone after her. They must have slipped into the house while she was outside on the patio.

Clenching the golf club with both hands, she eased up the stairs, careful not to make a sound. She stopped on the landing midway up the staircase. Her heart pounded in her chest as she strained her ears, trying to determine from which room the sounds had emanated.

She heard footsteps again.

In the master bedroom.

Steadying her grip on the golf club, she crept up the remaining stairs into the hallway. The master bedroom door stood ajar. Fear rippled down her spine as she placed her hand on the middle of the door and nudged it the rest of the way open.

The room was empty. The sounds now coming from the master bathroom.

Raising the sand wedge above her head, she sneaked toward the open bathroom door. She caught movement out of the corner of her eye. Glimpsed the figure of a man.

Ashley leapt through the doorway, swinging the sand wedge with all of her might.

CHAPTER SEVEN

Ashley could hear her heart pounding in her ears as she shot through the master bathroom doorway swinging the golf club straight toward the unknown man who had invaded her home.

Brett jumped backwards just outside the arc of her swing.

The head of the club struck hard, punching a hole in the bathroom drywall directly between the twin mirrors hanging above the vanities.

"Are you crazy?" Brett yelled at her.

Ashley caught her breath. Shocked to find her fiancé standing half dressed in the bathroom, his face red.

"You're not supposed to be home yet," she explained. "I thought you were a burglar."

"Did you forget about the silent auction?" he asked, his tone unforgiving.

The auction to benefit the children's wing of the hospital. Brett's father, a pediatric oncologist, was on the hospital board and had agreed to host the event at his home. Yes, with all of the current upheavals in her life, she had forgotten.

"I'm sorry, Brett. It completely slipped my mind." Had she remembered, she wouldn't have charged into the bathroom and made a fool of herself.

Brett pulled the golf club from her hand and checked it for damage. Anger gleamed in his eyes. Ashley realized that by letting her imagination get the best of her and almost attacking her fiancé, she'd split the fissure between them even wider.

Now more than ever, she wanted to confess her marriage to Ethan, explain everything she'd gone through, and beg Brett's forgiveness for keeping the secret for so long.

"Brett –"

"Get dressed," he ordered, leaving her standing alone in the bathroom.

Ashley stared at her reflection in the mirror. She somehow appeared older now than she had just a week ago. Dark circles had formed under her blue eyes from lack of proper sleep and her skin seemed to have dulled. The happy young woman who'd moved in just five short months prior, her future bright and full of promise, no longer existed.

She washed her face with cold water and reapplied her makeup. In an attempt to appear more sophisticated, she twisted her hair up on top of her head. Struggling with pins and different hair clips, she just couldn't achieve the effect she desired. In the end she gave up, leaving her hair loose to cascade across her shoulders, the style her fiancé preferred. In the closet, she found the full-length navy gown Brett had picked out for her a few weeks earlier. He'd purchased the dress specifically for the charity event. How could she let herself forget?

Maybe because she dreaded spending the evening with his family. She felt so out of place among the elite of Belle Haven, a mansion-filled enclave for the wealthiest of Tennessee's residents. And Brett's childhood home.

When she'd finished dressing, she met her fiancé in the family room. He looked so handsome in his tux. His dark hair perfect, his shoulders broad and well defined and his waist narrow. She used to believe they made quite a striking couple. Now, she wondered whether the term "couple" and all that it implied was still accurate.

At least he's still acting like a gentleman, Ashley thought as Brett opened the SUV door for her and waited until she was safely ensconced in her seatbelt before climbing into the driver's seat.

"Where did you go this morning?" he asked, catching her off guard.

She wondered how he'd known that she left the house. Had he tracked her phone? Was he that suspicious of her now?

"This morning?" she hedged, wondering how much he already knew, not quite certain what to say.

"I left a client's folder behind, so I circled the neighborhood and came back. You were already gone."

After leaving the parole hearing, she'd stopped at the bakery to pick up a list of options available for their wedding cake. She wouldn't be lying if she told him about that.

"Just running errands," she said, trying to sound nonchalant, upbeat. "I went to Hoagland's. Picked out the flavors for the cake tasting. Do you still want triple chocolate for the groom's cake?"

Brett hesitated.

"I don't know," he finally replied, keeping his gaze fixed on the road ahead.

The brashness in his tone made her wonder whether it was the flavor of the cake he was undecided about or whether he was unsure that he still wanted to be a groom.

She needed to find out where he stood.

"Brett, about the whole thing with Ethan –"

"Now's not the time, Ashley," he cut her off. "I don't want to be arguing when we get to my parents' house. Let's just get through this evening. It's important to Dad."

She ached for him to talk to her. To hash out his feelings so they could repair their relationship. But with anger apparent on his face, she decided to do as he asked and let the subject drop.

They drove the remainder of the twenty-five-minute trip in silence.

***

As they pulled into the driveway of Clark and Miranda Holbrook's three-story southern colonial estate, Ashley felt her stomach flutter. Today of all days, she did not want to have to face Brett's parents or his younger sister, Bianca. Let alone all the other high society members she knew would be in attendance.

She took her fiancé's arm as they walked along the brick herringbone pathway leading onto the back lawn. Eyeing the dozens of guests who'd already arrived at the black-tie event, Ashley knew she was completely out of her league. The sight of the women with their professionally styled hair and expertly applied makeup, their perfect bodies draped in expensive designer gowns, their necks and ears dripping with gemstones, overwhelmed her. She felt like a cubic zirconia in a sea full of diamonds.

Scanning the lawn adorned with white canopies erected above tables with white cloths and centerpieces of red Peruvian lilies, she spotted her future mother-in-law in the midst of a group of women from the garden club.

Miranda turned and met Ashley's gaze.

Why was a simple glance from her fiancé's mother so unsettling? It always felt as though she was being scrutinized, even from across the lawn.

She watched as Miranda approached wearing a black silk gown, her dark hair pulled into a perfect chignon. She greeted Brett first.

Her fiancé kissed his mother's cheek.

"Just as gorgeous as always, Mom," he told her. "Where's Dad?"

"I believe he's with Doctor Simmons," she said, flashing her son a warm smile as she motioned toward the tent where the auction items were displayed.

Miranda's face turned stoic as she eyed Ashley.

"You look … lovely, dear," she said, the comment sounding more like a subtle dig than a compliment.

The gown Ashley wore might be off the rack, but it had been expensive. Her shoes as well. And the small diamond studs gracing her ears had been a Christmas present from Brett. She wondered what part of her outfit her fiancé's mother had found lacking.

"Thank you," Ashley began her reply, but Miranda had already pulled away to talk to another guest before she could get out, "so do you."

Brett touched her arm, seemingly unaware of his mother's slight. "I'm going to go talk with Dad for a minute, check out the auction items, then we'll meet back up when it's time to eat, okay?"

She knew her fiancé wanted to mingle, but Ashley wished he'd stay by her side. At least for a little while, just to give her a chance to get her bearings. Although with the group here this evening, she realized that was a near impossible task.

Standing alone, feeling more like one of the hired-help than a guest, Ashley accepted a glass of champagne from the tray carried by one of the serving attendants. She surveyed the growing crowd and noticed Bianca – tall and dark-haired like Brett – dressed in a red designer number that hugged every one of her perfect curves. Her fiancé's sister stood talking with her best friend, Wendy, near the catering tent.

Ashley had always felt intimidated by Brett's sister and her friends. It was as though she was an imposter among them. Never really knowing what to say or how to act around the sophisticated young women. Always feeling as though they were silently judging her. Knowing there was no way she could ever measure up to their standards.

Deciding she should at least make an effort to fit in, Ashley strolled toward the two women.

"How are the wedding plans coming?" Wendy asked her. The cost of the Hermès purse on the arm of the willowy blonde was most likely equivalent of two months of Brett and Ashley's mortgage, if not more.

Ashley hesitated, not sure how to respond, remembering her conversation with Brett on the way to the auction.

"Good," she finally replied.

The planning part was going fine. The problem was her groom-to-be wouldn't even talk to her, making her wonder whether there would even be a wedding. Other than that, things were great.

"Just make sure you pay attention to the old saying," Bianca taunted, a wicked gleam in her eye. "First comes the marriage. *Not* the baby carriage."

Wendy and Bianca both erupted in laughter.

The words stung Ashley. She felt her face growing hot. Was her fiancé's sister implying that she would have to become pregnant in order to get Brett to go through with the wedding? Had he spoken with his sister about their relationship problems? Did Bianca know something that Ashley didn't?

"So in other words, I shouldn't do things the way you did," Ashley retorted, letting her nerves get the better of her, referencing the fact that Bianca's wedding had taken place only eight and a half months before her son was born.

Bianca stopped laughing and glared at her.

The second the words spilled out, Ashley knew she never should have said them. She needed to get far away from her fiancé's sister before the situation escalated.

"Excuse me," she said, choler still evident in her tone. "I need to use the restroom."

Ashley placed the untouched champagne on top of one of the tables and darted toward the house. Entering through the back French doors, she hurried past the first powder room and circled around to the other side of the home. Choosing to retreat to the bathroom next to Clark Holbrook's study, the one on the first floor that was farthest from the activity.

She locked the door and sank onto the antique Georgian settee in the vanity area as tears welled in her eyes.

Her relationship with Brett might be rocky at the moment, but she would never try to trap him into a marriage. Would never use the precious gift of a child as a weapon.

Ashley wished she could transport herself back in time and start over with her fiancé. If she'd told him everything about her life – all of her secrets – from the beginning, they wouldn't have argued and could have faced the parole hearing together. Knowing everything, Brett may not have asked her to marry him in the first place. But if he had, if he'd still loved her in spite of her past, their relationship would be solid now.

Rising from the settee, she stood before the mirror and dabbed her eyes with a tissue, careful not to ruin her mascara. She had to pull herself together. Go back to the party, find Brett, and force herself to endure the evening for his sake.

She heard her phone chime. The text message ringtone.

Pulling her cell from her small shoulder bag, she checked the screen. It was a text from Kyle. There was no message, just a link to an article on a Nashville television station website. She unlocked her phone and tapped the link. Ashley's breath caught in her throat when she saw the headline.

Prison Break: Middle TN State Penitentiary

Her heart began to pound as she read the news article. His mugshot stared back at her, his cold eyes boring into her soul. Her worst fear was now a reality.

Ethan had escaped from prison.

CHAPTER EIGHT

Knowing she was about to faint, Ashley collapsed onto the antique settee in the downstairs bathroom of Clark and Miranda Holbrook's southern colonial mansion. With the room spinning around her, she pressed her eyes shut and forced herself to take several deep breaths.

Ethan's mugshot loomed before her, seared into her mind. The accompanying news article she'd read on her phone terrified her to the core. Somehow deep in her soul, she'd known the worst would happen – that her ex-husband would escape from prison – and now her premonition had come true.

He would be coming after her; Ashley knew that for certain. He could even be at her house now, hiding in the shadows, waiting for her to come home. He might be planning to kidnap her and hold her hostage for testifying against him, first at his trial eight years ago, and then again that morning at his parole hearing.

A chill ran through her as she realized he could even be here at the charity auction disguised as one of the catering staff. He could surprise her anywhere at any time.

Why hadn't the police notified her of the prison break? She'd given them all of her contact information at the hearing. Were they just going to wait until after he'd committed another crime against her before they took her plight seriously? She had to make them understand the magnitude of the situation. That the lengths Ethan would resort to in an attempt to get his revenge were limitless. That her life was in jeopardy.

Ashley needed to get to the police station. Now.

But what would she say to Brett? What excuse could she give for leaving the benefit early? Surely he would understand if she told him she felt sick. Which she most definitely did.

Forcing herself from the settee, she stood at the vanity sink, her legs shaky, and splashed cold water onto her face. The reflection in the mirror – a pale ghost of herself – shocked her. She had to get her nerves under control. In order to convince the police that Ethan posed a severe threat against her, she had to appear level-headed. In control of her emotions. She couldn't risk looking like an erratic ex-wife who'd become unhinged for no good reason.

After applying fresh power to her face from the compact in her purse, she left the bathroom. She wound her way through the crowd on the back lawn searching for Brett. She finally found him in the auction tent, bidding on a Florida resort golf package, Miranda and Bianca at his side.

"Brett, I need to leave," she told him. "I'm not feeling well."

"What's wrong?" he asked, turning away from the auction table.

She paused for a moment, not wanting to lie. "I almost passed out in the bathroom."

He clasped both of her hands in his, worry filling his eyes. "Let me tell Dad; I'll take you home."

"No. You stay. I know how important tonight is," she said, squeezing his hands.

He hesitated, searching her face as though he was trying to determine the seriousness of her condition. Was that concern she saw in his expression now, or was it a hint of doubt that she felt ill? She couldn't tell.

"I'll be okay," she assured him, hoping he wouldn't protest. "Promise."

Bianca scowled at her. "Not enjoying the company?" she asked, motioning toward herself and her mother.

Ashley wanted to wipe the smirk right off of Bianca's face. She refused to let her fiancé's sister gall her any further.

"It's a lovely benefit and I hate to leave early," she said, the comment directed more toward Miranda, "but I'm feeling sick at my stomach."

She turned back toward Brett. "Don't worry about me," she said. "Enjoy the auction and I'll see you at home later."

Although she could tell he had reservations about letting her leave alone, Brett finally nodded in agreement.

Ashley felt all eyes on her as she walked across the lawn and back up the brick path to the driveway. Knowing the event was important to her fiancé and his father, she felt terrible for leaving early. Even worse, she hated herself for not being completely honest with Brett. Her stomach was in knots – that much was true – but she wished she could explain the reason to her fiancé. Wished she had confessed everything to him earlier.

After adjusting the driver's seat and strapping herself in, Ashley steered the SUV out of the Holbrooks' driveway and headed toward Briarwood. With no way of knowing whether or not Ethan had help escaping or whether he had a vehicle, she kept an eye on the rearview mirror as she drove, making sure she wasn't being followed. By the time she reached the police station, the sun had set.

Ashley hurried into the modern gray and white building, glancing over her shoulder as she went.

"I need to speak to someone about Ethan Barrett. He just escaped from prison," she told the red-haired female officer manning the information desk encased behind a wall of bullet-proof glass.

"Your name?"

"Ashley Hope. I'm his ex-wife."

The officer keyed the information into the computer on her desk and then asked Ashley to wait in the lobby.

Ashley perched on one of the modern pewter-hued chairs, finding it impossible to relax. With Briarwood being rated as one of the best places to live in the state, she was surprised by the number of people waiting along with her. Two women – who appeared to be mother and daughter – with a little boy in tow, a man dressed in a business suit, another man wearing cargo shorts and a pullover shirt, and an elderly couple in the corner, a worried expression on both their faces. The old adage that crime never rested must be true. Even in Briarwood.

She studied each of the waiting individuals in turn, wondering what misfortune had brought them here. And what were they imagining about her – the pale ghost in the full-length navy evening gown?

Hearing the elevator ding, she turned her attention to the corridor across from the lobby. When the doors slid open, a dark-haired man in his early thirties dressed in a light-blue oxford and navy slacks, a badge pinned at his waist, emerged. His gaze was focused on a tablet, his fingers swiping back and forth across the screen.

"Ashley Hope?" he called out.

"I'm Ashley," she announced as she leapt from the edge of the chair.

"Detective Daniel Lansing." As he shook her hand, his inquisitive blue eyes swept over her, seeming to assess her all at once. "Please come this way."

As she followed the detective to a door labeled *Reporting Room B*, she wondered what kind of impression she'd made, what conclusions he'd already drawn. He was probably thinking her attire seemed rather odd for a visit to the police station. Had he assumed correctly that she had just left a party, or did the dress lead him to believe that she was unstable?

The detective opened the door and directed her to one of the black and chrome chairs next to a table with a black laminated top.

"You're the ex-wife of Ethan Barrett?" he asked once they were both seated.

"Yes. And I don't understand why I wasn't notified when he escaped."

Detective Lansing referred to his tablet. "You still live in Chattanooga?"

"No, I live here in Briarwood now. I gave all of my contact information to an officer at the prison this morning."

The detective nodded. "Sorry for the confusion. Your updated information hasn't come through yet. We called your old number. Totally our fault."

Although Ashley was aggravated by the snail's pace at which the paperwork traveled in the justice system, at least law enforcement had tried to get in touch with her.

"It was my testimony that put Ethan in prison," she explained. "He wants revenge. I know he's coming after me."

She looked directly into the detective's eyes as she spoke, determined to make him understand the gravity of her situation. He returned her gaze, his expression compassionate, seeming to comprehend her fear.

"We got a lead on his location. It's nowhere near Briarwood," he told her, his voice reassuring. "He was spotted near the Alabama state line."

Alabama? Ashley knew Ethan had numerous relatives living in the neighboring state. She'd traveled with her ex-husband to visit a few of his cousins right after they were married. Still, she had trouble believing that he wasn't headed straight for her.

"Are you sure?"

"We got three separate reports. A statewide manhunt's in progress. Both here in Tennessee and in Alabama."

Maybe Ethan's plan was to get help from one of his relatives. Money and supplies. A car. But once he'd gotten what he needed, she knew he would travel straight back to Tennessee to terrorize her.

"At his parole hearing, he screamed that he'd make me sorry for testifying against him."

“I understand. And I know you’re scared. But everything’s being done by the book. We’ll catch him.”

Although the police were skilled at conducting manhunts, they’d never had to track her ex-husband before. He was cunning. He knew the backroads between Tennessee and Alabama well. And he knew how to live off the land. Finding him would not be an easy task.

“Will you notify me if you get any more leads?” she asked.

“Of course,” the detective promised. “He tries to contact you, don’t wait. Call me first thing.”

“I will.”

The detective seemed to believe that Ethan’s focus was centered on evading capture rather than seeking revenge against her. She wasn’t convinced. She knew her ex-husband possessed a twisted mind. And he’d never once failed to follow through on a threat.

As she crossed back through the main door of the police station, Ashley scanned the parking lot, looking for anyone who seemed out of place. Even if Ethan had traveled to Alabama, there was still a definite possibility that he’d hired someone else to hunt her down.

Satisfied there were no people lurking in the lot, she ran to the SUV and climbed inside. As she drove toward home, her thoughts turned to the charity auction and the smirk on Bianca’s face when she’d warned Ashley not to get pregnant. Her fiancé's sister would probably love to see the wedding canceled. Mr. and Mrs. Holbrook would likely be happy to see their son’s relationship end as well. Even if the wedding went ahead as planned, Ashley knew Brett’s family would never truly accept her as one of their own.

Her house popped into view as she turned onto Marigold Court. Her stomach tightened when she noticed a light burning downstairs in the study.

Brett was already home.

CHAPTER NINE

A wave of dread hit Ashley as she pulled into her driveway and pressed the button to open the garage door. She never imagined Brett would arrive back at their home first.

When she walked from the garage into the house, she met her fiancé standing in the hallway. He'd already changed from his tux into shorts and a T-shirt, so he didn't just arrive. He'd obviously been waiting for her.

"First, tell me nothing's wrong with you," he said, concern visible on his face. "That you're okay."

She nodded. "I'm fine."

"Did you go see a doctor?"

"No."

A fire lit in his eyes.

"So then where have you been?" he demanded.

She stared at him, a knot forming in her stomach, trying to figure out a way to explain.

"I left the auction early," he spat out, "worried sick about you and you weren't even here."

He braced his hands on his hips, his face red. "I called you several times. Straight to voicemail. I even called the hospital. You could have been dead for all I knew."

Before leaving the auction, she'd told Brett that she had almost fainted. He had no way of knowing that it was her nerves that had caused her lightheadedness and not an illness. Of course he'd been worried. If she had passed out while driving, she would have crashed – could have died. She should have called him when she reached the police station. Without telling him her exact location, she could have let him know that she'd arrived back in Briarwood safely.

"I'm sorry," she finally uttered.

"Who were you with?"

"Not who you think."

She could tell that he no longer trusted her. That he suspected she'd been with Ethan. It was time to tell Brett the truth. He deserved to know. Especially now that her ex-husband had escaped from prison.

"There are some things I need to tell you – should have told you a long time ago," she admitted. "You're going to want to sit down."

Brett followed her into the family room. Instead of sitting next to her on the sofa, he chose the chair opposite, leaving a wide distance between them. Ashley could feel the hostility radiating from her fiancé and knew he'd reached his breaking point.

Their entire future together hinged on his reaction to the revelation of her past.

Now that she was ready to tell him about her ex-husband, she didn't quite know how to begin. She decided it would be best to keep her story as short and simple as possible. Just reveal the details he needed to know.

"I was seventeen when I met Ethan," she began. "He was my first real boyfriend. In the beginning, things were wonderful between us. I thought I was in love."

She paused and took a deep breath, dreading her next words.

"The day after I turned eighteen, we eloped."

Brett's eyes narrowed. "You've been married to someone else? How could you keep something that important from me?"

Incensed, he shot up from the chair.

"Brett, just hear me out," she plead, rising beside him.

Ashley couldn't let him walk away. She needed to make him understand.

She touched his arm. "Please, sit back down."

There was more than just anger evident on his face. An emotion she couldn't quite discern. Almost as if he expected her to announce that she was leaving him for her old flame. He hesitated for a moment then returned to his chair.

She eased back onto the sofa, perching on the edge.

"I wasn't married long," she assured him. "Ethan became very abusive. And then one day he snapped."

She paused, gathering her strength. "He knocked me unconscious. Then he threw me into a pit in the forest. He left me there to die."

Brett appeared stunned. "He – he did what?"

"He tried to kill me."

Her fiancé shook his head. His expression of indignation had morphed into anguish at the torture she'd endured.

"The guy's obviously a lunatic," he said. "I wish you'd told me all of this sooner."

"I wanted to – I tried several times. I hated keeping the secret from you, but it was just too painful to talk about. And when Shane brought up Ethan's name, I worried that if I told you about my first marriage – after waiting for so long – you might wonder if I was hiding something else."

"Are you?"

Ashley nodded, bracing herself for Brett's reaction to the worst part of the news.

"Ethan was convicted of attempted murder eight years ago," she said. "Yesterday he escaped from prison."

Her fiancé appeared shell-shocked as the hits kept coming.

"You have an ex-husband who's now an escaped convict," he stated as though trying to digest the information.

"He's coming after me – after us," she warned. "You asked where I went yesterday. Before the bakery, I went to the prison. Ethan was up for parole, and I testified against him at the hearing. He wants revenge."

Brett stood, crossed his arms, and paced across the family room. He seemed to be considering their options.

"Eight years is a long time, Ashley. He probably just wants his freedom. And if he came here, he'd risk getting caught."

"That's what the detective said."

"Detective?"

"That's where I went when I left the charity auction. To the police station."

Brett nodded, as if her actions the past few days were all starting to make sense. His expression remained grim. Now that he knew the truth about her past, she hoped they could rebuild their relationship. That it would end up being stronger than before.

"Do you forgive me for not telling you?" she asked, her heart aching.

He hesitated, stared at the floor, then met her gaze.

"I love you, Ashley. But it's a lot to take in," he said. "I need some time."

She nodded, wondering how she could gain back his trust.

"I'm tired," he told her. "Calling it a night. I'll sleep in the guest room."

Tears stung Ashley's eyes as she watched Brett walk from the family room into the foyer. What could she do to keep her world from crashing down around her? She knew she was on the cusp of losing the one person she cared about the most. The man she loved more than life itself. She hoped that he would be calmer in the morning. That she'd be able to talk to him. Get him to understand that their relationship was more important to her than anything else.

Ashley headed upstairs to the master bathroom. She washed off what was left of her makeup, dried the tears streaming down her face, and changed out of her dress and into a satin nightgown. She walked over to the window and stared out into the night, wondering how much time Brett would need to sort through his feelings.

At least she no longer carried the burden of keeping her first marriage a secret. For that, she was thankful.

Glancing down at the patio to her right, in the glow of the moonlight she spotted what appeared to be a package next to the back door. There were still a few items she'd ordered for the wedding that had yet to be delivered, but in the past, their postman had always left their packages on the front porch. She wondered what the reason was for the change. It seemed unlikely in their neighborhood, but maybe there had been reports of porch pirates in the area.

Pulling on her robe, Ashley ambled down the stairs and turned off the security alarm using the keypad in the foyer. Figuring the package most likely contained the sample cocktail napkins for the wedding reception, she made her way through the family room. She peered out onto the patio making sure no one was lurking in the shadows before she opened the back door.

The box seemed far too large for the napkins. The return address label bore the name of the company she'd ordered them from, but somehow it looked off. Like the label had been torn and put back together.

Stumped, she stared at the box.

What if Ethan had stolen her real package and replaced it with one of his own? He could have peeled off the label and reused it. The box might contain a bomb. Maybe she should call 911. But if she called the police and the package only held the napkins, she'd look foolish. And like the boy who cried wolf, Detective Lansing might not believe her if she ever did receive something from her ex-husband.

She knelt down and placed her ear against the box. Did bombs tick, or was that only in the movies? Not hearing anything, she clasped the sides of the box with her fingertips and eased it upward. The weight felt right for the napkins. Maybe the company had enclosed them in bubble wrap, making a large box necessary.

Ashley realized she had reached the point of being paranoid. Just as her earlier package had contained the invitations she'd ordered, this box would contain the napkins. Not all labels were perfect.

She brought the package inside and placed it onto the coffee table. She took a deep breath and then ripped off the packing tape.

As she folded back the flaps of the cardboard box, fear raced down Ashley's spine. She recognized the item inside. A souvenir from her past.

A weathered pink teddy bear.

The bear Ethan had won for her at the carnival. On their first date.

CHAPTER TEN

Terrified by the knowledge that Ethan had found her – that he had actually stood at her back door – Ashley shoved the box containing the pink teddy bear into the rear corner of her closet. Unable to stand the sight of the stuffed toy her ex-husband had won at the carnival all those years ago, her first impulse had been to throw the entire package into the trash. But based on her studies in forensic science, she knew the evidence needed to be preserved. That a small clue might exist somewhere inside the box that could help the police capture Ethan.

The bear was a warning. Her ex-husband's twisted way of telling her that he knew where she lived and could come for her at any time. The fact that he'd positioned the package at the back door instead of leaving it on the front porch was a message in itself. It implied intimacy. He'd crossed the boundary into her private space as if he owned it. The way he'd once thought he had owned her.

Ashley grabbed her purse from the closet shelf and dug inside until she found Detective Lansing's card. Although it was after nine p.m., the detective had stressed that she shouldn't hesitate if Ethan contacted her. Lansing had instructed her to call him immediately.

She tapped the number into her cell. The call transferred to the detective's voice mail.

"This is Ashley Hope," she said, struggling to keep her voice steady. "Ethan Barrett was at my house tonight. Please call me."

Her ex-husband could still be there. Lurking outside her home. Waiting for the opportunity to break in. A chill rushed through her as she imagined him watching the house. Spying on her as she'd retrieved the package from the patio.

How much time had passed since he left the box at her door?

Before retreating upstairs, she'd checked that all the blinds were closed and had switched on all the exterior flood lights. But if her ex was still there, she knew it would take more than a few outdoor lights to scare him into leaving. She doubted the presence of law enforcement would deter him either. He most likely expected her to call the police. Would probably derive pleasure from watching them arrive.

Thinking the detective may send an officer to the house right away to pick up the bear, she pulled on a pair of jeans and a turquoise cotton top. She needed to wake Brett and show him the bear.

As she closed the closet door, her cell rang. Detective Lansing returning her call.

"Ethan was here," she told him, urgency in her tone.

"You saw him?"

What difference did it make whether or not she had laid eyes on her ex-husband? That didn't change the fact that he had found her.

"Well … no," she admitted. "But he left a package at my back door. Inside is a teddy bear that he gave me on our first date."

The detective paused a moment, as if he was checking something.

"We got another report about an hour ago," he informed her. "A sworn statement. Ethan Barrett was seen outside a bar in Pruitt, Alabama."

Ashley had never heard of Pruitt.

"How many miles are there between Pruitt and Briarwood?" she asked.

"Enough that he couldn't be in both places."

"I know that he was here tonight," she insisted. "The man at the bar has to be mistaken."

The detective hesitated, as if he was pondering the situation.

"Your ex wants to mess with your head. Probably got a buddy to leave the bear at your door."

She supposed that could be true. With all the sightings that had been reported, it was possible that Ethan was in Alabama. For now, anyway.

"What if this person comes back?" she asked the detective.

"It's probably just a one-time thing. But keep your doors locked. Don't go anywhere alone," he instructed. "You have a security system?"

"Yes."

"Good. Make sure it's armed. I'll request a patrol car for your neighborhood. But we just got hit with a massive budget cut. We're stretched thin. My boss might not approve it."

If Ethan wanted to get to her, she knew having an officer on patrol wouldn't stop him anyway.

"What should I do with the teddy bear and the packaging?" she wanted to know. "Do you need to send it to the crime lab for testing?"

"Hold onto it for now."

She heard a man's voice in the background, someone talking to the detective.

"I have to go," he told her. "But Ashley, if you need anything. Call me. Day or night."

As she disconnected the call, Ashley flipped off the bedroom light, walked to the window and peeked through the blind. She scanned the patio and back yard wondering who had delivered the bear to her doorstep. If Detective Lansing was right and Ethan was hours away, that meant he had someone else helping him. Was it one of his relatives? Or was it someone he'd met in prison? Either way, she was still in danger.

She heard a noise in the hallway.

Telling herself not to panic, she nudged open the bedroom door and peered out. Brett stood near the doorway leading to the hall bathroom.

"Was that your phone ringing?" he asked.

"It was the police detective," she said. "I'm glad you're up. There's something I need to show you."

Brett followed her into the master bedroom. Ashley rushed to the closet and pulled out the package containing the stuffed animal and presented it to her fiancé.

"I found this on our patio just a few minutes ago," she told him. "It's the bear Ethan gave me on our first date." She hoped that now her fiancé would understand the level of hatred Ethan still held for her. That they were both in danger.

He stared at the box, his eyes wide. "What did the detective say?"

"That he'd try to send a patrol car, but because of budget cuts, they may not have any officers available."

"Yeah. I read about the cuts online."

"Maybe we should check into a hotel on the other side of Nashville and stay there until the police catch Ethan," she suggested.

Hiding out seemed like the safest option. Maybe they should even leave the state.

Brett shook his head. "No. I don't think running is a good idea. We can't let this guy think we're afraid of him."

He cupped Ashley's shoulders, looked into her eyes.

"I won't let him hurt you," he promised. "We'll hire a private security firm. The one Dad used for the benefit concert last year. I think I've still got their card in my desk."

As she gazed into Brett's eyes, Ashley's hopes soared. He hadn't left her. Didn't walk away from the mess she'd made of her life – of their lives. Instead, he wanted to protect her. Wanted to tackle the problem together.

"I'll call them now," he told her. "They'll be here within the hour."

CHAPTER ELEVEN

"Do you still want to marry me?" Ashley asked Brett once the security firm's video surveillance tech had finished his work, leaving the couple alone in the study. She gripped the back of the leather chair next to her fiancé's desk, fearful of his response. Although Brett had promised to do everything in his power to keep her safe, including hiring the best – and most expensive – private security service in the state, she worried their relationship teetered on the edge.

Her fiancé closed his laptop, sighed and started to speak, but was cut off by the familiar melody of Ashley's cell phone ringing on the side table.

She met his gaze, knew he was sharing the same thought: *who could be calling her at this late hour?*

They had discussed the possibility of Ethan obtaining her number and calling to harass them.

With trepidation, she scooped up her cell and checked the caller ID.

"It's Detective Lansing," she told him before answering, hoping the police had captured her ex-husband.

She put the call on speaker so Brett could hear.

"Have you found Ethan?" she asked the detective instead of saying hello.

"No, sorry. And no new sightings," Lansing informed her. "We're pretty sure your ex is still in Alabama. I hope it's not too late to call. I just drove by and saw your lights on. Saw the Steel Armor Security truck in your driveway. Everything okay?"

"Yes, nothing else has happened since I received the bear," she told him. "Brett thought a security guard would be a good idea."

"Steel Armor's the best. They should be able to handle things."

Ashley was glad the detective had confidence in the security company.

Lansing continued, "I'm still trying to get a patrol approved. But there's a lot of flak from the higher ups."

"I appreciate your effort."

"Anything else happens – call me," he said before disconnecting.

Even though there was no further news regarding Ethan, she was thankful the detective had taken the time to drive by and check on them. She hoped that he was right, that her ex-husband really was hiding in the neighboring state.

With the protection of an armed guard and Detective Lansing keeping her informed regarding the manhunt, Ashley was beginning to feel a little better about their decision to stay at home rather than moving to a hotel. Now if she could only begin to mend the damage she'd done to her relationship with Brett, she'd be able to rest easier tonight.

She moved behind his desk, putting her hand on his shoulder.

"You didn't answer me before," she reminded him. "Do you still want to marry me?"

Her fiancé pulled away, stood and walked toward the newly installed video monitor situated atop the bookcase in the corner near the front window.

"Let's just get through the next few days, Ashley," he said, avoiding her eyes. "We can talk about everything else later."

Her heart sank. She could understand him being angry that she'd kept her first marriage a secret. If she found out he was hiding an ex-wife somewhere, she'd be irate as well. But her circumstances were far from normal. He should try to see things from her perspective.

She started to voice her opinion, stand up for herself and try to make him realize that she'd thought she had no choice. But for now, she decided not to press the subject. She'd let it wait until morning. After a night's sleep, maybe he would be in a better mind space to understand.

At least he hadn't ended their relationship right then and there. Hadn't yet dashed all her hopes.

She watched Brett fiddle with the brightness and contrast of the monitor hooked to their new surveillance cameras. One view focused on their front porch while the other image was of their patio.

Ashley trembled as she imagined Ethan standing at their back door.

At least now if her ex-husband decided to break into their home, they would be warned before he could get inside. But if he did come for her – and she was certain he would – she hoped the guards would be able to stop him.

To her surprise, the night guard, Steve, a former marine, had arrived less than an hour after Brett made the call to the security firm. An entire team descended on their home shortly afterward, installing the video cameras and equipment along with several motion activated lights around the perimeter of the house.

Brett readjusted the angle of the monitor, positioning the screen so that it could be viewed both from his desk and from the doorway leading to the foyer.

The chiming of the doorbell startled Ashley.

She followed her fiancé through the foyer to the front door.

It was the guard, Steve. Ashley liked him. Even if she hadn't been told that he was ex-military, she could have guessed it. He still wore his blonde hair close-cropped, his torso was a solid wall of muscle, and he was both well-mannered and well-spoken.

"Sorry to disturb you, Mr. Holbrook," he said when Brett opened the door. "I just need to give you this two-way radio; it's been reprogrammed to a secure channel which means that no one else will be able to intercept our communications. Keep it close beside you at all times."

Brett thanked Steve. After closing and locking the front door, he handed the radio to Ashley.

"I'm beat," he told her. "I'm going to turn in."

Exhausted as well, she nodded and followed him up the stairs. When they reached the hallway, he turned right and headed toward the guest room.

Pain sliced through her heart. Ashley had thought that Brett would choose to stay with her in the master bedroom. That after the incident with the bear, he wouldn't want her to be alone.

"You can't hate me for having a past, Brett," she said to his back.

Her fiancé stopped and turned toward her. "Who said I hate you?"

"That's how I feel. I just think you should be more sympathetic. It's not my fault that I was Ethan's victim. And you act like I still care about him. Which would be impossible."

"I don't blame you for your past. I blame you for hiding it all from me."

She wished she could explain her fear that revealing certain details of her life would likely hurt him. Especially one secret in particular.

Ashley hadn't known it at the time, but she'd been pregnant when Ethan threw her into the hole all those years ago.

"Can't you understand why I would?" she countered.

He stared at her. Sighed. "I'm trying. But you have to understand how blindsided I feel. You dumped a lot on me. I have to sort it out."

Rooted in the hallway, she watched as he closed the guest room door behind him. She longed for the closeness they'd once shared. They'd been so happy together before moving to Briarwood. Before her past came back to destroy her.

Tears flowed down her cheeks as she turned and walked into the master bedroom. She changed into her nightgown, climbed into the bed, and stared at Brett's pillow. Would he ever forgive her?

Ashley jumped as a motion light clicked on outside, the glow partially illuminating the room.

Ethan. In the backyard.

She sprang from the bed and ran to the window, her heart pounding. She peeked through the blinds and scanned the lawn. Steve appeared beneath her, circling the house on his patrol. He'd most likely triggered the light. But to be safe, she grabbed the two-way radio from the nightstand.

"I saw the light come on," she said, her voice shaky. "Is everything alright?"

"A-OK," Steve answered.

It would be difficult not to panic each time the light flashed on as he rounded her side of the house. She was grateful he'd given them the radio.

"Thank you. Goodnight," she said into the mic, feeling foolish for bothering the guard. If anything had been amiss, he would have alerted them.

Ashley placed the radio back onto the nightstand and crawled beneath the bedcovers. Even as exhausted as she felt, sleep wouldn't come easy. It would be a long night.

Ethan was out there somewhere, plotting against her.

She felt certain capturing him would be a difficult feat even for the most seasoned of law enforcement. A skilled woodsman, he could thrive in conditions other men would likely not survive. He was an expert at playing mind games. Calculated and cunning, he knew how to strategize. And he knew all of Ashley's weaknesses.

Regardless of what the detective thought, she still worried Ethan had left Alabama. That he was close by.

He had a plan for vengeance. And he would never give up.

CHAPTER TWELVE

Steve Pulliam adjusted the Bluetooth earpiece connected to his two-way radio as he began his three a.m. circuit of the perimeter of the Holbrooks' home on Marigold Court. They seemed like a nice couple. The job a cakewalk. It was about time he'd received an easy assignment. He'd just come off the tour of a young country music star, had battled crazies every night as they stalked her across the nation, following her tour bus, fighting to get close to her. At more than one stop, he'd had to get physical with a few of the ardent fans, holding them until the police could haul them away.

After his grueling time spent on the road, protecting the Holbrooks from an abusive ex felt like a vacation. His numerous assignments within the music industry coupled with his military experience in the Middle East had prepared him for just about anything. How much trouble could a lone man cause him?

From his previous experiences, he knew that most wife abusers were only comfortable going up against women. They tended to wilt like the true cowards they were when faced by a man. Especially one who was armed.

Moving in a clockwise direction, he walked past the front porch and crossed the driveway. He was used to guarding celebrities and their multi-million-dollar mansions. This home was not quite a mansion, but it was large and inviting, and located in an exclusive neighborhood. The kind of place he'd like to buy if he ever struck it rich. As he rounded the south corner of the attached garage, he caught the flash of a motion light on the north-west side of the house.

Probably just a cat or maybe a raccoon. He didn't really expect the ex to show up, especially not with the truck emblazoned with the Steel Armor logo parked out front.

He ran to the area bathed in light but found nothing there.

Thinking the animal that had triggered the sensor had gone on its merry way, Steve continued his circuit. The lot the house sat on was especially nice. He liked the row of evergreens lining the back of the property. Wished his own tiny yard had a green barrier between him and his neighbor. When he reached the patio on the north side of the home, a motion light at the east side flashed on.

He rushed to the east end of the house, but again, no one was in sight.

He shined his Maglite out past the far edge of the lawn, searching for an animal that could have tripped the sensor. Nothing caught his eye. No discernable reason for the light to come on.

Holstering his Maglite, he headed south, back toward the front of the property. He cursed as the motion light on the north-west side came to life again. He ran to the area.

This time he saw something. In the middle of the lawn.

He drew his Glock 22. Glancing side to side, he advanced toward the cylindrical object. The hairs on the back of his neck prickled.

It was his coffee thermos.

He'd left it locked inside the cab of the truck.

So the ex had decided to show up after all. And it seemed he liked playing games.

You want to play, tough guy?

Steve knew he should follow protocol and radio for backup, but the guy had broken into his truck. Had taken something that belonged to him. He wanted to find the ex and teach him a lesson before he called in reinforcements.

A marine could defeat a wife beater any day of the week.

First, he'd check the truck for damage and then he'd find the ex. As he headed toward the front of the house, the east light flashed on again. His Glock ready, Steve raced toward the light, hoping to catch sight of the ex before he had time to flee.

When he reached the east side of the house, the wife beater was already gone, but he'd left something behind. Steve recognized the decorative metal pole standing in the middle of the side lawn. It belonged in the Holbrooks' back yard. The hook from which a bird feeder once dangled. But the feeder had been replaced by a piece of paper.

As he shined his Maglite on the paper, a shiver ran the length of Steve's spine.

It wasn't an ordinary piece of paper; it was a photo of his girlfriend. The one she'd given him earlier that evening. The ex had taken a knife to the photo, carving holes where his girlfriend's eyes once were.

Was this a threat?

"Huge mistake, tough guy!" Steve yelled into the air, hoping the ex would come out and face him.

He had placed the picture in the center console of the truck, right on top of his mail. He shuddered as he realized the wife beater now had his name and knew where he lived. He pulled out his cell. Opening his favorite contacts, he tapped his girlfriend's name.

Voicemail.

"Vicki, you need to go to your mom's house," Steve said into the phone. "Leave as soon as you get this. I can't explain now, but it's not safe at my place."

As he disconnected, he hoped his girlfriend would wake and get the message quickly.

A line had been crossed. The game had now become personal.

When he caught the ex, Steve planned to beat him to a bloody pulp.

He walked to the patio, pulled out his phone and opened the security app. He clicked on the schematic of the house. Whenever a motion sensor was tripped, a red dot would appear on the map in the app. When a light came on, it would stay on for thirty seconds before turning back off. The current status of each light was mirrored on the app.

He studied the screen and noticed that the lights were now being triggered in a pattern. First the north-west light, then the east light, and finally a south-west light. The guy was steering clear of the cameras at the front and rear of the house. Steve realized he could cross over into the neighboring yard, circle around onto the street, and cut the ex off at the south-west corner.

Then he'd beat the shit out of him.

Timing his jaunt, Steve waited for the east light to flash on.

Drawing his Glock, he ran west across the lawn. He crouched next to a magnolia tree in the neighbors' yard watching the Holbrooks' house. When the south-west light triggered, Steve scanned the yard, but couldn't see anyone or anything that would have been responsible for activating the sensor. As the north-west light switched on, he ran south toward the street.

Steve circled around and flew toward the garage, knowing that if the pattern held, whoever had initiated this game of lights was now behind the house. His Glock poised, he edged between the garage wall and a row of boxwoods, careful not to trip any of the motion sensors himself.

As he neared the end of the wall, he heard a faint noise.

Steve froze.

A twig snapping? He wasn't sure. Goosebumps danced down his arms as he stood with his back glued to the wall.

He didn't have much time. He had to move before the wife beater made it back around to the south side of the house.

Steve crept toward the large azalea bush where he would hide and wait for the crazy ex.

Panic hit him as he caught movement out of the corner of his eye. As he jerked toward the left raising his Glock, powerful arms clamped around him from behind.

He felt the cold steel of a blade rake across his throat.

The Glock slipped from his fingers as darkness overtook him.

CHAPTER THIRTEEN

Ashley woke from a troubled sleep and stretched toward Brett's empty side of their king-sized bed. Pulling his pillow to her cheek, she breathed in the scent that still lingered on the case. His cologne. Noticing it was light out, she glanced at the bedside clock. It was almost five-thirty. She wondered if he was awake. Lying in the guest room thinking about her the way she was thinking about him. Under normal circumstances, her fiancé would sleep until seven.

But nothing had been normal lately.

At least the night had passed without a visit from Ethan. He'd plagued her dreams, taunting her, screaming that he would even their score. She'd shaken herself awake once, sure he was standing next to her bed, but it had only been a shadow.

Where was he now? How much time did she have before he appeared at her doorstep?

Knowing she wouldn't be able to fall back asleep, Ashley slid out from under the covers. After a quick shower, she retrieved the two-way radio from the nightstand, left the master bedroom and crossed the hallway to the guest room. She stood outside the closed door listening for Brett's familiar snore. She wondered whether he'd given any more thought to their wedding. If there would still be a wedding. Hearing nothing, she trudged down the stairs and into the kitchen.

With her stomach doing anxious somersaults the past few days – causing her to throw up more than once – she hadn't been eating as much as she should. She'd picked over her dinner last night and still had no appetite now. But she could use some caffeine. Brett wouldn't be up for a while and he hated stale coffee, but Steve might like a cup. He deserved it after guarding the house all night. Grinding enough beans for four cups, she loaded the coffeemaker and switched it on.

While she waited for the coffee to brew, she checked the news on her phone. A Nashville television station had posted an update on the prison break. According to their report, the manhunt continued to be centered in Alabama. Law enforcement still thought Ethan was hiding out in the neighboring state.

Ashley wished the police's hunch was true – that her ex-husband was far away from Briarwood – but she had trouble believing it. It just didn't feel right. Somehow, she knew Ethan was closer to home.

Pulling two sixteen-ounce mugs from the cabinet, she filled them with the fresh coffee. Steve was probably out front near his truck. She grabbed one of the mugs and headed through the foyer. As she passed the door to Brett's study she glanced inside.

Fear gripped Ashley's heart. She stopped short, almost spilling the coffee.

The video monitor in the study was on and the image from the front door appeared normal. But the image from the patio had turned solid black. The way it had looked before the cable was connected.

The feed had been cut.

Ashley ran back into the kitchen, put down the mug and grabbed the two-way radio from the counter.

"Steve, something's wrong with the video camera at the back door," she said into the mic, hoping that it was just a malfunction. That he would tell her everything was under control.

She waited. There was no answer.

"Steve, are you there?" she asked, panic rising in her chest.

Still nothing.

Ethan had cut the cable. She knew it.

The hairs bristled on the back of her neck as she inched toward the back door. Ashley peered through the glass and saw Steve sitting in one of the teak chairs next to the outdoor dining table, his back toward her.

Why didn't he answer the radio?

"Steve, can you hear me?" She tried again.

The guard didn't move. Something was very wrong. One thing malfunctioning was possible. But both the video feed and the radio being out was not a coincidence.

She searched the lawn but didn't see anyone else. Ethan could have drugged Steve. He might need medical help. She turned off the security alarm.

After checking again to make sure no one else was outside, Ashley pulled open the back door. She stepped onto the patio.

"Steve?"

The guard still didn't answer or move. Her heart began to pound as she circled around in front of him

Ashley screamed at the sight of the blood covering the guard's neck and shirt.

Steve was dead.

CHAPTER FOURTEEN

Ashley couldn't stop trembling as she sat on the sofa in her family room next to Detective Lansing, repeating the events of the morning for the third time. Going over everything that had taken place just before she'd found the guard's body on her patio. She was still having trouble grasping the reality of what had happened.

Ethan had murdered Steve.

She'd known her ex-husband was a monster. That he seemed to lack a conscience. He'd left her to die in the pit. But in the back of her mind, she'd always thought – hoped anyway – that maybe he would have reconsidered. That after a day or two, he would have gone back to the forest and pulled her from the hole himself. Since she'd been found by hunters the very next morning, she had no way of knowing for sure.

But now he had killed Steve with his own hands. He'd sliced the throat of a man he didn't even know. Had no quarrel with. Just to terrorize her.

An innocent man lay dead. How many more would follow?

Although she hadn't wielded the knife, Ashley felt as though Steve's blood was on her own hands. She should have warned the guard about Ethan. Should have stressed how crafty her ex-husband could be. If she'd given Steve more details about her ex's nature, maybe he would still be alive.

Brett sat in the chair across from her, his face pale. He seemed almost as shaken as Ashley felt. She realized it could have been her fiancé who was killed during the night. He was no doubt thinking the same thing.

She looked up as a uniformed officer entered the room from the foyer, an evidence bag in his hand.

"Think we've found the murder weapon," the officer said as he handed the bag to Detective Lansing.

Ashley gasped. Through the clear plastic, she could see a folding knife with the Briarwood Country Club logo stamped in gold on the ebony wood handle.

Brett's knife.

“You recognize this?” Lansing asked.

“It’s mine,” Brett spoke up. “I won it in a golf tournament last month. It was in the garage cabinet.”

The uniformed officer looked at him. “We found it in your mailbox.”

Ethan had broken into their garage and stolen the knife. Had he been inside their home as well? Ashley remembered the dream she’d had. Hovering in the state between sleep and wakefulness, she’d thought she had seen her ex-husband standing next to her bed. Was it just a dream, or had it been real?

“I think Ethan may have been inside our house last night too,” she told Detective Lansing.

“Anything taken? Or left behind?” he asked.

She could see guilt in the detective’s eyes. He’d already apologized twice for not being able to send a patrol car to their home. She got the impression that he felt partially responsible for Steve’s death.

“No, he didn’t take anything, but I think I saw him in my bedroom. At first I thought I was dreaming, but now …”

“Alabama Highway Patrol says your ex is still in their state,” Lansing said as though trying to reassure her that Ethan was miles away.

“The Alabama police are wrong,” she declared. “Ethan did this – he killed Steve. He’s probably been hiding right here in Briarwood ever since he left the teddy bear at our door.”

“They’ve got sworn statements,” the detective reminded her. “Your ex can’t be in both places. He’s got a partner here.”

Ashley didn’t doubt that Ethan had someone else helping him. But his partners were in Alabama. Her ex-husband was in Briarwood.

“I don’t know who the police in Alabama are chasing – it could be one of his relatives, one that looks a lot like him – but I’m positive it’s not Ethan.”

The detective swiped his fingers across his tablet. She couldn’t tell whether he believed her or not.

“Have your officers found any bubble gum wrappers?” she asked.

The detective looked at her. “Gum wrappers?”

“Ethan is addicted to Buster’s Grape Bubble Gum like some people are addicted to cigarettes.”

Most of the men Ashley knew from Mettler Ridge dipped tobacco. But her ex-husband chewed gum.

Lansing motioned for the officer to go back outside, probably to check whether they'd come across any of the wrappers. Then he turned his attention back to Ashley.

"You said the guard had a radio?" he asked.

"Yes, he gave us a two-way radio so we could keep in touch with him. Just in case something ..." her voice started to break, a knot forming in her throat. The radio had not been able to help Steve. And she feared that nothing – and no one – would be able to help her and Brett now.

"The guard didn't have it on him. It's missing," Lansing said.

A chill ran down Ashley's spine. Her ex-husband had Steve's radio.

"That means Ethan was listening to me this morning – the whole time I was trying to find Steve. This is all a sick twisted game to him."

The radio's signal range couldn't be more than a few miles which meant that her ex-husband had still been close by when she'd called out to the guard. He may have even been in her garage. Hiding and waiting for her to find Steve's body.

Ashley heard Detective Lansing's cell ring.

He checked his phone's screen. "Alabama HP," he announced.

The detective stood up and paced behind the sofa as he spoke on his cell. From his side of the conversation – mostly one-word affirmations – she couldn't decipher what the police officer on the other end was saying. Maybe they were telling him what Ashley already knew. That Ethan was back in Tennessee.

After Detective Lansing disconnected the call, he eased back onto the sofa, an encouraging expression on his face.

"Got a new report," he told her. "Ethan Barrett's in Newsome, Alabama. He was spotted an hour ago. At a campground."

Ashley felt the color drain from her face.

"Quail Falls?" she asked, already knowing the answer.

"Yeah. You've been there?"

"That's the campground where Ethan and I spent our honeymoon. Don't you see what he's doing? This is all a big set up – a fake sighting in order to send me a message. To play with my mind."

Her ex-husband was using the details from their past to torture her. Reminding her that she'd made a vow to love, honor, and obey him. A vow consummated at Quail Falls.

The detective appeared perplexed. He tapped on his tablet.

"You're getting a patrol," he said. "Even if I have to go over my sergeant's head. They can't stay parked here. Not with the budget cuts. But they can drive by every couple of hours."

Ashley appreciated the detective's efforts to keep them safe, but she knew a police patrol wouldn't make a difference. A twenty-four-hour armed guard hadn't been enough. How could a police drive-by help?

She thanked Detective Lansing and walked him to the front door. Brett followed, slipping his arm around Ashley's waist. The first time he'd touched her since finding out about her first marriage.

"I'll call the manager of Steel Armor again," her fiancé told her after the detective had left. "See if he's found another guard."

With the news of Steve's murder spreading like wildfire, the manager of the private security firm had informed Brett that he was having trouble finding someone else willing to take the assignment.

Her fiancé headed toward his study as Ashley walked back into the family room. She wandered to the back door and stared through the glass at the yellow crime-scene tape cordoning off the patio.

Ethan planned to make her suffer. He was playing the ultimate mind game and had every intention of winning. Making a sport of spilling innocent blood, she knew he would drag the game out as long as he could. How many people would he kill? Would Brett be next?

It didn't matter whether or not the security firm sent out another guard. She knew it was time to take matters into her own hands. She had to stop her ex-husband.

Ashley refused to allow another innocent person to die.

She needed to protect Brett, her family, and herself. She had to think like Ethan. Get inside his head. She had to beat him at his own game.

But in order to do so, she would need a gun.

And she knew just where to get one.

CHAPTER FIFTEEN

Ashley banged on the front door of the Appalachian farmhouse, alarmed that her father had failed to answer, wondering where he could be. The red Ford pickup he drove was parked in its normal spot, but there was no sign of Spencer Hope. And his Bluetick hound, Ace, hadn't run to greet her when she'd pulled into the driveway.

She rattled the doorknob. It was locked. Also unusual in the daytime. Both Kyle and Shane worked at the auto shop until five. But per his doctor's orders, her father had taken an extended vacation. He should be home.

The house sat still and quiet.

Too quiet.

The first thought that hit her: her father had suffered another heart attack and had been rushed to the hospital. But if that were the case, either Kyle or Shane would have called her. And it wouldn't explain Ace's absence.

Her next thought …

Ethan.

Fear raced through her as she imagined her father lying helpless and bleeding inside the house. She scolded herself for not phoning him that morning with the news that her ex-husband had murdered the security guard. She should have warned her father that Ethan was now a cold-blooded killer.

She stifled the urge to call out to Spencer. If her ex-husband was lurking somewhere on the property, she didn't want to alert him. Instead, she crept to the window on her right and looked inside. From what she could glimpse through the curtains, nothing seemed out of place in the living room. No overt signs of a struggle. But her view was limited by the armchair wedged next to the window.

Her father was old school; he only had a landline. She pulled out her cell and tapped in his number. If he was hurt, maybe he could crawl to the phone. The muffled ringing echoed through the closed living room window. She counted fifteen rings before disconnecting the call. He was either not inside, or … She didn't want to consider the alternative.

The porch steps squeaked as Ashley made her way back down. She slinked along the side of the house to her father's bedroom. It was impossible for her to peer inside the window – the draperies shut tight. Another red flag. Her father loved waking to the first rays of morning sunlight. He preferred to keep his curtains open.

Panic mounting in her chest, she skulked around the end of the house and crossed to the back door. She twisted the knob. It was locked as well. If her father was inside, he could be dying.

She had to break in.

The shed located in the side yard housed Kyle's workbench. He tinkered with all types of vehicles: cars, motorcycles, boats – anything with a motor. He must have some type of tool she could use to force open one of the doors.

After scanning the boundaries of the yard, making sure she was alone, Ashley ran toward the shed. Just as she reached the door, she heard a rustling in the underbrush at the edge of the woods. A chill hit her.

It could be Ethan.

She dropped to a squat and backed around the corner of the shed. She waited and listened.

After a few seconds, a familiar bark split the air. It was Ace. She jumped up and saw her father's dog loping out of the forest. Spencer trailed behind carrying a fishing pole and a mess of smallmouth bass dangling from a stringer.

Ashley had never been so relieved in her life. She felt a huge smile cross her face.

"I was wondering where you were," she said, hugging her father. "I was worried sick that something had happened to you."

Though some of his color had returned, Spencer still didn't look well.

"Don't be fretting 'bout me. Fine as frog hair."

She wished she could believe him.

"You shouldn't be outside alone, Daddy," she said. "Ethan killed a man last night – at my house in Briarwood."

"Brett's kin?"

"No, he murdered an armed security guard."

Spencer nodded, his lips a thin line. "Don't surprise me none. Devil's in that boy."

"I'm afraid he'll come after you, Kyle, and Shane," she said. "Ethan will do everything he can to make me regret testifying against him."

"We done been expecting him. Counting on it," Spencer said, a smile spreading across his face.

Ashley should have figured as much. Her father was most likely itching to meet up with her ex-husband, had probably rehearsed the encounter in his mind a hundred times. She realized the locked doors and drawn curtains were part of his preparations. She had to be prepared as well.

"I need a pistol, Daddy."

Her father stared at her, a worried glint in his eyes. "You come on back home. Won't nothing happen to you here."

She could tell he was afraid that she might not be able to handle a weapon.

"I can't leave Brett and I know he'd never agree to come here," she explained. "We're staying at a house that belongs to one of his old friends. It's out in the middle of nowhere."

When the security firm had been unable to supply them with a new guard, her fiancé had contacted an old college buddy who owned a house on a private lake. A friend he hadn't seen in years. It would be hard for Ethan to connect the two, making tracking them more difficult.

"I need to be able to protect him," she continued. "And myself."

"Russ can spare Shane at the shop a while. He'll go take care of y'all," he told her, as if the matter was settled.

She shook her head. "Brett would never go for that idea either, not in a million years."

"He ever shoot a gun?"

Ashley tried to recall whether her fiancé had ever mentioned any firearms.

"I don't think so," she said after a moment.

Spencer hesitated, a concerned look on his face. "You sure this is what you want?"

Although she had no experience with a pistol, she knew she could learn. She was her father's daughter after all.

"I wouldn't ask you if I hadn't already thought it through."

He nodded, as though he'd decided to give in. He shifted the stringer of fish to his left hand and pulled up his shirt, revealing the gun holstered at his side.

"Forty-five like this 'un here's a mite big for your hand," he told her and then paused a moment. "Think I got something better up at the house."

Ashley was thankful that no permit was required to conceal carry in Tennessee and that firearms needed no registration. She could leave her father's house with a pistol without breaking any laws.

She followed Spencer through the back door into the kitchen, where he stowed the bass, and then to the gun safe in his bedroom.

"This here's a nine-millimeter," he said as he pulled a pistol from the safe. "Should do you just right."

When she was a teenager, she'd fired a shotgun into the air to scare a fox prowling around their chicken coop, but she'd never fired a pistol. The Smith & Wesson was heavier than she'd expected. Felt foreign in her hand.

Knowing she needed proper instruction, she'd traveled to her father's house rather than purchasing a firearm from a dealer. Without Spencer's help, she'd feared killing herself or some innocent person by accident.

"Can you teach me how to shoot it?" she asked, handing the gun back to him.

Her father smiled. "Come on outside."

Spencer retrieved a box of ammunition from the top shelf of the gun safe and relocked the door. When his back was turned, Ashley pulled out the ten one-hundred-dollar bills she had folded in her pocket and slid them onto the top of his dresser, knowing he would never accept the money if she offered it to him outright. She figured the amount should cover the cost of the pistol, the ammo, and his time. Then she followed her father to the backyard, to the area near the edge of the forest where Kyle and Shane practiced their aim.

Spencer and Ashley worked together lining up empty beer and soda cans on a two-by-four stretched atop two rusty barrels. She enjoyed spending time with him and judging by the smile on his face, it appeared he felt the same.

Her father held out the pistol. "Push this here button, the magazine pops out."

She watched as he loaded the magazine with rounds and snapped it back inside the grip of the pistol.

"This here's the slide. Push it back like so," he said, demonstrating. "Round's chambered. Good to shoot."

After showing her how to work the safety and how to line up the sights, he handed the weapon to Ashley. Gripping the pistol the way her father had instructed, she closed her left eye, fixed the front sight on the middle of a red can, pulled the trigger …

And missed.

Surprised by the intensity of the recoil, she almost stumbled backward. She had known the shot would be loud, having grown up in a family of hunters, but she hadn't realized how amplified the sound would be when holding the weapon in her own hands.

Spencer laughed. "You done gone all tense," he said. "Relax. Breathe in deep. Breathe out slow. Then squeeze."

She nodded. Standing with her feet apart, she focused her vision on the front sight, took a deep breath, exhaled, and then squeezed the trigger.

The clink of metal hitting metal sent a bolt of adrenaline rushing through her.

"I hit it!"

"Yep. Sure did," her father said, his eyes twinkling.

Ashley took her stance again and aligned the sights. When she pulled the trigger, another can fell.

"Good job!" Spencer proclaimed in a loud voice.

The look of pride on her father's face reminded her of her high school graduation. He'd worn the same expression when he'd watched her walk across the stage to receive her diploma.

He met her gaze. In that single moment, they shared a closeness she hadn't felt in years.

The rush of emotion that flooded her must have thrown off her aim, because the next two rounds she fired, she missed.

She remembered all the times she'd watched Kyle and Shane practice. Hitting the target was harder than her brothers had made it look. Of course they'd been shooting since they were children. So had her father.

Not interested in hunting, she'd never wanted to be taught before. Now it was going to take her a while to get the hang of it. The ability to shoot well obviously wasn't hereditary.

Ashley fired off several rounds, missing almost as many cans as she hit. About halfway through the box of ammo, she realized she'd become comfortable with the pistol. Liked the weight of it in her hands.

“Thank you, Daddy,” she said, grateful not only for the lesson, but also for the time they’d spent together.

“You stay for supper. Let me fry us up some fish.”

“I wish I could,” she said – and meant it. “But I have a few errands to run before I meet Brett back at the lake house.”

“Don’t you be out after dark,” Spencer said, giving her a hug. The gleam in his eyes telling her that he was proud to have her as a daughter.

As they walked back toward her father’s house, Ashley thought about her fiancé and hoped he was safe. He’d had an appointment scheduled with one of his biggest clients and it was too late to cancel. He’d texted her earlier – right as she pulled into her father’s driveway – confirming he also had dinner plans with the client. Brett didn’t expect to be back at the lake house before eight. Not wanting to worry her fiancé, she hadn’t told him where she’d gone. She’d left him a note just in case he arrived back at the house first.

Ethan would be searching for them. She was worried he may have already located Brett’s parents, thinking they might go there. She’d risk her own life to protect her fiancé and his family members. But she realized shooting at aluminum cans couldn’t prepare her for the ordeal of firing at flesh and blood.

If she came face-to-face with her ex-husband – if it was her life or his – would she be able to pull the trigger? Could she actually kill another human being?

If she had to shoot Ethan in order to defend someone she loved, she hoped she could muster the strength. But even if she found the courage to pull the trigger, she feared she lacked the skill to hit the target.

“Goodbye, Daddy,” she said, hugging him again. She looked into his eyes, “I love you.”

“Love you, too, baby girl.” She could feel the warmth of truth in his words.

Ashley hopped into her sedan and buckled the seatbelt. She returned her father’s goodbye wave as she pulled out of his driveway. She hadn’t told him that one of the errands she needed to run was in Mettler Ridge. That she planned to turn the tables on her ex-husband.

Now it was time for Ashley to track Ethan.

CHAPTER SIXTEEN

The sedan rocked as Ashley's tire hit a rut on the gravel lane leading into the trailer park that was once her home. Her stomach tightened as she remembered the night that she'd packed her things and fled, thinking she would never return. Not much had changed since then. Although the occupants were likely different, the trailers seemed the same. Weatherworn and tired, yards littered with children's toys and rusty outdoor furniture.

Dodging potholes, she rounded the curve and drove past the rental office toward the rear of the park. To the trailer at the dead end.

The home she'd shared with Ethan.

As she pulled along the side of the lane to park, she noticed that their old place hadn't fared as well as the other trailers. The roof sagged and the wooden front stoop appeared ready to collapse. She wondered about the people living there now and hoped their lives were happier than hers had been.

But she didn't come to inspect her old home; she'd driven here to see Jesse. She'd heard from one of her cousins that Ethan's old drinking buddy and his girlfriend, Lou Ann, still lived in the park after all these years. Ashley could recall many nights when Ethan had stumbled through their bedroom door – so drunk he could hardly stand – after hitting the local bar with their neighbor.

In a normal relationship, most wives would resent a man for keeping their husband out until the wee hours, but looking back, Ashley realized she had actually been grateful to Jesse. While they were out, she was allowed several hours of quiet peace. And when Ethan did manage to come home, he'd be too far gone to perform sexually, passing out almost as soon as his head touched the pillow.

Ashley had been friendly with Lou Ann and had considered her to be a kind-hearted person, but the two women had never had the opportunity to become close. Ethan had made sure of that. He'd invented a slew of daily chores that kept Ashley far too busy for a social life.

A green pickup truck and a white coupe sat next to the couple's trailer signaling they were likely both at home. Just like they were the night the sheriff's deputy had driven Ashley back to her trailer to collect her things. Jesse and Lou Ann had watched in silence from their front porch.

Fighting to push aside the images of her last night here, Ashley took a deep breath and counted to ten. Her memories cut deep, but to have any hope of winning Ethan's game, she would have to face certain parts of her past.

She climbed the porch steps and knocked on Jesse's door. Music mixed with explosions and gunfire leaked from the trailer's walls. She wasn't sure whether the sounds emanated from a television show or a video game.

After a few seconds, the door cracked open and Lou Ann's head popped out. Surprise flashed in her eyes.

"Ashley, is that you?" she said, stepping onto the porch. "I ain't seen you in ages."

Her old neighbor seemed stuck in time. The thirty-something woman's straight red hair still flowed to her narrow waist as it had all those years before, and her makeup-free skin appeared creamy and smooth. *Coconut oil*, Ashley remembered. Lou Ann had sworn it was an anti-aging miracle and evidentally she'd been right.

"How have you been, Lou Ann?"

"Been doing fine. Still working at the diner," she said, studying Ashley's face. "Damn, girl. You sure do look different. I can tell by your eyes you ain't that same meek little thing who hightailed it out of here with the deputy that night."

Ashley assumed the comment was intended to be a compliment. "Yeah, that was a long time ago," she said.

"What brings you to these parts? Heard you was a city girl now."

"I'm trying to find Ethan."

Lou Ann wrinkled her nose. "He ain't been here," she said, her eyes letting Ashley know it was the truth.

Her old neighbor had never liked Ethan, even before she learned of his abusive ways. It was as if she'd sensed the evil in him and knew to stay away. Although Jesse traveled on the wrong side of the law, he'd always seemed to treat Lou Ann well. With respect.

"I was hoping I could talk to Jesse and find out if he's heard anything."

Just because her ex-husband hadn't shown up on their doorstep didn't mean he wasn't in contact with his old buddy.

Lou Ann glanced back over her shoulder at the open door. “He’s playing C.O.D.”

“C.O.D?”

“Call of Duty,” she smiled. “Been trying to level up all day.”

Neither Ashley nor Brett played video games, but she knew some people reveled in them, spending all their free time in a virtual-reality world.

“Is he still … in the delivery business?” she asked her old neighbor.

The delivery business was code for how Jesse made his money. A couple of times a week he’d travel to Chattanooga with an order to steal a certain type of car. Then he’d deliver the car to a chop shop near the county line.

Lou Ann laughed. “Afraid so. He’d go straight if there was work. But ain’t none around here. Not that pays anything.”

Ashley nodded. “Would you please ask him if he’ll talk to me for a minute? I’ll make it worth his time.”

A light came on in Lou Ann’s eyes when she realized Ashley was willing to pay for the information.

“I guess I could.”

She disappeared inside the trailer, pushing the door closed behind her. Ashley couldn’t hear their voices, but after a few minutes, the rumbling from the video game stopped.

Jesse ambled out onto the porch. Time had not been as kind to him as it had been to Lou Ann. His brown hair had thinned on top, and he’d gained a few pounds in his midsection.

“You looking for Ethan?” he asked.

She nodded. “I was hoping that maybe you would know where he’s at.”

He looked at Ashley, his eyes squinting as a half-smile crossed his face.

“I might,” he said. “But I might not.”

She couldn’t tell from his expression whether he had any actual information, but she had no other leads, no one else she felt safe contacting.

“I’ll give you a hundred dollars if you’ll tell me what you know.” It was all the cash Ashley had left on her.

He stepped toward her. “What’s to stop me from just taking it?” he asked, a wicked glint in his eyes.

She reached for the pistol at her waist, lifted her shirt just enough so he could see the weapon nestled in the new holster she'd just purchased.

"Whoa, hold up there, girl." he said, stepping back, his palms raised toward her. "I was just playing."

From what she remembered of Jesse, she doubted he would have actually tried to rob her, but he most likely thought the threat would be enough to net him the cash. The fact that he'd tried the tactic made her suspect that he had no idea of Ethan's whereabouts. No information to trade.

"Can you help me or not?" she asked.

He rubbed his chin. "I don't rightly know where he is now. But I seen him."

A seed of hope sprang up in her chest. "When and where?"

"Last night. About nine or so. On Fenton Hill Road near your daddy's place."

He must have gone to her father's house after leaving the bear on her patio. Finding out she wasn't at home, he may have thought she was in Mettler Ridge.

"Are you sure it was Ethan and not someone else?"

"Yep. It was him. I didn't know he'd broke out yet when I seen him. He was crossing the road and my truck lights hit him. Looked straight at me. Then ran off in the woods."

"Do you have any idea where he could be hiding out?"

He shook his head. "Naw. Maybe with some of his kin?"

Ashley knew that the police would have checked Ethan's relatives' homes first. One or more of them were probably helping him, but he was too smart to hide on any of their properties. They were a tight-knit group. She knew they wouldn't give her any information and seeking them out could even be dangerous.

She pulled a one-hundred-dollar bill and a slip of paper from her pocket. "I've written down my phone number. If you hear anything, or see Ethan again, call me and I'll make it worth your while."

Taking one last glance at the decrepit mobile home that still tortured her dreams, Ashley climbed back into her car. As she circled the dead end of the lane, her cell phone rang. She checked the screen.

No Caller ID

Whoever was calling her had blocked their number.

She stared at the phone, wondering if she should answer. It was probably just a telemarketer.

"Hello?"

At first she thought there was no one on the other end. She was about to hang up when a voice broke the silence, chilling her to the bone.

"See you soon," the caller said and then disconnected.

It was a voice she knew well.

Ethan.

Ashley scanned the trailer park, her pulse racing. Did her ex-husband know she was in Mettler Ridge? She had to make sure she wasn't being followed. And she had to get back to the lake house – fast.

CHAPTER SEVENTEEN

Still shaken from hearing Ethan's voice on the phone, Ashley traveled up the tree-lined driveway to the lake house. She'd contacted Detective Lansing on the way and had filled him in on both the call from her ex-husband and his sighting in Mettler Ridge. With reports continuing to mount in Alabama, the detective believed Ethan was no longer in Tennessee. And there was no physical evidence tying her ex-husband to Steve's murder which made Lansing think his killer-partner theory was viable.

Ashley wasn't convinced.

As she approached the house, her headlights cut through the darkness illuminating the carport. The space was empty. She glanced at the clock and saw that it was almost nine. Brett was running an hour late.

When her sedan rolled to a stop, she pulled out her phone and fired off a text to her fiancé.

Are you okay?

She refused to allow herself to believe that Ethan was the reason for Brett's absence. Maybe the client had wanted to go for drinks after dinner. Or Brett could have stopped back by his office.

As she grabbed her purse, her phone chimed. It was her fiancé answering her text.

On my way.

Relieved to hear from him so quickly, she gathered a few of the bags of groceries she'd bought and headed into the house. Built in a style she would call modern rustic, the house featured lots of wood and glass. There was a security system, a thick grove of trees on each side, and the lake with a dock in the back. The nearest neighbor lived at least a mile down the road.

Although they no longer had a guard for protection, the fact that they were ensconced in the woods in the middle of nowhere with no way for anyone to connect them to the property, made Ashley feel safer than she had in Briarwood.

And now she carried the pistol.

The holster hung lodged inside the waistband of her jeans. As long as she wore her shirt untucked, the weapon should go undetected. And the lake house afforded her a place to practice her aim. She'd purchased a pack of paper targets and additional ammunition at the firearms store in Mettler Ridge. Now she just had to break the news that she'd acquired a gun to her fiancé. She wasn't quite sure how he'd react.

Heading back to the car, she brought in the remainder of the groceries and stocked the fridge. She wandered out onto the front porch, sank onto the top step, and waited in the darkness for Brett.

Two questions had plagued her on the drive to the lake house: how had Ethan obtained her cell number, and how had he managed to locate her address in Briarwood so soon after escaping from prison? She guessed he could have found out Brett's name from one of her ex's relatives in Mettler Ridge, but where would they get the information? She knew her brothers and cousins wouldn't give anyone even remotely connected to Ethan the time of day. She hadn't kept in touch with anyone else from her past and to preserve her privacy, she didn't post on social media. And yet, he'd found her.

Her ex-husband's ability to obtain her phone number stumped her even more. She'd switched her cell company when they'd moved to Briarwood. Brett had added her to his account, changing her number. She hadn't given it to anyone outside her immediate family.

Until today.

She'd written it on the slip of paper she'd handed to Jesse. But not more than five minutes had passed between the time she'd given him the number and the time Ethan had called. Had her ex-husband been hiding in her old neighbors' trailer?

Lou Ann had seemed so convincing when she'd said Ethan hadn't been to their home. Ashley remembered the scowl on her face and the look in her eyes at the mention of his name. No, she didn't believe her ex-husband had been there. Ethan must have another source.

Someone was feeding him information. But who?

Headlights flashed at the end of the driveway. Ashley watched as the beams cut through the trees heading toward her. Her breath caught in her throat as she realized the silhouette of the vehicle didn't match Brett's SUV. It was a sedan.

She sprang from the porch steps and slipped around the corner of the house, ducking behind a boxwood shrub. With a clear view into the carport, she hid and waited. She wondered if it was Brett's old college friend. But it seemed rather late in the evening for him to check on them.

The sedan pulled into the carport. When the door opened, the car's interior light switched on, illuminating the driver. Her fiancé climbed out lugging his laptop bag across his shoulder. He had a white box in his hand.

Ashley emerged from her hiding spot.

"Where's your SUV?" she asked him.

He smiled in the moonlight. "At the airport. I rented this car to throw your ex off our trail. We should get you a rental in the morning."

It was a good idea. Ethan had been inside their garage. He'd seen the vehicles they owned.

"He called me today," she announced.

"He what?" her fiancé asked, shock on his face. "What did he say?"

Ashley trembled as she remembered Ethan's words. "He said, 'I'll see you soon,' and then he hung up."

"Did you tell the detective?"

"Yes, but there's no way of knowing where Ethan was calling from. He blocked the number, and he was probably using a burner phone anyway."

Her ex-husband wasn't stupid enough to give away his location. He'd known the call couldn't be traced.

Brett nodded.

"I brought you something from the restaurant," he said after a moment, handing her the box.

Knowing her fiancé, it was likely dessert.

"Thank you," she said, smiling.

Brett walked behind her into the house. She headed to the kitchen, stashed the box in the refrigerator, and then returned to the living room.

Her fiancé dropped his laptop bag on the sofa. "My day's been hectic," he told her. "Think I'll get some sleep."

Brett had left his suitcase in the living room earlier when they'd first checked out the lake house. He grabbed it from the corner and strolled down the hallway. Both guest rooms were upstairs. He was heading toward the master bedroom.

Ashley followed.

"Does this mean that you're claiming this bedroom?" she asked. "Or …"

"I'm still hurt," he said, his expression serious. "But I love you, Ashley. Maybe we can work things out."

Hope filled her heart. "I'm sorry for everything – for dragging you into this mess."

"I know."

He pulled back the bedcovers and began to undress, his eyes appearing heavy. The way he looked, he'd fall asleep the minute he lay down.

Ashley felt dusty from her day of shooting. She realized she'd forgotten to tell him about the pistol. Since he seemed tired, the discussion could wait until morning.

"I'm going to take a shower," she told him as he slipped into bed.

In the master bathroom, she noticed a large jar of lavender bath salts next to the whirlpool tub. A hot soak might be just what she needed. She opened the faucets, adjusted the water temperature, and dumped a scoop of salts into the tub. When she returned to the bedroom to get her hairbrush, she heard Brett snoring. She envied his ability to fall asleep so fast. Smiling, she pushed the bathroom door closed to keep the light from bothering him.

She sank into the warm water and switched on the jets. Just as she started to feel the tension leaving her body, she heard her cell ring.

A pang of dread hit her. It could be Ethan.

She grabbed her phone from the stool next to the tub and checked the caller ID. She was relieved to see Detective Lansing's name on the screen. Given the late hour, she knew the call must be important.

She answered before the second ring. "Hello?"

"Ashley, it's Lansing," he identified himself. "You know a guy named Ray Wilson? From Chattanooga?" the detective asked her.

She was familiar with the name, but she could only remember seeing the man once – maybe twice.

"He and Ethan are cousins," she said, "but they've never been close."

"You sure?"

She paused, wondering which statement he was questioning. "I'm sure that they're related and I'm also sure Ethan doesn't like Ray."

"They spend time together?"

She thought for a moment. "If they did, I wasn't aware of it. There's a lot of hostility between the two of them. It all goes back to the day Ethan's father, William, died. He and Ray's father, Doug, were out drinking. Doug was supposed to pick Ray up from football practice

– both Ray and Ethan were in high school at the time. Anyway, William decided to ride along with Doug. And they never made it. They crashed into a tree."

"Killed them both?"

"Yes. And Ethan feels like it's Ray's fault. He's always said that Ray owes him."

Lansing paused a moment. "Looks like he might have paid up."

She wondered what Ray had done that made the detective think the score had been evened. Had Ethan somehow talked his cousin into helping him escape from prison? Was Ray supplying him with money and a place to hide out?

"What do you mean?"

"You ever meet Ray?"

"I know he was at a family reunion that Ethan and I attended not long after we were married. I may have seen him once after that, but I'm not sure."

"He's a ringer for your ex."

She tried to picture Ray's face in her mind. Her memory was fuzzy, but she recalled that their bone structure was similar. With Ethan's hair cut short now, they probably did look a lot alike.

"Do the police in Alabama think that Ray is the person they've been chasing?" she asked, certain that she already knew the answer.

"Looks like it."

"Do they know where Ray is now?"

"Alabama HP found him earlier today. Near Quail Falls Campground."

"Did they bring him in for questioning? Does he know where Ethan is hiding?"

The detective hesitated a moment.

"Ray's dead," he said.

CHAPTER EIGHTEEN

Doctor Charles Fisher stripped off his bloody scrubs, along with the surgical cap covering his salt-and-pepper hair, and tossed them into the locker room hamper in the labor and delivery unit of Cedar View Medical Center.

"Heard you had a rough night," Doctor Gains – the skinny intern who reminded Charles of Bob Denver from Gilligan's Island – commented as he pulled a bag of chocolate chip cookies from one of the lockers.

The rumor was true; it had been a difficult night. Called in for what he thought would be a routine birth, Charles had instead encountered a life-endangering hurdle.

"I had to perform an emergency Caesarian," he said. "The umbilical cord prolapsed – became compressed between the fetus and the mother's cervix. Almost cut off the baby's oxygen supply."

The infant's heartrate had plummeted, and Charles feared they would lose her. To his relief, now at two a.m., both the newborn and her mother slept in comfort, unharmed by the near-fatal complication.

"Glad I wasn't shadowing you tonight," Gains said.

The intern held out the bag of cookies.

Charles shook his head.

As he dressed into his long-sleeved shirt and slacks, his thoughts turned to his own daughter, due to give birth in just two short weeks. The pending arrival of his first grandchild thrilled him more than he ever believed possible. A baby boy his daughter and her husband had named Jacob Charles. The honor of having his name passed down warmed his heart and filled him with pride. His wife of thirty-one years, Cindy, was just as excited. The joy on her face had mirrored his own when they'd first heard the news. And helping their daughter prepare for their new grandson had become Cindy's primary focus over the last nine months. His family was indeed his greatest blessing.

Thunder rumbled in the distance as Charles pushed through the physicians' access door, exiting into the storm-washed night. Rain no longer fell from the sky, but the thick air clung to him like a wet blanket. He trudged down the sidewalk lined with orange cones that blocked off the main section of the staff parking area. With a repaving project underway, he'd been forced to park in the lot around the corner from the labor and delivery wing.

When the sidewalk ended, he stepped out of the bright lights surrounding the physicians' entrance and onto the dimmer-lit pavement. Dodging puddles, he navigated his way past a row of blue dumpsters.

Hearing a noise behind him, he looked back over his shoulder.

Footsteps?

He was almost certain he'd heard someone walking near the dumpsters, but now could see no one behind him.

The hairs on the back of his neck sprang upright.

It was possibly a destitute person who'd been digging in the trash. But he knew that not all of the homeless were harmless. A mentally ill vagrant had murdered one of the hospital's nurses the year before.

He increased his pace and rounded the corner of the building.

Stunned, he stopped and stared at the empty space between Doctor Lee's SUV and Doctor Singh's convertible. Hours earlier, Charles had parked his Audi sedan between his two colleagues' automobiles.

Someone had stolen his car.

He reached into his pocket and pulled out his cell. He hated to wake Cindy, but he needed to let her know about the theft. He'd have to file a report, and it might take a while for the police to arrive.

Hearing another noise behind him, he swung back around toward the medical center.

"Hi Doc."

A burly man with a buzz cut, dressed in hospital scrubs, stood in the shadow of the building. A knife in his hand.

Charles's heart pounded in his chest. First his car, now his money. But neither was worth his life.

"If you want my wallet, you're welcome to it, just let me go back inside the hospital."

"Your phone," the man ordered.

"Of course; it's yours."

He tossed his cell toward the man expecting him to catch it, but the guy stood motionless as the phone crashed onto the pavement. His cell was the latest model – worth over a grand – but the man had made no attempt to save it.

Panic swept through Charles as he realized the encounter was more than a simple robbery.

"What do you want?" he asked the man, trying to hide his fear.

"You killed my kid."

Charles had been fortunate. He'd only delivered three stillborn infants during the course of his medical career. The faces of all three of the babies' fathers were etched into his memory. The man standing before him now was a stranger.

"I think you have me confused with another doctor."

"Gonna carve you up," the man said. "Same way you cut up my kid."

Cut up? Did he mean an abortion? Charles had never performed an abortion. He had to calm the man down. Reason with him.

"I don't know what you're talking about, but I'll help you," he said. "Come inside the hospital and we'll find out what happened to your child."

"Don't need help," the man said, wild eyed. "You do."

The man lunged toward him.

Charles raced behind Doctor Lee's SUV. A tall chain-link fence bordered the parking lot, trapping him on three sides. To escape, he'd have to get past the guy with the knife and run back to the medical center.

As the man bounded around the side of the SUV, Charles flew in front of Doctor Singh's convertible. He slammed both his fists down on the hood. The car alarm erupted – blared into the night. He doubted the siren could be heard inside the medical center, but it was worth a shot.

Seeming surprised by the alarm's squeal, the man hesitated, granting Charles an opening. The doctor bolted toward the hospital.

As he neared the corner of the building, his foot hit a puddle. He slid across the slick pavement and tumbled backwards. Landed hard.

On the ground, his gaze snapped back over his shoulder. The crazed man marched across the parking lot – laughing.

Fear rising in his chest, Charles pushed himself to his feet. Pain shot through his coccyx. He'd also sprained his right ankle. In his condition, he couldn't outrun the man. Would never make it to the physicians' entrance in time.

He'd have to find a place to hide.

Charles limped around the corner of the medical center. He headed for the row of blue dumpsters. If he ducked behind the bins, he'd be caught. He lacked the proper keycard to open the service door located at the top of the ramp to his right. But the guy chasing him couldn't know that. Although the man wore scrubs, he wasn't a hospital employee. He wasn't wearing a badge.

Charles pushed up the lid of the dumpster closest to the building, squared his palms on the edge of the opening and jumped inside. As he pulled the lid closed, the stench from the rotting garbage in the bags beneath him wafted upward. His stomach churned and a knot formed in his chest as he waited in the darkness.

After a few seconds, he heard footsteps.

He strained his ears as the man circled the bins and then strode up the concrete ramp.

Silence as the guy paused. Maybe he was checking the door, probably noticing the keycard reader on the wall.

Footsteps again as the man stepped back down the ramp and walked a line in front of the four dumpsters. Charles heard the lid of one of the bins creak open. Rustling. Then a metallic clank as the lid slammed back down.

Sweat soaked his shirt. Dripped from his forehead. As he listened to the second dumpster being searched, Charles dug his hands under the plastic bags beneath him and lifted them up on top of his body. Careful not to make a sound, he covered himself with as many bags as he could without cutting off his air supply.

The second lid clanked shut.

The man moved to the third bin. Charles heard the creaking of the cover as it opened, but then there was silence. No sounds of a search. Was the dumpster empty? Or had the guy decided to stop?

The third lid crashed down.

Charles held his breath. Heard the man move in front of the final bin. His senses shifted into overdrive, his pulse racing.

The lid of the dumpster groaned open.

He felt the slight rock of the bin and the weight shift of the bags being rearranged on top of his body.

Cool air hit him as the guy lifted the bags from his head and chest.

Terror gripped Charles as he stared into the cold eyes of a madman.

"Bye, Doc."

As the maniac raised the knife, the faces of Cindy and his daughter flashed into Charles's mind. He didn't want to abandon the loves of his life. He threw up his arms in defense, but the man struck hard.

Charles felt a jolt of pain as the blade severed his aorta. Then the darkness rushed in to claim him.

CHAPTER NINETEEN

"Ethan killed another man – his cousin," Ashley told Brett as he stumbled into the kitchen of the lake house, appearing still half asleep.

She was glad her fiancé had been able to rest. It was only seven o'clock, but she'd been up for almost two hours. A nightmare had woken her – Ethan standing beside her bed again – and although she'd tried, she couldn't fall back to sleep.

"Are you serious?" he asked, his eyes opening wide as though the information had jolted him awake. "His own relative?"

It seemed that getting his revenge was more important to her ex-husband than the life of someone who shared his own blood.

Ashley nodded. "All those sightings in Alabama weren't of Ethan. It was his cousin, Ray, and now he's dead."

She'd warned Detective Lansing that the police were chasing a look-a-like, and she'd been right.

"When did it happen?"

"Sometime yesterday. A hiker found him at the foot of a cliff near Quail Falls Campground."

Ray must have been hanging out there waiting for further instructions. Evidently, her ex-husband had decided he no longer needed his cousin's help.

"Ethan pushed him?"

"Well, Detective Lansing said the police think it's possible he may have accidentally fallen, but I don't buy that for a second. Ethan did it."

She realized her ex-husband had made sure no one could conclusively link him to either of the two murders he'd committed.

Ashley handed Brett a cup of coffee and then carried two plates topped with scrambled eggs and toast to the kitchen table.

Her fiancé slid into his chair. "So Ethan really is in Alabama now?"

"Well, he was. I mean he'd have to be to kill his cousin, but that was yesterday. I'm betting he's back in Tennessee by now."

Her ex-husband was probably searching for them in Briarwood. Or in Belle Haven where Brett's parents lived.

Her fiancé nodded and then shoved a fork laden with eggs into his mouth.

"What time did you want to go to the rental car agency?" she asked him, wondering if they opened early.

She needed to tell him about the pistol, hoped he would go outside with her and watch her practice shooting. But she didn't know how he'd react to the idea of her carrying a gun and she wanted to time the conversation right.

He appeared to think for a moment. "There's some work I need to take care of first. Let's go after lunch."

She was glad Brett had decided to stay away from the office for a few days. When Ethan realized they'd fled from their home, the building where her fiancé worked would likely be the first place on his stakeout list.

Nodding, she swallowed a bite of toast. But as soon as it went down, her stomach knotted. The food threatened to come right back up. Her anxiety had killed her appetite the past few days. She'd probably lost five pounds.

She pushed away from the table.

"You okay?" Brett asked.

"It's just my nerves; they're making me nauseous."

She ran to the master bathroom, raising the lid of the toilet just in time. When she'd finished throwing up, she took a washcloth from the linen closet and drenched her face with cold water. Her reflection still reminded her of a ghost – pale skin and haunted eyes. She knew she wasn't getting enough rest with her sleep constantly being interrupted by nightmares. At least when she woke, she could curl up next to Brett again.

When she trudged back through the living room, her fiancé was sitting in the armchair next to the fireplace typing on his laptop. Ashley definitely couldn't interrupt his work to tell him about the gun. She'd wait until they returned from the rental agency. She headed for the kitchen to clear the breakfast plates. When she got there, she found the task already done. Brett had rinsed the dishes and placed them into the dishwasher. His considerate act reminded her once again how much she loved him.

Ashley scooped her tablet and cell phone from the counter, padded through the living room – careful not to disturb her fiancé – and slipped out the sliding glass door onto the covered back deck. A thunderstorm had blown through during the night ushering in morning air that felt fresh and clean. She plopped onto a lounge chair and woke her tablet.

She scanned the Nashville news sites checking for updates on the manhunt for her ex-husband. Finding nothing, she had decided to change her search to Alabama when a headline caught her eye.

Cedar View Doctor Murdered

When she tapped the link, the doctor's photo popped up. Ashley felt a chill run through her. She recognized him. Guilt filled her heart. She was sure Ethan had struck again. An innocent man – with a loving family who needed him – had been murdered. And again, she was to blame. She grabbed her cell and called the detective.

"Lansing," he answered after the second ring.

"Hi, it's Ashley. I just read an article about a murder in Cedar View – Dr. Charles Fisher," she told him. "It happened last night. I think Ethan did it."

"Yeah? Why?" Lansing asked.

She took a deep breath, bracing herself for the questions that would likely follow.

"When Ethan went to prison … I was pregnant," she said. "Dr. Fisher was my OB/GYN."

The detective paused. "That's it?"

Ashley knew he was likely thinking the doctor had hundreds of patients. That she was connecting dots that didn't exist.

"Hear me out," she said. "After Ethan murdered Steve, he could have killed Brett and me – there was no one to stop him – but he didn't. He's toying with me. Throwing our past together in my face. First the teddy bear and then the fake sighting at Quail Falls Campground. Now this."

"Maybe. But why the doctor?"

She sighed, not wishing to go into the details. "Because Ethan wanted a child. He might think that it's Dr. Fisher's fault he doesn't have one."

"Okay. I get it."

She doubted the detective understood. Figured that she'd jumped to the wrong conclusion.

"No, I don't think you do, but that's not important. Just please, contact the Cedar View police and ask them to check whether Ethan was seen at the hospital last night."

She knew they must have surveillance cameras mounted all around the building.

"All right. Consider it done," the detective relented.

"Thank you."

She hoped the Cedar View PD would take the information seriously. At least she knew the tip would carry more weight coming from a detective rather than a concerned ex-wife.

"You should fly to Aruba. Or Tahiti," Lansing said. "Stay gone until your ex is caught."

The idea sounded wonderful. She'd like to leave tonight. Take her father and brothers along with them, but her fiancé wanted to stay in Tennessee.

"If I could get Brett to agree, I'd go in a heartbeat," she told the detective. "But he thinks we're safe here at the lake house."

"Hope he's right. Think it over."

"I will."

Ashley disconnected the call. She knew Ethan had murdered Dr. Fisher. Could feel it in her bones. She wished she could have anticipated her ex-husband's last move. If she'd been able to figure out his plan, she could have warned Detective Lansing. The doctor might still be alive.

Who would Ethan target next? Brett seemed unlikely. Her ex-husband had passed on his first – and likely easiest – chance at her fiancé the night he killed Steve. He was probably planning to save Brett for last. Knowing how much the loss would hurt her.

Maybe he would attack her father or brothers. She wasn't sure.

One thing she did know for certain. Now that Dr. Fisher was dead, she couldn't postpone the conversation she'd dreaded any longer. Her past was catching up with her – fast. And she feared Brett would be crushed by the fallout. She had to dampen the blow. Ashley couldn't let him find out about the tragedy she'd suffered from someone else. She needed to come clean with her fiancé.

Open her old wounds. Confess everything.

All of her secrets.

CHAPTER TWENTY

Prepared to rip open her deepest wound, Ashley forced herself up off the deck chair and through the sliding glass door into the living room of the lake house. Regardless of the amount of pain her memories thrust upon her, she had to recall them. Brett deserved to know everything about her life. Especially now.

But along with the anguish she felt reliving her past, she also feared her confession would shatter what remained of her relationship with her fiancé. Just when he seemed on the verge of forgiving her. She took a deep breath and then strode across the room toward Brett's chair. Instead of looking up, he kept his eyes glued to his laptop's screen as his fingers danced across the keyboard.

"I need to talk to you," she said. "It's something that can't wait."

Brett met her gaze. "Another murder?"

"Yes," she said, struggling to keep her composure, aware her distress showed on her face.

"Not your dad?"

Ashley shook her head. "My family's alright for now," she assured him.

Her fiancé closed his laptop and slid it onto the side table, giving her his full attention.

She perched on the edge of the ottoman in front of his chair.

"Ethan killed a doctor last night … my doctor," she said.

A puzzled look sprang to his face. "Your doctor? Why?"

Images of the night she'd awoken in bed – her stomach cramping and her sheets soaked in blood – flooded Ashley's mind. Tears gushed from her eyes and flowed down her cheeks. Brett wrapped his arms around her.

"Ashley, it's okay," he said. "You're safe. We're safe."

She realized he assumed her tears were caused by fear. Not knowing that her heart was being torn apart again, just as it had been all those years ago. She pulled away, needing to look into his eyes, to see his expression when she told him the truth. She wiped her face with the backs of her hands.

"Nine years ago, when I was still married to Ethan …"

A sob hit her, forced her throat closed. Despite what she'd been told, the ache in her soul hadn't diminished over the course of the years. It was just as strong now.

"Take your time," her fiancé said, his voice soft.

Brett's compassion made revealing her secret even more difficult. She feared learning that she'd carried another man's child might hurt him. One of the reasons she'd waited so long. She'd always hoped she would be able to spare him the pain of finding out.

Ashley caught her breath. Wiped her tears again.

"There's no easy way to say this. Nine years ago … I found out I was pregnant."

She'd tried to convince herself that once the words were out that she'd feel better, that she could be more objective, but instead the wound felt even fresher.

A stunned look crossed her fiancé's face, followed by ire. He shot up from the chair.

"You're telling me you have a child?" he yelled.

She shook her head. "No, I don't."

"How could you hide this from me?"

Brett paced in front of the fireplace as though he hadn't heard her denial. Was he even listening to her?

"I don't have a child," she repeated, a new wave of tears hitting her. "My baby died."

The loss of her daughter had cut Ashley to her core. Leaving a gash in her heart that would never heal.

Her fiancé continued to pace as though he'd tuned her out completely.

"Did you hear what I said?" she asked him.

She was baring her soul to him, recounting the darkest hours of her life, and he wouldn't even respond.

He stared at her; his eyes narrowed. "I heard you."

She took several deep breaths in an attempt to calm down, and then rose from the ottoman. She needed to explain about the murder.

"I think Ethan blamed Dr. Fisher –"

"You know what, Ashley?" he interrupted. "I'm sick of this. You just keep betraying me."

She hated that he saw the omission as a betrayal. Hated herself for causing him pain.

"I'm sorry I kept my pregnancy from you, but can't you see how much it hurts me to talk about it?"

She wished he could understand. Could realize that recalling her miscarriage shredded her soul even now. As though it was happening all over again.

"That doesn't matter."

"Are you kidding me? Do you really think it doesn't matter that I lost a child?"

How could he be so callous?

"That's not what I meant," he said.

She couldn't believe he was discounting her feelings as though they weren't important.

"Every time I think about what happened – about my baby – I feel a part of myself die."

She felt it now, as though a chunk of her heart was disintegrating.

He folded his arms across his chest. "You still should have told me."

It appeared as though he wasn't even willing to consider her side of the situation.

"You make it seem black and white, but it's not," she told him. "I've spent years trying to forget that time in my life. To put my past behind me and move forward. Can't you understand that I wish those days had never happened?"

"But they did," he said. "And you didn't tell me. I don't know who you are anymore."

If she had told him about her miscarriage when they'd first started dating, would it have changed anything? Would it have kept him from falling in love with her?

She nodded. "You're right, I can't wish those days away – they did happen. And they scarred me for life. But everything I've gone through has made me the person I am right now. The same person you fell in love with. I haven't changed."

He stared at her, shook his head.

"I have to get out of here," he announced.

Brett marched from the living room down the hall and into the master bedroom. Ashley followed. Watched him grab his carry-on suitcase.

She didn't understand his reasoning – why he'd decided to run away rather than staying and talking through their problems like an adult.

"It's not safe for you to leave – not with Ethan still out there." she said.

He threw his suitcase onto the bed. "I don't give a damn about your ex-husband."

She couldn't just let him go. The risk of Ethan finding him was too great.

"If you need space for a while then let me leave. I'll go to my dad's house, and you can stay here where it's safe."

Brett shoved a stack of shirts into his carry-on.

"I don't care what you do, Ashley," he said. "Go. Stay. Whatever. It doesn't matter. I'm still leaving."

He continued to pack.

She wished he'd change his mind. If he stayed at the lake house, Ethan would have a harder time locating him.

"Where are you going?" she asked.

He didn't reply. He closed his suitcase and jerked it from the bed. She followed him down the hallway and into the living room, wishing he would talk to her.

"So you don't want to tell me where you're going?"

He could at least have the decency of letting her know where he'd be in case something happened.

"I don't know yet," he finally said. He crammed his laptop into its carry bag, flinging the strap over his shoulder.

She followed him out the front door and onto the porch, wondering if there was anything she could say that would change his mind and get him to stay. Not being able to think of any words that would make a difference, she watched him throw his bags into the rental car. He climbed inside the driver's seat and slammed the door.

As Brett sped down the driveway and onto the road, tears sprang to Ashley's eyes and spilled over her cheeks. Did he plan on coming back? Or was this the end?

She'd never dreamed their relationship would reach this point. How could a love that had felt so strong in the beginning end up being so fragile? Brett had complained that he didn't know who she was anymore. But in Ashley's eyes, he was the one who had changed. He wasn't the same man now as he'd been when he asked her to marry him.

The change had been gradual, but she'd first noticed a difference in him about a month after they'd moved to Briarwood. They used to spend almost as much time talking over dinner as they did eating, but their conversations had dwindled. He'd stopped sharing the events of his day. He'd even stopped sharing his dreams for their future together.

And every time Ashley had pressed him – asked him what was wrong – he'd always laughed it off and had changed the subject to something mundane. She'd chalked his behavior up to stress from working at a new location. Figured he was just trying to settle in. But the tight bond they'd shared in Chattanooga had started to unravel not long after they'd unpacked their boxes.

Wiping her tears, she trod back inside the house. Her face felt hot, and her throat dry from crying. She headed into the kitchen for a bottle of water. When she opened the refrigerator door, the aroma from the tuna salad she'd bought for Brett wafted out.

As soon as the odor hit her, Ashley's stomach somersaulted, making her want to throw up. She grabbed the water, sat down at the kitchen table, and took a small sip. What was wrong with her? Why did her nerves have the power to make her feel so sick? She'd been having trouble eating for the past few days. Now just the smell of food had made her nauseous.

That hadn't happened since …

Springing up from the table, she rushed out to the deck where she'd left her phone. She tapped open the calendar app, swiped back a month, and counted the days.

Stunned, she sank onto the lounge chair.

Ashley's period was late.

Was she pregnant? There was no way she could wait to see a doctor. She had to find out – now.

CHAPTER TWENTY ONE

With shaky hands, Ashley ripped open the pregnancy test box and placed the contents on the vanity in the master bathroom of the lake house. Although she longed for a child, now seemed like the worst possible time for her to find out she was expecting. Her life had careened out of control, and she had no idea where it was headed.

Her future with her fiancé dangled by a thread. How would he feel if the test came back positive? Would he think she was trying to force him into proceeding with the wedding whether he wanted to or not? She remembered Bianca's words at the charity auction. *First comes the marriage* ... His sister would likely try to convince Brett that Ashley had planned the pregnancy.

But her relationship woes paled in comparison to the real threat she faced. Ethan still roamed free. The police seemed no closer to catching him now than they had been the day he'd escaped from prison. In that time, he'd murdered three people. And he'd warned Ashley that he planned to see her soon. How could she protect an unborn child when she wasn't even sure she could protect herself?

The box contained two test sticks. Wanting double confirmation of the results, she peed on both of them. She perched on the vanity stool and drummed her fingers on the countertop, jittery with anticipation. This would likely be the longest three minutes of her life.

As she stared at the wood-framed clock hanging on the wall next to the shower, she heard her cell ring in the master bedroom. She hoped it was Brett calling to tell her he was safe. She'd texted him earlier, before driving to the drug store, but he didn't respond.

She hurried into the bedroom and picked up the phone. Detective Lansing's name flashed on the screen.

"Hi, Detective," she said, eager to hear whether the police had any new leads or sightings of Ethan.

"Got some news about your doctor," Lansing told her. "Looks like you were right. Surveillance video caught an image of a person matching your ex's description at the hospital. The picture's fuzzy. But we think it could be him."

Ashley's stomach fluttered. She'd known Ethan would prove to be the killer.

"Did the police see anything on the video that can help them find him?"

"Maybe. We think he stole the doctor's car. We'll search it when it's located."

She laughed, knowing that would never happen.

"If my ex-husband stole that car, there's no way you'll ever find it, Detective," she said.

"Because?"

"Ethan has some relatives who work for a chop shop in Laurel County. I can guarantee you that car is in a million pieces by now."

Depending on the make and model of the doctor's vehicle, her ex-husband had probably netted a tidy sum of cash which he could use to stay hidden.

"Good to know." He paused. "But there is something else. You might have information that could help us."

"What kind of information?"

She'd already told the detective everything she knew in order to help him find Ethan.

"Things from your past. You think your ex is playing mind games. Where will he go next?"

Ashley had asked herself the same question, wondering who Ethan would target. The simple fact that the detective would query her on her past meant that the police were no closer to catching Ethan than they had been at the beginning. They obviously had no leads on his whereabouts.

"I had no idea he would kill Dr. Fisher, or I would have warned you. And other than my family – my father, brothers, and Brett – I can't think of anyone else he'd want to harm. Except maybe Brett's family in Belle Haven."

"Belle Haven PD has been filled in. And Mettler Ridge PD's been on alert since day one."

She was thankful her fiancé's parents lived in a gated community with their own security, and that her father and brothers were armed and ready.

"I'll call you right away if I remember anything else that might help."

As she disconnected the call, she wondered whether Brett had gone to his parents' house. Or maybe he'd checked into a hotel. She just hoped he'd picked a spot where Ethan couldn't find him. She decided to text him again.

Please let me know you're safe.

She watched the screen waiting for the word *Delivered* to pop up. An uneasy feeling spread through her as the seconds ticked by. Had he turned his off his cell? Or had he blocked her? She switched to her favorite phone contacts and tapped his name. The call went straight to voice mail. She didn't bother leaving a message; he obviously wasn't interested in speaking with her at the moment.

She checked the time. Her three minutes were up.

Taking a deep breath, she returned to the bathroom. She picked up one test stick and then the other. Double confirmation.

Ashley was pregnant.

A mixture of both joy and worry flooded her heart, making her feel like laughing and crying at the same time. She wished her fiancé was here, that she could share this discovery with him. But what if he didn't want a baby – at least not now, not with her? If that were the case, she'd raise the child alone. She loved Brett and wanted him in her life, but if she had to, she could make it without him.

Nothing, and no one, mattered more to her than her baby.

Now, with her child's safety at stake, it was even more important for the police to catch Ethan. She wished she could figure out what his next move would be. Contacting his family in Mettler Ridge and Alabama would be too dangerous, and she knew they wouldn't give up any information anyway.

Then a thought struck her. Maybe there was someone else who could help. Who might know her ex-husband's plan.

And Ashley was determined to make him talk.

***

Ashley slid onto the hard metal stool bolted to the floor of the visiting room at the Middle Tennessee State Penitentiary feeling as though she was under a microscope. Before being let in, a drug dog had sniffed her, and a female corrections officer had grilled her and patted her down. Now, not only were the guards scrutinizing her, the eyes of several of the inmates had followed her to her seat. She'd been stripped of her purse and cell phone as well, instilling a sense of vulnerability within her that she hadn't expected.

Folding her hands together, she placed them on the metal table in front of her so they could be seen. She stared at the door where the prisoners entered wondering how long Vincent Lomas would make her wait. Her cousin, Clarence, a corrections officer at the prison, had pulled a few strings to get her onto the visitor list for Ethan's cellmate.

Clarence had warned her to be careful. The man who'd shared a living space with her ex-husband had received a life sentence.

For murder.

With no idea what Vincent looked like, she met the gaze of each prisoner who trudged through the door. Probably not a wise decision. Three inmates eyed her and then passed her by. The fourth man who swaggered into view appeared more ominous than the previous three. His muscular frame crowded the doorway as he crossed the threshold. Dark stubble topped his shaved head, and a tattoo of a cobra covered the side of his face. His coal black eyes bore into her as a slight smile flickered across his lips.

"Vincent Lomas?" Ashley asked as he approached her table.

The prisoner nodded and then plopped onto the stool across from her.

"My name is Ashley Hope."

He put his arms on the table and leaned forward.

"I know who you are," he said, as though he was trying to make his voice sound sultry. "I've seen lots of pictures."

Repulsed, she wanted to slap the lascivious grin from his face. Instead, she ignored the innuendo, knowing that she had to play nice in order to gather information about her ex-husband.

"If you know who I am, then I guess you have a pretty good idea of why I'm here."

"Something about your old man."

She nodded, deciding to get straight to the point. She didn't want to spend any more time with her ex-husband's cellmate than necessary.

"Did Ethan ever talk about what he planned to do when he got out?" she asked.

Vincent laughed and sat back. "Why would I tell you?"

She realized the inmates lived by a strict code and snitches weren't tolerated. However, she wasn't in law enforcement, and she wasn't asking him to reveal the details of a crime. Maybe she could appeal to his human side – if he had one.

"I think my life could be in danger."

He stared at her. "So?"

The coldness in his eyes chilled her, making her appreciate the attentiveness of the guards. She'd have to try a different approach. One with universal appeal.

"I can put money into your prison account."

A smile crossed his face. "How much?"

"It depends on what you can tell me."

He shook his head as if taking control. "A grand," he said. "That's what it will take."

His terms struck her as being more than reasonable if he had information that could stop another murder.

"Okay, I'll put a thousand dollars into your account today," she told him.

He nodded. "Come back tomorrow," he instructed and started to rise.

"No – wait," she said, panicking. "Please, I need the information now. It's more than just my life that's at stake. My entire family is in danger. I promise you that I'll deposit the money into your account as soon as I can get to my phone."

She looked at him with pleading eyes. She couldn't let him walk away; she had to make him believe her.

Vincent hesitated a moment, then fell back onto his stool.

He tapped his fingers on the table. "Your old man talked about you. Nonstop. Every damn day."

She knew her ex-husband hated her but didn't realize he'd been that obsessed.

"What kind of things did he say about me?"

"You destroyed his life. And he was gonna destroy yours."

Ethan never could take responsibility for his actions. It was his own fault he'd been sentenced to prison.

"Did he ever say how he planned to ruin my life?" she asked.

He shook his head. "No details. Just that you wouldn't see it coming." He leaned toward her. "He gets inside your mind."

Ashley realized she wasn't the only person Ethan had played psychological games with.

"You hate him, don't you?" she asked.

Vincent stared at her, his lips curving into a smile.

She knew the inmate didn't care what happened to her, but she guessed that he'd like for Ethan to fail. For her ex-husband to be captured. Or worse.

"He knows where you live," Vincent told her. "Where you go to school. Everything."

So Ethan had already collected all of the information he needed on her before he ever broke out of prison.

"How did he find out?" she asked.

"Some guy on the outside kept tabs on you."

"He had someone keeping tabs on me? What – what does that even mean?"

"This guy was watching you. Followed your every move. Your ex talked about it all the time."

The news hit Ashley like a lightning bolt, stunning her and sending shivers down her spine. How long had this been going on? Months? Years? How long had Ethan been planning his escape? She'd felt safe while her ex-husband was in prison. But someone could have been stalking her the entire time. Following her everywhere she went. She wondered whether it was Ray.

"Did he ever tell you this person's name?" she asked.

Vincent rubbed his chin as though trying to remember.

"I don't think so," he said after a moment.

Ashley sighed, still reeling from the fact that her life had been invaded without her knowledge. It was high time she turned the tables on her ex-husband.

"Can you think of anything Ethan might have said that could help me find him?" She hoped that maybe he had mentioned a hiding place.

The inmate met her gaze. "You don't want to find him," he told her. "You need to get out of town."

The tone of Vincent's warning prickled the hairs on the back of her neck.

"Destroying your life is not all he wants," he said, pulling his arms back from the table.

She watched the prisoner rise to his feet, his cold eyes still fixed on her.

"Your old man wants you dead."

Vincent turned and then walked back through the door leading to the prison cells, leaving Ashley feeling like she was caught in a whirlwind. How much information had her ex-husband really uncovered? Did he know everything about Brett's life as well? Would he be able to find the lake house?

She had to figure out where Ethan was hiding. Before it was too late.

CHAPTER TWENTY TWO

Vincent's words haunted Ashley as she drove back to the lake house. Ethan yearned to see her dead. But first he wanted to destroy her life. He probably planned to make her suffer through the deaths of the people she loved – Brett, her father, Kyle, and Shane – before executing his final kill. She guessed he would save her fiancé for last, thinking his loss would hurt her the most. His first target would likely be one of her brothers. She was thankful that both Kyle and Shane knew how to take care of themselves.

She maneuvered the sedan up the tree-lined driveway hoping to spot Brett's rental car in the carport, but the space was empty. She'd texted him again before leaving the prison and he still hadn't answered. How long would it take him to cool down? She hoped that wherever he'd gone, he was taking precautions. And that Ethan wouldn't be able to find him.

As she headed into the living room, she pulled her cell from her purse. She wanted to check in with Kyle and make sure her family was still safe. Her brother answered on the third ring.

"Hey, Ash," he said, sounding rushed.

She could hear the whirring of air tools in the background and realized he was at the auto shop. She glanced at the clock, surprised to see it was only four-thirty. Somehow it felt later.

"How's everything going there? Are all of you okay?" she asked.

"We're good," he assured her.

She knew they were waiting for Ethan, that they had plans in place to counter her ex-husband's moves.

"Have you heard any rumors about where Ethan might be hiding out?"

"Nope. His kin's clammed up. Ain't talking to nobody."

Ashley wasn't surprised that her ex-husband's family had banded together. For the most part, they were close knit. She tried to remember whether he had any relatives who disliked him. Who might turn on him and reveal his location. The only person she could think of was Ray. And he was dead.

But Ray had a younger brother.

"When's the last time you saw Neil Wilson?" she asked Kyle.

Ashley hadn't known Ray at all, but she'd gone to school with Neil. He'd been one grade ahead of her. He'd always struck her as being different from the rest of his relatives and she remembered that he'd graduated at the top of his class. Of course, that didn't mean a whole lot in Mettler Ridge.

"It's been years," her brother said. "He moved to the city."

"Chattanooga?"

"Nah, Nashville. Heard he went to college. Got a fancy job."

She wondered whether Neil had kept in touch with his family or if he'd completely broken away from life in Mettler Ridge.

"Why do you care?" her brother asked, suspicion in his tone.

Knowing Kyle would worry if he found out she was running a mini-investigation, she decided to pass her inquiry off as simple curiosity.

"When I found out Ray was dead, I just wondered what had happened to his brother. Whether he was still around."

"Uh huh." Kyle sounded unconvinced.

"I'll let you get back to work," she said, wanting to get off the phone before her brother figured out what she was up to.

"You be careful," he told her, as if he already knew.

Ashley disconnected the call and opened her laptop. She clicked on her browser and searched for Ray's brother. She couldn't find an account for him on any of the social media sites. She'd have to dig deeper. At one of the websites selling background checks, she finally found a listing for a Neil Wilson that fit. The age seemed correct, and his former address was Mettler Ridge.

He now lived in Briarwood.

Was that just a coincidence? Probably. She and Brett had only moved to the suburb five months ago. Neil could have been living in Briarwood for years. Without paying for a full background check – which she didn't have the time for – there was no way to know.

Now that Ethan had murdered his brother, she hoped Neil would become her ally. That he could talk with his relatives and get them to divulge information that would lead to the capture of her ex-husband. But Detective Lansing had told her the Alabama police thought Ray's death had been accidental. What if his brother believed that theory?

If she visited Neil, would she be walking into a trap?

It was a chance she had to take. It was her only shot at stopping Ethan from killing her family. At least now she had the pistol for protection.

Ashley headed out of the lake house, hopped into her sedan, and drove toward Briarwood.

***

With apprehension building in her chest, Ashley drove past the home owned by Neil Wilson and then looped around the neighborhood. The subdivision appeared to be only one or two years old with houses still under construction. The homes were attractive and mid-priced. She wondered what line of work Neil had chosen. He had escaped the poverty of Laurel County and had done well for himself. It was too bad that Ray had gone in the opposite direction and had gotten mixed up in Ethan's scheme. She only hoped his younger brother had steered clear of her ex-husband. But what if Neil had completely cut ties with his family? If that was the case, she could be wasting her time. He might not be able to provide her with any information. Either way, she had to find out.

Wanting to dodge Ethan's radar, she pulled her sedan into the lot at the model home instead of parking in Neil's driveway. She'd stopped at a discount store on the drive to Briarwood and had purchased some hair clips and a baseball cap. She checked her reflection in the visor mirror, tucking the strands of hair that had slipped loose back underneath the hat. It wasn't much of a disguise, but it was better than nothing.

Neil lived in a traditional brick two-story on Peach Lane, one block over from the model home. Keeping her gaze focused toward the ground, Ashley strolled down the street, trying to look inconspicuous. There wasn't much traffic. The only sounds were the birds that flittered in the trees.

Making the turn onto Peach Lane, she wondered whether Neil had a family of his own. Other than his relatives from Mettler Ridge, the background search website hadn't listed any names linked to him. Although the neighborhood would probably appeal to a single man due to its location – close to the business park – it seemed more like the kind of place you would choose to raise children. She hoped that was the case with Neil. For some reason – and she knew it didn't really make sense – Ashley felt that if he did have a wife and a few kids, it would be easier to convince him to help her. Maybe her feeling had something to do with the fact that she was now expecting a little one of her own.

As she topped a small rise, Neil's house popped into view. Before traipsing up his driveway, she scanned the other homes and their lawns, both to the sides and across the street. No one else was around. Not that she could see anyway.

With trepidation, she angled up the sidewalk and mounted the porch steps. The house seemed quiet. Through the ripple-textured glass front door she had an obscure view into a small foyer. A light glowed from an adjacent room.

Ashley rang the doorbell.

The chime echoed on the other side of the front door. She waited, listening for footsteps. Hearing none, after a few seconds, she pressed the bell again. Still no answer or indication of movement inside. She checked the clock on her cell. 7:04 p.m. Not knowing where Neil worked, it was hard to guess his schedule.

She wondered whether he'd gone to Mettler Ridge to take care of Ray's funeral arrangements. She tapped her phone and pulled up the website for the only funeral home in Laurel County. Ray's visitation was scheduled for Friday night with the burial to follow on Saturday. With the arrangements already made, maybe Neil was here in Briarwood after all. Considering the time, he'd probably gone out for dinner.

She could wait. At least for a couple of hours. Her conversation with Neil was too important for her to leave now.

After glancing again at the neighboring homes, making sure no one was watching her, Ashley left the front porch and crossed back in front of the attached garage, this time edging closer to the windows. Through the spaces between the slats of the blinds she could see a blue sedan parked inside. Maybe the car belonged to Neil's wife.

Ashley veered around the side of the house. The lawn backed up to an empty lot. She didn't see any children's toys or play equipment in the back yard. Nothing that would indicate the size of the family living here.

A wooden deck stuck out from the rear of the home. She climbed up the stairs and peered through the curtain-free window into the living room. The furniture appeared sparse. She could see a sofa and a large television mounted onto the wall. What appeared to be a documentary about the solar system flashed on the screen. There were no other furnishings in the room. No tables, no artwork, no photographs.

The lack of décor led her to believe Neil was likely a bachelor. Maybe he had moved here from a small apartment and hadn't yet had time to decorate. The overhead light was on. That was the glow she'd seen earlier from the foyer.

But if Neil lived alone, who did the car in the garage belong to? And if he'd gone out for the evening, why had he left his television on?

She moved to the back door. Through the glass she could see a pair of leather loafers. The kind of shoes often used for everyday wear. She looked up at the second floor. Although the sun had not yet set, lights appeared to glow in the upstairs windows.

Something was off. The whole scene just didn't feel right. Everything pointed to someone being home.

Ashley rapped on the back door and waited. She counted off thirty seconds and then knocked again – louder this time. There was no answer and no sign of anyone inside. Maybe Neil was home, in one of the rooms upstairs, but didn't want to be disturbed.

Or maybe Ethan had gotten here before her.

A chill danced down the back of Ashley's neck. Neil could be hurt or dying. Or already dead, like his brother.

She gripped the doorknob. To her surprise, it turned.

Ashley nudged the door open.

She hesitated, rooted at the threshold. Should she go in? She didn't feel right just waltzing into someone else's home without permission. But if Neil had been attacked, if he was clinging to life and she didn't try to help him, she'd never forgive herself.

Taking a deep breath, she crossed through the doorway.

The television volume was turned down low. The muted voices were the only sounds that met her ears.

"Hello?" she called out. "Neil, it's Ashley Hope. Are you home?"

Silence.

She touched the pistol holstered in her waistband, just to assure herself that it was waiting there – ready in the off chance it was needed.

"Neil?" she called out again.

The house was still. She didn't sense the presence of anyone human. However, she detected the ammonia-like odor of a litterbox, so she expected to be ambushed by a furry creature at some point in her tour. Unless the cat was shy and in hiding.

She wondered if what she was doing was legal. Was it breaking and entering if the door was unlocked? What if Neil really was out somewhere and came home and caught her? She could end up spending the night in jail.

Ashley was torn. On the one hand she knew she shouldn't be here. But she couldn't leave until she was certain that Neil didn't need her help.

The kitchen lay to the right of the living room. A small white wooden table surrounded by four chairs sat next to the window. The set reminded her of something you'd see at Ikea. The refrigerator compressor kicked on, startling her. The low hum sonorous in the still house.

Leaving the kitchen, she passed through an empty formal dining room and then headed up the stairs. When she reached the top, it became apparent that the second floor housed the litterbox. And it really needed to be cleaned.

"Neil? Hello?" she shouted once again.

To the left, a partially open door called to her. She inched her way inside, expecting a cat to jump out of the shadows and hoping it wouldn't try to claw her to sheds. But the bedroom was empty. So was the closet.

The foul odor hit her hard as she stepped back into the hallway. She realized it wasn't a litterbox. The odor conjured up a memory of something she'd smelled before, when she was a child. When she'd stumbled onto a wild boar that had been caught in a trap in the woods.

Fear shot through Ashley's body.

It was the scent of rotting flesh.

Her brain screamed at her to run. To get out of the house as fast as she could. Instead, she froze. She directed her gaze down the hallway. Three more rooms. All three doors ajar, the same as the first room she'd entered. She knew she should heed her instincts and leave, but she couldn't. Not until she found the source of the odor.

Ashley drew the Smith & Wesson nine-millimeter from her holster.

With her heart racing, she moved to the room closest to her. Her pistol ready, she inched the door the rest of the way open. It was a bathroom. No one was inside. Nothing unusual. She turned her attention to the next room, several feet down on the right.

She crept down the hall and stopped in front of the door. A thin beam of light from the room leaked into the hallway. The smell was stronger here. Nauseating.

Ashley used her left hand to pull her shirt up over her chin, covering her nose. Then she gripped her pistol, pushed her foot against the door and nudged it open. On the other side lay a bedroom that had been converted into an office.

Neil sat slumped over the top of a metal desk.

His brains splattered the wall behind him.

CHAPTER TWENTY THREE

Ashley fought the urge to vomit as she stared at what was left of Neil Wilson. Her nausea stemmed not just from the sight of blood, mangled flesh, and splattered brains, but from the stench. The odor that permeated the room Neil had used as an office could best be described as rotting fruit, decaying meat, and feces, all mixed together. It was the worst smell she'd ever encountered, and she knew it was one she'd never forget.

Although it was uncomfortable, she kept the front of her shirt pulled up over her nose. Not that it helped much. Now she understood the stories she'd heard about cops smearing Vicks VapoRub under their noses before entering a location that contained a dead body. But she felt certain that even the pungent aroma of Vicks wouldn't be enough to mask the putrid odor.

The thought of calling 9-1-1 danced through her mind. But nothing could be done to save Neil. Rushing to inform the police of his death was not only unnecessary; it could prove to be a fatal mistake in her search for Ethan. The fact that Ray's brother was dead increased the urgency of her investigation. A major lead had no doubt been extinguished. And she knew that until her ex-husband was stopped, the body count would continue to rise.

The loss of the four lives stung her heart, filling her with guilt. The police had made no headway in their search for her ex-husband, wasting valuable time concentrating their efforts in Alabama. Every day that Ethan remained free offered him a chance to take another life. She couldn't allow his reign of terror to go on. It was time to take matters into her own hands. If there was a clue here as to her ex-husband's whereabouts, she needed to find it.

From what she'd learned from studying forensic science, Neil appeared to have died several hours earlier. Maybe even sometime during the previous night. Although the air conditioning was on and the temperature felt like it hovered in the mid-seventies, the body had already begun to decompose. Hence the smell of gases and chemicals being released.

Neil had been shot – that much was obvious. The top of his head had exploded, leaving a hollowed out red mess on top of an intact lower jaw. Although she remembered his hair color had been dark brown which matched the hair remaining at the nape of his neck, with his face disintegrated, she wouldn't be able to swear the body actually belonged to Neil. But since this was his house, it was a safe assumption.

Ashley felt her stomach drop and her vision began to blur as the reality of the sanguineous scene hit her. She leaned back against the doorframe, steading herself, fearing she might faint. Even though she had studied graphic photographs of crime scenes in class, the pictures she'd observed hadn't prepared her for finding Neil. The photos had in no way dampened the horror of witnessing the aftermath from the fatal gunshot. She pressed her eyes closed and waited for her lightheadedness to pass.

When she opened her eyes again, she tried to focus her gaze away from the cavernous wound and onto the desk and the area around Neil. His right hand gripped a revolver. It appeared to be a much larger caliber than the weapon Ashley now held. From the way his body slumped forward with both arms folded at the elbows in front of him, he must have been leaning over the desk when he'd pulled the trigger.

If he'd pulled the trigger.

Holstering her Smith & Wesson, Ashley made her way further into the room and moved around the side of the desk. She glanced at the screen of the laptop situated on the corner. No apps were open. Neil had chosen a mountain waterfall scene as his wallpaper. Maybe it reminded him of his old home in Mettler Ridge.

A white piece of paper peeked out from beneath his left arm. There was handwriting on the paper in black ink, but too much was hidden for her to make out what it said.

A suicide note?

Or was it just a ruse? Had Ethan committed another murder, setting the stage to make the wound appear self-inflicted? Except for his mistake of being caught on video surveillance at the hospital, he'd managed to eliminate the physical evidence that would tie him to the previous deaths. Why should this one be any different?

What would motivate her ex-husband to murder Neil? Maybe Neil had teamed up with Ray and was helping to orchestrate the fake sightings of Ethan in Alabama. After his brother's murder, he could have threatened to go to the police and spill her ex-husband's location.

Or maybe Ethan had just held a grudge against him and wanted him eliminated. The answer might be on Neil's computer – the most obvious place – but any important files he had would probably require a password to open.

Although she knew nothing should be disturbed, the urge to search through Neil's desk drawers tugged at her. What could it hurt? She would be careful – would put things back exactly the way she'd found them.

But if Ethan was the killer – if he'd been here, would he have been foolish enough to leave evidence behind? Not likely. He would have stolen the laptop if he thought anything of value was on the hard drive. And he would have removed any information contained in the desk drawers.

On the other hand, what if Neil really had killed himself? The key to locating her ex-husband could be right here in this room. The computer password – if there was one – could be hidden in the desk.

Now that the home was a crime scene, Ashley needed to worry about fingerprints. If she touched the computer keys, they'd have to be cleaned. She'd already left her prints on doors and doorknobs. She'd have to go back and wipe down everything before she left. Then she'd call Detective Lansing. But what would she tell him?

Hey, Detective, guess what? I let myself into another person's home and when I found him dead, instead of calling the police, I searched through his things.

Somehow, she knew that wouldn't fly. She'd figure out what to tell the detective later.

For now, exploring the desk was her priority.

She grabbed a tissue from the box next to the body. Then she caught herself. What if there was microscopic back spray on the thin paper? Would the police be able to tell a tissue had been taken after Neil fired the gun?

There were times when a master's in criminal justice proved to be a curse.

Without the training, she wouldn't be second-guessing everything. She would just act. But what did it matter if the police realized a tissue was missing? They wouldn't know who had taken it. Not unless she confessed to Detective Lansing.

Using the tissue as a barrier to prevent leaving her prints, she pulled open the file drawer at the bottom right of the desk. Alphabetical tabs in a rainbow of neon colors organized the contents. She flipped thought the hanging files to the letter *B*, looking for a folder for Ethan Barrett. There wasn't one. But she did find a yellow folder labelled *Briarwood.* A map and other general information on the area were inside. Normal literature for someone looking to purchase a home.

Moving on, she scanned through *C*, *D*, and *E*. When she hit the letter *F*, her breath caught in her throat.

She stared at the file. It read: *Dr. Charles Fisher*.

Why would Neil need an OB/GYN? She stuck her tissue-wrapped index finger inside the folder. She found documents detailing the doctor's work schedule, the names of his family members, his address, and a map to his home.

The realization hit hard. Neil had been the person supplying Ethan with information on Ashley. She glanced at the cold body to her left. Did Neil regret helping her ex-husband? Could his remorse have caused him to fire a bullet into his own head? She couldn't think of any other explanation for the file on Dr. Fisher still being here. Ethan never would have left it behind.

She flipped forward, skipping the *G* section, moving instead to *H*. Just as she'd suspected, two files met her gaze. One labelled *Brett Holbrook* and the other bearing her own name, *Ashley Hope*.

For now, she decided to skip past her fiancé's file and dig into her own. She wanted to know exactly what information Neil had collected on her and how he'd uncovered it.

Ashley's heart skipped a beat when she heard Neil's doorbell chime.

Adrenaline running through her, she pushed the file drawer closed and crept out of the office and into the hallway. She peeked around the corner and down the staircase trying to see the person on the other side of the front door. Due to the textured pattern of the glass, she could only make out a dark silhouette. Maybe a door-to-door salesman. At least that's what she hoped.

The bell rang again, reverberating through the house.

Frozen in the hallway, she heard a fist pound against the door, followed by a deep baritone.

"Briarwood PD. Open the door, Mr. Wilson," the voice ordered.

Shit. Ashley was trapped with a dead body in a home she'd broken into. And she was carrying a concealed weapon. There was no way she could make it down the stairs without being seen. No possible avenue to escape. If the cop continued to get no answer, would he leave? Or would he come in through the back door the same way she had?

Neil had been dead for a while. What if his employer had called in a welfare check? If that was the case, the police officer wouldn't leave until he made sure everything was okay inside the house. Even if it meant breaking in.

There were only two choices. Number one: hide and run the risk of being found in the house with a corpse (which wouldn't look suspicious at all). Or, number two: open the door, explain the situation, and hope for the best.

"Mr. Wilson?" the baritone voice called out again, followed by another pounding knock.

She had to make a decision – fast.

Ashley forced her feet to move. With her heart thrashing in her chest, she navigated her way down the stairs.

What have I gotten myself into?

Her mind raced as she tried to figure out what she could say – how to explain. As she crossed the small foyer a vision of herself in handcuffs flashed before her eyes.

Ashley took a deep breath and pulled the front door open.

CHAPTER TWENTY FOUR

The textured glass in Neil's front door had obscured Ashley's view of the police officer waiting on the other side. When she pulled the door open, she came face-to-face with Detective Lansing. The fear of being arrested still loomed in her mind, but with the detective aware of her situation, the threat had lessened – but only just a tad.

"Ashley, why are you here?" he asked, eyeing her ball cap, surprise evident on his face.

She'd almost forgotten she was wearing the flimsy disguise.

"I came to see Neil," she stammered.

That much was apparent, she knew. But she needed to figure out how to explain that Neil's dead body lay upstairs without implicating herself in a crime – such as breaking and entering. Stating the obvious was a way to buy some time, but she had to think fast.

Lansing looked at her as though wondering what kind of game she was playing.

"Are you two close?" he asked.

"No, I haven't seen him in years," she stated. "I'm here because I wanted him to help me find Ethan. I thought he'd be willing now that Ray's dead."

She decided it would be best to start at the very beginning and then lead up to the point where she'd discovered the corpse. But there was the huge hurdle of how she'd managed to get inside uninvited.

The detective tried to look past her into the house.

"I need to talk to him," he said, impatience spreading across his face.

She stood rooted at the threshold, blocking Lansing's entry. He couldn't come inside – not yet. Not until she could justify her reasons for traipsing through the unlocked back door.

Think, Ashley. Think.

"The door was open when I got here, so I came on in," she started explaining, leaving out the key detail that it was the back door she'd entered – not the front like a normal visitor would. "I called out to Neil, but he didn't answer me."

"Was he expecting you?"

The question cut right through her pretext. She should have known better than to try and talk her way around the fact that she'd technically broken in.

"Not exactly," she admitted.

Lansing nodded. "He's dead?"

The detective's abrupt assessment stunned her.

"How did you know?"

"The look on your face when you answered the door, for one thing. Like a deer caught in headlights. And I'm pretty sure that smell's not cat urine."

It made sense that the detective had recognized the odor. He was sure to have encountered many decomposing bodies in the past. And the stench had seemed to float down the stairs once she'd opened the door to Neil's office.

"I'm not the one who killed him," she was quick to say. "He's been dead for a while."

She hoped Lansing believed her. She had no motive to kill Neil.

She stepped back allowing the detective to shoulder his way through the door.

"When did you get here?" he wanted to know.

"Just a few minutes ago. I was getting ready to call you when the doorbell rang."

Going through Neil's files was her way of getting ready. She would have phoned the detective as soon as she was finished searching the house.

"Uh huh," he said. His expression told her he knew she'd been snooping. "Where's the body?"

"He's in the upstairs bedroom on the right."

Lansing pulled a pair of latex gloves and some protective shoe covers from his inside jacket pocket and slipped them on. He proceeded to mount the stairs with Ashley at his heels. He stopped and turned toward her.

"Where do you think you're going?" he asked.

"I've already been inside the room and have seen everything there is to see. There's no reason to keep me out now."

The detective sighed, relenting. "Fine."

He pulled out another pair of shoe covers. "Put these on," he instructed.

Ashley stretched the covers over her shoes and made her way up the stairs behind Detective Lansing. The putrid odor hit her full force again and she was tempted to pull her shirt back up over her nose. But with the detective there, she decided to soldier through the stench.

She was anxious to get Lansing's take on the scene. Did Neil shoot himself, or was the suicide staged? She followed as the detective entered the room, watching his expression. He moved around the body, going in the same direction she had gone. Glanced at the computer screen just as she had done and also noticed the note under the corpse's left arm.

"Was he murdered?" she asked.

He looked at her. "You tell me, Nancy Drew."

The reference to the fictional female sleuth solidified her belief that Lansing knew she had embarked on her own investigation.

"I think he most likely killed himself," she replied.

"Why?"

She could tell he wasn't just quizzing her on her forensic knowledge; he was questioning what she'd been up to before he'd arrived.

"Mainly because evidence was left behind that Ethan would have taken. Like the computer."

"What all have you touched?"

Or in other words, have you contaminated the scene? She didn't think so. She wondered whether she should tell him about the files she'd seen on Dr. Fisher, Brett, and herself. She hadn't technically touched them; she'd used a tissue. If she told him, how mad would he be?

"I left the laptop alone. I only touched doorknobs and doors," she said.

"You're sure?"

"Yes – I'm positive."

The detective pulled out his cell, a frustrated look clouding his blue eyes. She listened as he reported the death, requesting both the medical examiner and a forensics team.

A possible 10-56, he'd said into the phone.

From her studies in criminal justice, she knew that was police code for suicide.

"So, Nancy," Lansing said after ending the call, "why did he do it?"

She realized if she told him her theory, she'd have to admit to snooping through Neil's files. She hoped he wouldn't be too irate.

"I think he gave Ethan the information on Dr. Fisher and maybe he felt guilty about it. You know, after the murder. He probably killed himself early this morning. With all the construction going on, the neighbors likely didn't even notice the sound of the gunshot."

"You came to this conclusion because?"

She hesitated for a moment and then pointed toward the file drawer. "I didn't touch them with my fingers, but I found files on Dr. Fisher, Brett, and myself in Neil's desk."

The detective didn't seem surprised. "You find anything else?"

"No, I didn't have time to look anywhere else."

Lansing nodded, his lips pressed into a thin line. She knew he was pondering the situation. And like Ashley, he was likely wishing there had been a way he could have prevented Neil's death. But she couldn't tell whether the detective was angry with her or if he was just frustrated with the case.

"Anything else you need to tell me?" Lansing asked.

She thought for a moment. She was about to say no when she glanced at the gun in Neil's hand. "I should probably let you know that I'm carrying a pistol."

He nodded. "I know."

Of course he knew. He'd been trained to spot hidden weapons.

Lansing held out his hand. She pulled the gun from her holster and placed it on his palm. He checked to make sure there was no round in the chamber and then shoved the pistol into his pocket.

"You'll get this back later," he told her.

She didn't really want to surrender the weapon, especially now that she had a baby to protect. Ashley hoped *later* meant tonight – when she was ready to leave Neil's house – and not a week from now.

"Have the police in Alabama finally realized that Ethan killed Ray? Is that the reason you wanted to question Neil?" she asked.

The detective looked at her as though he was considering his words before he spoke. "I'm here off the books – or, at least, I was."

She guessed that meant he was investigating on his own time – not being paid by the police force.

"Are you here during your time off because of the budget cuts?" she asked.

"Partly." He rubbed his chin. "But mainly because AHP thinks Ray's death was an accident. They won't investigate further. I found out Ray had a brother. And like you, I thought Neil might crack. Give me a lead on your ex."

She was glad Detective Lansing had been assigned to Ethan's case. There most likely weren't many detectives who would go that extra mile and work on their day off.

"So you believed me when I told you Ethan killed Ray?"

"There's a good possibility."

Finally, the detective was listening to reason.

"It's more than just possible – that's why I have to find Ethan and stop him."

Lansing motioned to the pocket where he'd stashed her pistol.

"This can get you killed." he told her, his face grim. "You need to trade in your P.I. gig for a plane ticket. I don't want to investigate your murder."

She knew he was concerned for her safety, but Ashley couldn't run away. Not now. Too much was at stake. She had to make sure Ethan would never be able to harm her child. Or anyone else she knew. But she wasn't going to argue. It was best to let the detective believe that she might choose to take his advice.

Ashley stared at the file drawer.

"I didn't get to look inside my file," she said, hinting, hoping he'd pull it out and let her read it.

"I can't touch it yet. The forensic guys have to do their thing first."

She wondered whether he was telling her the truth, or if it was just an excuse to keep her from finding out what Neil had uncovered. Maybe he thought she'd be embarrassed with her past on display in front of him.

Disappointed, she nodded. "I just wonder how Neil managed to find out my cell phone number."

"You don't know?"

She shook her head.

"Neil Wilson worked as a data security analyst for Osselton Cybersecurity."

"So that means he would know how to hack into my cell provider's database."

It made perfect sense. If Neil had been an expert in cybersecurity, he would have possessed the knowledge and skill to hack into just about any company he'd wanted in order to find information on her. Who else would be in a better position to do Ethan's dirty work?

Lansing nodded. "He moved here a month after you did."

"So Neil actually followed me and Brett to Briarwood?"

"Looks like it."

Ashley felt even more creeped out than she had before. In addition to electronically tracking her, she wondered whether Neil had ever followed her physically. Goosebumps erupted on her arms.

But there was one thing she didn't understand. Why would an intelligent man with a successful career agree to stalk her? It couldn't be due to a personal grudge against Ashley; she hadn't known Ethan's cousin all that well. What could her ex-husband have possibly offered Neil? What would have convinced the computer expert to risk it all?

The sound of car doors slamming echoed through the window from outside. Reinforcements had obviously arrived. Detective Lansing had instructed them to keep their sirens turned off during the drive to Neil's home. She assumed he wanted to keep the discovery of the body quiet as long as possible.

"Time for you to go downstairs," he told her.

She glanced around the room one last time before heading into the hallway. It was a shame that Ethan had sucked Ray's brother into his plot. Neil had given up a life that seemed to have a promising future.

Lansing followed her down the stairs.

"Wait in the living room," he said before pulling the front door wide open, letting in a trio of evidence techs wearing white protective coveralls.

"As long as you promise to fill me in on what your team finds out, I don't really need to stay," she said.

He shook his head. "You can't leave."

There was nothing more she could add to the investigation. Staying would serve no purpose, and with the strenuous proceedings of her day stacking up, she felt exhausted.

"I've already told you everything I know," she said. "Going through it again won't help."

The detective stared at her. "You don't get it."

She knew how the police worked, that they liked to hear witness's stories more than once to check for any inconsistencies, but frankly she just wasn't in the mood to repeat the events that had led her to find Neil's body ten times.

Ashley sighed. "What is it that I don't understand?"

"The process. Evidence has to be collected. All of it."

He was right; she didn't understand. She had no idea why it would be necessary for her to stay while the forensic team sorted through the evidence.

"What does that have to do with me?" she asked.

Lansing stepped toward her. "The medical examiner determines the manner of death, not me."

She was well aware of that fact; it was criminology 101. First, there was the cause of death which in this case would be a gunshot wound. And then there was the manner of death which would be suicide. Murder was still a possibility, but she believed Neil had most likely killed himself.

Ashley shot the detective a confused look. "But why do I have to stay?"

"You're a suspect," he said.

CHAPTER TWENTY FIVE

"Am I under arrest?" Ashley asked Detective Lansing as they stood in Neil's foyer. Police officers streamed back and forth through the open front door next to her, but they were nothing more than a blur. She had tunnel vision. All she could see was her future self – nine months pregnant and locked behind prison bars.

How could the detective possibly believe that she'd murdered Neil? She had no motive, no reason to want Ray's brother dead. In fact, it was just the opposite. Losing Neil meant losing an opportunity to find Ethan.

And Neil had died several hours earlier. No less than twelve, based on her forensic studies. If she'd killed him, she would have fled. She wouldn't have stuck around for the police to find her.

Lansing motioned toward the doorway leading into the living room. She complied, moving out of the foyer. A knot formed in her chest as she waited for his answer. Following his direction, she headed toward the sofa but remained standing.

"I'm not arresting you," he said, his eyes soft. "But procedure has to be followed."

She stared at him wondering what that meant exactly.

"Normally, you'd have to go down to the station," he explained. "But everything can be done here."

She realized he was trying to make the process easier for her, but she was unsure of what the procedure entailed.

"Are you going to have me fingerprinted?" she asked.

He nodded. "That's part of it. And your fingers will be swabbed for gunpowder residue."

A memory of her father teaching her to shoot flashed into her mind.

"I fired my pistol yesterday at my father's house in Mettler Ridge."

"Okay. Anything else you need to tell me?"

Ashley thought for a moment. "I came in through the back door – but like I said before, it was unlocked. Are you going to charge me with breaking and entering?"

"No." He looked directly into her eyes. "Did you touch the body? Or brush up against it?"

Making sure she didn't come into contact with Neil's body had jumped to the forefront of her mind as soon as she'd found him.

She shook her head. "I only touched the things I've already told you about. And I used a tissue to open the file drawer in the desk."

He seemed satisfied with her answer.

"Your clothes need to be tested for blood spatter," he told her. "You'll have to wear some of my things home. Unless you've got a change of clothes in your car."

That was the reason he'd asked whether she'd rubbed up against the body. In case they found blood or tissue on her clothing. She was safe in that department.

"No, I don't have anything else with me to wear."

He nodded. "Just sit tight. One of the techs will be with you in a minute."

Ashley sighed and sank onto the sofa as Lansing disappeared into the foyer. Her fishing expedition had turned into a nightmare. Neil had been shot, and she'd recently fired a gun. It had been foolish for her to be concerned about a breaking and entering charge when in reality she could be arrested for murder. She'd studied court cases where innocent people had been convicted of heinous crimes. She couldn't become another statistic. She had a baby to protect now.

Feeling restless, she rose from the sofa and wandered through the doorway into the kitchen. A man inside taking photographs stopped his work and shot her a warning glance. *Stay out of the way*, it said. She ducked back into the living room and was met by a pretty middle-aged brunette wearing a white Tyvek suit.

"I'm Maggie," she said. "Ashley, right?"

"Yes, that's right."

"I need to collect a few samples from you," the forensic tech continued. "But we can't do it in the house."

Ashley followed Maggie outside to a white van parked in Neil's driveway. When the doors were opened, she was astonished to see a work-table, stools, multiple storage doors and drawers, and even a sink inside.

"Have a seat." The tech motioned to a stool next to the white table that folded down from the wall. "I'll swab your hands first, and then take your prints."

Feeling like a criminal, Ashley nodded. The sun had already set, but the light beaming down on her inside the van was intense. She guessed it had to be in order for the techs to perform their jobs.

Hearing a noise outside, she looked up. Detective Lansing appeared at the open door.

"I know these are too big," he said as he placed folded clothing and a pair of athletic socks and shoes inside the van, "but it's all I've got."

"I don't mind. Thank you."

He nodded and then closed the van door.

Ashley was grateful that the detective had allowed her to be processed here rather than taking her to the police station. She felt humiliated enough as it was. If she'd been forced to go to the station, the police officers there would likely have assumed she was guilty and treated her as such. She wondered whether Maggie thought she was capable of murder. But more importantly, did Detective Lansing believe she had killed Neil?

Earlier when they'd been in the office discussing Neil's death, she'd thought the detective believed it was a suicide. But now, she wasn't so sure. She knew the police were trained to pretend they were on the suspect's side in order to get a confession. Had she misread Lansing? Had he been playing her?

After her prints were taken, Ashley changed out of her clothes and into the orange University of Tennessee T-shirt and gray fleece shorts that the detective had loaned her. The shirt fit like a dress, but at least the shorts had a drawstring she could adjust. She'd taken one look at the size twelve cross trainers and had decided to go barefoot. They had let her keep her undergarments which she counted as a blessing.

Once she was dressed, Detective Lansing reappeared. He glanced at Maggie, as though he was telling her he needed to speak with Ashley in private. The tech gave her a polite nod and then exited the van.

Ashley was glad they were alone. She wanted to set the detective straight.

"I didn't kill Neil," she said, her voice firm.

He looked her straight in the eyes. "The truth will come out. It always does."

What did that mean exactly? Was he saying her innocence would be proved? Or did he really believe she was guilty? She studied his face but couldn't get a clear reading.

"You saw the note, right?" he asked her.

The question ignited a hope that the forensic team had found a lead. Was Lansing actually about to spill some of the information they'd discovered?

"The one under Neil's left arm – yes, I saw it. Do you know what it says?"

"He confessed to helping Ethan. You were right. He blamed himself for the security guard's death. And he mentioned Ray. He felt guilty for not saving his brother. There was nothing in the note about the doctor's murder. He probably didn't know about it."

If he hadn't yet found out about Dr. Fisher's murder, then that meant Neil could have been dead even longer than Ashley had originally suspected.

"So you believe Neil committed suicide?"

"The note will have to be checked against his known handwriting. But, yeah. I do."

At least she could stop worrying about being arrested for murder.

"Does that mean that I'm free to leave now?" she asked.

"Uh huh."

The detective reached into his pocket and pulled out her pistol.

"Be careful with this," he warned, handing her the weapon. "Just because you don't need a license to carry, doesn't mean you should."

She nodded.

"Where's your car?" he asked.

"I parked it at the model home."

"Come on," he said. "I'll drive you over."

The model home was only a block away, but since night had fallen, she was grateful not to have to walk. She was pretty sure Ethan didn't know about Neil's death yet or he would have swooped in and destroyed the files and the suicide note. But he could still show up at any time.

Ashley climbed into the passenger seat of Detective Lansing's car.

"Don't leave the state until the ME's ruling comes in," he told her.

She hadn't planned on it. She had no idea where Brett was, and she wouldn't leave without him.

"I'll be staying at the lake house unless something happens."

She curled the dangling drawstring of the shorts around her finger. It wouldn't be long before her waist would begin to expand. She hoped that Ethan would be back behind bars before that day arrived.

The detective pulled his Ford up next to Ashley's sedan.

"Thank you for the ride, for the clothes, and for saving me the hassle of going to the police station," she said, pushing the car door open.

"No problem."

She paused before getting out. There was one thing she wanted to clear up, for her own peace of mind.

"Did you know that I was innocent before you read the suicide note, or not until after?" she asked Lansing.

He smiled, his blue eyes sparkling. "What do you think, Nancy?"

She returned his smile, realizing that he had figured out what had really happened as soon as he'd laid eyes on Neil. That was his job after all.

Ashley stepped out of the detective's car. The concrete that had been baked by the sun during the day still felt warm beneath her bare feet. She slid into her sedan and strapped on her seatbelt. She watched Lansing's taillights disappear from her rearview mirror before unlocking her cell phone. The clock on the screen glowed 10:27 p.m.

Tapping her contacts, she called Brett again. Her call went straight to voice mail. She checked the text messages she'd sent earlier, looking for the *Delivered* tag. It wasn't there. He still had his phone turned off, meaning he was still angry. She guessed he wouldn't be at the lake house when she returned. Sighing, she dropped her cell onto the center console.

The second the phone escaped her fingers, it rang. Maybe it was Brett. She snatched it back up and looked at the screen. Fear raced through her.

No Caller ID

Her ex-husband had blocked his number when he'd called her. Just like the person calling now.

"Hello?"

"I got a surprise for you," Ethan said. Then the call disconnected.

CHAPTER TWENTY SIX

With a penlight clasped between his teeth, Ethan Barrett rammed the flathead screwdriver into the track underneath the rear sliding glass door of the townhouse. In one fluid motion, he pressed the screwdriver down with his left hand and jerked the door handle up with his right.

A soft *thump* and the door slid open. *Easy as pie*.

Pocketing the screwdriver in his black cargo pants, he crept across the threshold. He glanced at the security system keypad glowing green on the wall beside the door. Unarmed. Rich people were stupid. Always spending money on things they never used.

The penlight cut through the darkness illuminating the living room. Gray walls. A white sofa and two matching chairs. A vase stuffed with fresh flowers on the coffee table. He pulled a pink bloom from the bunch. Wondered what the flower was called. Probably something fancy. He swirled it beneath his nose. It smelled like a funeral parlor. He thought about the woman sleeping above him and smiled.

The staircase rose against the far wall. The flower still tucked in his hand, he aimed the flashlight and eased up the steps. His feet hugged the wall to his left where the treads were less likely to squeak. When he reached the top, music floated toward him. Slow and sorrowful. A female voice. The singer betrayed by her lover.

He followed the melody to the bedroom at the end of the hallway. He clicked off the penlight and stood still next to the open doorway, letting his eyes adjust to the darkness. The song reminded him of Ashley. The woman who'd turned on him, sold him out, and robbed him of his future. And she'd killed his kid.

Neil had lied for Ashley. He'd told Ethan that the baby died because something was wrong with it. But Ethan knew better. His wife made the doctor kill the kid on purpose – out of spite.

Ashley's actions had forced him to commit unspeakable deeds.

The blood he'd shed belonged on her hands, not his. He needed to make her understand. To compel her to see the error of her ways.

Her punishment fit her crime.

He stepped into the bedroom. Moonlight leaked through the blinds, streaming across the bed where the naked couple slept. The man on his back. The woman on her side, facing her lover. Her long blonde hair fanned around her head like a halo. Her body lay at an angle with the sheet bunched at her waist and her right foot dangling off the mattress.

He had watched the dark-haired man before, knew the woman's lover was a heavy sleeper.

Ethan stared at him. The idea of slashing the man's throat flickered through his mind, but he pushed the idea aside. For now, he'd stick to the plan.

As the music began to fade, he glanced at the phone plugged into the speaker dock on the nightstand. It was the woman's phone, on her side of the bed. The next song filled the air, slow like the first, but with a male's voice. He'd never heard either tune before – and didn't care to hear them again – but the music made his job easier.

If there was a struggle, it would help mask the noise.

Ethan dropped to the floor.

Holding the flower to his chest, he rolled onto his back and slid across the hardwood underneath the bed, his feet toward the headboard. He brushed the end of the flower's stem across the arch of the woman's dangling foot.

The woman jerked once and then settled back down. He paused a few seconds. Brushed the stem against her arch again.

The woman stirred. He watched her bare feet land on the floor next to his head. She shuffled around the bed toward the master bathroom.

Just as he'd expected.

He lay still on the floor and listened. The bathroom light flashed on. He counted off the seconds: *one ... two ... three ...* Then he slid out from beneath the bed, dropped the flower on the nightstand, and slipped across the room. With his back against the wall, he stood in the deep shadows next to the bathroom doorway.

Then he waited.

When he heard the toilet flush, his muscles tensed. Like a coil ready to spring. The bathroom light flipped off. As the woman stepped across the threshold into the bedroom, Ethan struck.

In a swift move, his arms cinched around her, lifting her up off her feet, his hand clamped tight over her mouth. She struggled for a moment and then dug her fingernails into his arms. Pain ripped through him as though he'd been clawed by the talons of a hawk.

Ethan flinched.

His hand almost slipped from her mouth. A muffled scream escaped the woman's lips. The wail was louder than he'd anticipated, rising above the melody that resonated through the room.

The man shifted his position on the bed, demanding Ethan's attention. Had her lover heard the woman's cry? Was he awake?

The woman squirmed in his arms, trying to break free. He squeezed her tighter. He had to end it now, before the man had a chance to stop him.

He pressed his lips against the woman's ear. "Ashley made me do it," he whispered.

With a quick jerk, he snapped her neck.

She fell limp in his arms.

Ethan froze, holding the dead woman in the shadows, waiting for the man to rise from the bed. After a few seconds had passed, he released his grip on the body, allowing it to slide to the floor. He inched toward the bed.

An overwhelming rage surged through Ethan's core at the sight of the dark-haired man, now curled on his side, but still bound by sleep. And again, the idea of slashing his throat bubbled to the surface. The man deserved to die for what he'd done. But simply killing him now would be too quick. What Ethan had planned would be a far more suitable punishment. He'd force the woman's lover to suffer. The man's fate would be worse than death.

Ethan scooped the woman from the floor. He arranged her naked corpse on the bed next to her sleeping lover, spreading her long blonde hair across the pillow.

He smiled again as he placed the fancy pink flower between her breasts.

CHAPTER TWENTY SEVEN

Ashley aimed the pistol and fired, hitting the paper target that dangled from the metal frame she'd set up behind the lake house. Her skill was improving. With each shot, she'd managed to get closer and closer to the bull's eye. Defending herself was more important now than it had ever been before. Her little one's life depended on it. She'd emptied three magazines of ammo from her Smith & Wesson Shield Plus – thirty-nine rounds. She holstered the pistol. It was time to end the practice session.

A weak smile crossed her face as she snatched the target from the stand. Learning to shoot a firearm had never ranked on the long list of things she'd wanted to accomplish in her lifetime. But life had a way of forcing you to adapt. Survival of the fittest and all that. She scribbled the date on the top corner of the target, so she'd be able to track her progress.

As she walked back toward the lake house, she glanced at her cell. 8:37 a.m. Brett still hadn't called and the last time she'd checked – just before breakfast – his phone was still turned off. She'd hoped that after a night's sleep, he'd be ready to talk. That he would return to the lake house. She wanted to see him in person. She wasn't going to break the news about their baby over the phone.

And she needed to know that Brett was safe.

Even though Neil was gone and could no longer help Ethan, her ex-husband's phone call the night before had affirmed that his plan was still in motion. Her blood ran cold when she wondered what his surprise would be. He possessed far too much information about their lives. There was no telling where he would strike next.

Neil's file drawer had contained a thick folder on Brett. With his hacking skills, Neil may have even uncovered the names of her fiancé's college friends. Ethan might already know about the lake house.

Entering through the deck door into the living room, Ashley dropped the paper target onto the coffee table and plopped down on the sofa. She tapped the message app on her cell. The long-awaited *Delivered* tag floated beneath the last text she'd sent to her fiancé.

Brett had turned his phone back on.

He'd finally received her texts, but he hadn't bothered to answer her.

Should she call him? Or should she send another text? He obviously wasn't ready to speak with her yet. If she called, he might turn his phone off again. But it was important for her to know he was somewhere safe, where Ethan couldn't find him.

She opened the Find My app. She'd never spied on Brett before, had always respected his privacy. But under the current circumstances, she felt no guilt in tracking him. It was the only way she could gain peace of mind. She needed to make sure he wasn't lying in a hospital bed, or worse – in the morgue.

A little blue dot popped up pinpointing her fiancé's location: 1751 Wiltshire Place in Briarwood. She wasn't familiar with the address. From the satellite view of the map, she could tell it was located in a residential neighborhood. He was likely crashing at the home of one of the guys from work.

Which could prove to be a bad move.

Ethan was sure to have all the names and addresses of Brett's colleagues. She needed to tell her fiancé about Neil and the thick files of data he had compiled on them. It was too much information to try and explain in a text. And he most likely wouldn't answer if she called.

Only one solution remained. She'd drive to Wiltshire Place, knock on the door, and hope Brett would agree to speak with her. She'd be honest about tracking his phone and explain that she'd only used the app because she was worried about his safety.

If she could get her fiancé to listen to her, maybe she could talk him into returning to the lake house. Once they were alone, she would find a gentle way to announce her pregnancy. She wondered how he would feel about the baby. Would the revelation that he was going to be a father rekindle his love for her? Or would the news push him even further away?

Ashley hopped into her sedan and plugged the address into the car's navigation system.

***

As Ashley turned onto Wiltshire Place, her heart jumped to her throat. Police cars blocked the end of the street in front of a row of expensive looking townhomes. Their blue lights flashed an ominous warning.

Please don't let it be Brett.

She parked her car on the side of the road and bolted out.

With her pulse racing, she ran toward the townhouse at the center of the action. The lawn had been cordoned off with yellow crime-scene tape. The white CSI van she'd been processed in the night before sat in the driveway. Even from a distance she could read the black house numbers emblazoned on the front porch column: *1751*.

Brett was inside. Was he still alive?

A uniformed police officer caught her as she approached the house.

"Sorry, Miss," he said, blocking her entry to the sidewalk. "No one's allowed in."

Tears welled in her eyes. "But you don't understand, my fiancé is inside, and he could be hurt. I need to see him."

At least his phone was inside the townhouse. There was no ambulance on the street. Could he have already been taken to the hospital?

The officer shook his head, ignoring her plea. "I'm sorry. You have to stay behind the line."

She was about to start screaming, about to demand that he let her through when she heard the front door of the townhouse swing open. She looked up and saw Detective Lansing descending the front porch steps.

His eyes locked with hers, his face grim.

"Please tell me that Brett's okay," she begged as the detective met her at the crime-scene barrier.

Lansing motioned for her to cross over the yellow tape and then follow him down the sidewalk, out of earshot of the police officers.

After taking a few steps, she decided it was far enough. She couldn't wait a second longer; she had to know.

"Is Brett dead?" the question shot out of her mouth, louder than she'd expected.

The detective's expression morphed from concern to confusion. He shook his head.

"No, he's fine. Didn't he call you?" Lansing asked.

Relief flooded through her. Brett was still alive. But something terrible had happened, of that she was sure. Had Ethan killed one of her fiancé's colleagues?

"I haven't talked to Brett yet," she said. Ashley didn't want to admit to the detective that she'd tracked her fiancé's phone. "Will you please tell me what happened?"

A strange expression crossed Lansing's face. It was as though he was having trouble finding the right words.

"There was a murder," he finally said.

A heavy wave of guilt washed through her soul. Another murder at Ethan's hands. Another death she hadn't been able to prevent. Had her ex-husband left any evidence behind? Could they prove he had committed the crime?

"Ethan did it," she stated, sorrow filling her voice.

The detective nodded. "The neighbor's security camera covers both back yards. Ethan Barrett was captured on video. He broke in at 3:18 a.m."

Ashley let out a breath. It seemed they had him this time. Proof that he had broken into the townhouse. Her ex-husband would most likely receive the death penalty.

The victim was someone linked to Brett – maybe a co-worker or one of his college friends. A person her ex-husband wanted to use to send them both a message. It could be anyone from her fiancé's past or present. If Brett was fine as Lansing had said, he may not have been staying here. He could have rushed over after receiving the news.

"Who did Ethan kill?"

She hoped it wasn't someone with young children. Most of Brett's co-workers had families. The murders her ex-husband had committed were already horrendous enough. Robbing a child of their parent would be even more heartbreaking.

The detective looked at her. "Do you know Cherie Donnelly?"

The image of a smiling pretty blonde sprang forth from Ashley's memory. She didn't actually know the woman, but she had met both Cherie and her husband once before, at an office party when she and Brett had first moved to Briarwood. As she'd suspected, the victim was her fiancé's colleague.

"She works as a financial consultant for Parker Stone."

After the words were out, Ashley realized she had used the present tense to describe Brett's co-worker. If Cherie was the victim … Lansing had said there had been a murder – singular. But Cherie was married. She might still be alive.

"Did Ethan kill Cherie, or did he kill her husband?" Ashley wanted to know.

"Cherie. The husband doesn't live here. They're separated."

Ashley's heart ached for the loss of the young woman. Another innocent life snuffed out. She was surprised to hear about the couple's break up. They'd seemed happy together at the party.

"How did she die?"

"I can't divulge that yet."

She nodded, wondering what had led her ex-husband to kill the financial consultant. Was he trying to cause a shakeup at Parker Stone? He wanted to ruin their lives. But if he'd just wanted to get her fiancé fired, there were a million easier ways to accomplish it. There was something deeper going on here. But what?

Ashley needed to figure out a way to piece Ethan's plan together. She had to work fast in order to prevent him from taking another life. Dr. Fisher had been someone her ex-husband might have held a grudge against, but Cherie's death seemed to come out of left field.

"Are you the one who called Brett?" she asked.

Once the detective had seen Ethan on the security footage, he should have contacted Ashley as well, but maybe he wanted to get her fiancé's take on the murder first.

Lansing hesitated. The strange look back in his eyes. He rubbed his jaw.

"Brett called us," he said.

If her fiancé had notified the police, that must mean he had been the one to find the body. He must have stopped by Cherie's house for some reason. Maybe to drop off something for work. Brett had promised to stay away from the office out of fear that Ethan would follow him back to the lake house.

"When did Brett find her?"

"Around seven."

That didn't make sense. Her fiancé never got out of bed before seven. Unless something had happened. Maybe Ethan had found a way to contact her fiancé like he had contacted her. Had possibly sent him a warning, giving him a head's up on the murder.

"How did Brett know to come here so early in the morning?" she asked.

Lansing sighed. "He was already here," the detective's gaze dropped to the sidewalk, "when your ex-husband broke in."

Stunned, Ashley stared at Lansing. Brett was here at three in the morning? Had he crashed on Cherie's couch? A seed of doubt sprouted in Ashley's chest.

"What are you not telling me, Detective?" she asked, trying to keep her voice from shaking.

"You should talk to Brett," Lansing said, avoiding her eyes. "He's inside. You can see him in a few minutes."

It wasn't fair to make her wait. Her whole world was crumbling around her. She needed the truth – now.

"If you know something, please just spit it out," she demanded. "After everything I've been through, I think I deserve the truth. What was my fiancé doing here at three o'clock in the morning?"

Detective Lansing met her gaze, a troubled expression on his face. "Brett and Cherie Donnelly were together … in bed."

CHAPTER TWENTY EIGHT

All of the air rushed out of Ashley's lungs as though someone had punched her in the stomach. Standing next to her on the sidewalk, Detective Lansing must have noticed she was struggling to breathe. He placed his hand on her shoulder, concern evident on his face.

"Are you okay?" he asked.

Ashley pressed her eyes closed and concentrated – inhaling deep, followed by a slow exhale. Once her lungs had decided to work again, she opened her eyes. She shook her head and shrugged in answer to Lansing's question, then stared up at Cherie Donnelly's townhouse.

Maybe she'd misunderstood the detective's words regarding Brett and his colleague. Her fiancé wouldn't cheat on her, would he? She swallowed hard, fighting back the tears that threatened to flood her eyes.

"Are you sure that Brett was in bed with Cherie?" she asked the detective.

Lansing nodded. "I'm sorry."

She could tell by the detective's expression that it pained him to deliver the news. But she was glad that it had come from him rather than from another member of the police force. A stranger who didn't care that her life was being ripped apart.

Everything she'd questioned about her relationship with Brett was starting to fall into place now. She thought back over the last five months since they'd purchased the house in Briarwood. The disconnection between them had sprung up just a few weeks after the move. She remembered the many times he'd called to say he was working late. All the client dinners that had taken priority over dinner with her. The last-minute meetings that had kept popping up. The late-night phone calls he'd stepped out of the bedroom to answer. All the days when he'd been too busy to meet her for lunch.

The things she'd glossed over – had brushed off as being normal – all made sense now.

An affair would also help explain his hostility toward her when she'd first told him about Ethan. At the time she'd thought he'd overreacted to the news that she had an ex. Maybe what he'd really been feeling was guilt. He'd known he was keeping a much bigger secret.

No wonder he'd jumped to the conclusion that she was still seeing Ethan. He was quick to suspect her of living a double life because that was exactly what he'd been doing. She wondered how long Cherie and her husband had been separated. Was Brett the reason they'd split?

Now it was easier for Ashley to understand why he hadn't made more of an effort to repair his relationship with her. He had someone else waiting in the wings. Had he been trying to choose between the two women all these months? Or was Cherie just some fun on the side?

Either way, Ashley felt her blood begin to boil.

"How much longer do I have to wait before I can see Brett?" she asked Detective Lansing.

"Come on inside," he said. "I'll check."

She followed the detective up the sidewalk. The neighbor had captured Ethan on the security camera footage breaking into the townhouse. But unless they had an image of her ex-husband actually committing the murder, then she guessed Brett was considered a possible suspect. He'd probably been subjected to fingerprinting and other processing the same way she'd been after Neil's death.

Lansing held the glass storm door open, allowing Ashley to enter first. She stepped across the threshold into the entry hall and noticed a console table to her left. Her soul shattered when she saw the photograph displayed on top. Brett and Cherie smiled up at her – dressed in a tux and evening gown. They sat together at a dining table, Brett's arm pulling the pretty blonde close.

Ashley recognized the hunter-green tablecloth and the wall behind them. The picture had been taken at the Briarwood Country Club's restaurant. Now she knew the reason Brett had never wanted to take her to any of the parties or functions there. She thought back, trying to remember whether the Spring Fling Gala at the club had coincided with one of his so-called business dinners. She wasn't sure. But the couple's attire suggested it wasn't an ordinary night out.

The expression on Cherie's face was one of true happiness. Her eyes glowed like someone in love. Had she known that Brett was still living with Ashley? Or had he deceived her as well?

She pried herself away from the photo, turned around, and glanced at Detective Lansing. He'd obviously been watching her when she'd discovered the picture and was giving her time to digest the hard fact that her fiancé had been cheating on her.

"Wait here," he said, walking past her. He stopped short and then looked back over his shoulder. "Don't touch anything," he added.

The detective disappeared through the doorway into what appeared to be the living room. From her angle, all she could see was a fireplace.

Lansing probably thought she'd smash the photograph into a million pieces once he'd left the entry hall. And if he hadn't warned her, she might have. After a few seconds, the detective poked his head back around the doorframe and motioned for her to follow.

A lump formed in Ashley's throat as she plodded into the living room. Decorated in crisp white and slate blue, the room looked like it had been plucked from the pages of Southern Living magazine. Brett sat slumped in one of the two white armchairs that flanked a matching sofa. His elbows rested on his knees, his fingers were laced together, and his head was down. He was wearing the same polo shirt and shorts he'd had on when he'd stormed out of the lake house the day before. She glanced at Lansing. The detective nodded at her and then headed up the stairs.

Just a few moments earlier, Ashley had wanted to scream at Brett, had wanted to slap him hard across the face. But now that she stood before him, all that she wanted was answers. For her fiancé to explain his reasons for betraying her.

"Is it true?" she asked, trying to keep her voice steady. "About you and Cherie?"

Although she already knew – had seen the photographic proof on the console table – Ashley wanted to hear the truth from Brett's own mouth.

He raised his head and looked at her. His eyes appeared red and puffy as though he'd been crying for hours. He dropped his gaze back to the floor without saying a word.

Brett's refusal to speak infuriated her. The urge to slap him surged through her again.

"Answer me, dammit. Were you sleeping with Cherie?"

"Yes," he admitted, his eyes still focused on the floor.

Even though she was expecting it, the answer sliced through her heart like a dagger.

"How long has this been going on?"

He shrugged, wouldn't look at her.

"When did it start, Brett? I deserve to know."

"Right after we moved."

So her guess had been correct. The distance she'd sensed between herself and Brett had been created by his relationship with Cherie. And this whole time she'd thought his pulling away had been her fault. That she'd done something wrong. That because of her background, she wasn't good enough to be his wife.

"We were in the middle of organizing our wedding – planning our future together. How could you do this to me?"

Her question was met with silence.

Rage bubbled up inside her. "I can't believe you were angry with me for not telling you about Ethan when you had a girlfriend on the side."

The man she'd believed to be near perfect was nothing more than a lying hypocrite.

She shook her head and continued, "You had the nerve to scream at me and then walk out of the lake house because of my past – because of things that happened before we even met. And yet, you were screwing around *after* you asked me to marry you."

"What do you want me to say, Ashley? That I'm sorry?"

She knew he wasn't sorry that he'd been with Cherie. If he'd regretted sleeping with his colleague, he would have stopped.

"I want you to tell me why you cheated."

He finally met her gaze. "It wasn't because I didn't love you."

If he'd still loved Ashley, he shouldn't have been unfaithful. He shouldn't have wanted to risk losing her.

"Then why did you do it?"

He hesitated. "It's hard to explain."

"Try."

What would have caused him to stray? Was it simple lust? The excitement of doing something he knew was wrong? The thrill of knowing he could be caught?

"There's something special about Cherie. I was drawn to her. I couldn't help myself," he confessed, his voice thick with emotion.

The dagger plunged deeper into Ashley's heart. It obviously wasn't just lust that had caused Brett's infidelity. She realized he had real feelings for Cherie. She felt compelled to ask the question that burned in her mind, but at the same time, she feared hearing the answer.

"Were you in love with her?" The words singed her tongue.

He lifted his head, looked into her eyes. "I think so."

The final slice of the dagger cut her heart to shreds. She thought about the life growing inside her and hoped her little one couldn't feel her pain. She looked at Brett – his head buried in his palms – and although she was still livid, she actually felt sorry for him. Maybe finding out he was going to be a father would help him deal with his loss. But now wasn't the time or the place to tell him he had a baby on the way.

"I'll be out of the lake house this afternoon," she said. "I'll leave the key underneath the flowerpot on the back deck."

Brett glanced up at her and nodded.

"Give me a couple of weeks to collect all my things from our house. After that, you can sell it or you can keep it – I don't care. I don't want anything from you."

He straightened in his chair. "Ash, we should talk first. Before you think about moving out."

Was he kidding? He'd just told her he'd been in love with another woman.

"What do we have left to talk about?" she asked.

He sighed. "Starting over. Both of us have made mistakes. But we can still make it work."

Why did she get the feeling that she was the consolation prize now that Cherie was gone? After the fight at the lake house, had he decided he no longer wanted to marry Ashley? Had he made the choice to spend his life with his lover instead? Or maybe he'd planned to go through with the wedding in spite of his infidelity – have Ashley be his safe place and raise his children – while he continued to see Cherie on the side.

She realized that he could have been stupid enough to allow himself to love two women equally at the same time. With his heart pulled in both directions, he might not have known which way was the right way. Ashley could never know for sure what he'd been thinking. At this point, it didn't really matter. Her path forward was clear.

She slipped the diamond engagement ring off of her finger and placed it on the coffee table in front of Brett.

"I'm starting over by myself," she told him. "And I never want to see you again."

Ashley swallowed the lump in her throat and held her head high as she marched out of the living room. She plastered on a brave face, but inside she was dying.

The perfect life she'd imagined with Brett would never be a reality. Instead, she was left to face her future alone. But where would she go?

For now, she realized she only had one option available. She'd return to Mettler Ridge.

CHAPTER TWENTY NINE

Tears stained Ashley's face as she wheeled her sedan up the hard-packed dirt driveway leading to her father's house. After ending her relationship with Brett, she couldn't hold back her emotions. The loss of her baby's father had hit her harder than she'd imagined. All of her dreams for her future – and the future of her child – had disintegrated with the revelation of Brett's affair. The fact that he'd been in love with another woman had crushed her soul.

She'd cried during the entire drive from Cherie's townhouse to the lake house. She'd forced herself to stop her whimpering and to be strong while she'd packed her things. But the waterworks had started up again as soon as she'd slid back into her car. She'd bawled all the way to Mettler Ridge.

But Ashley's tears weren't just for herself and her unborn child. She'd wept for Steve, Ray, Dr. Fisher, Neil, and Cherie. The five deaths weighed heavy on her heart. She blamed herself for not being able to find a way to prevent the murders.

When Ethan had first escaped from prison, she'd thought that he would try to kill the people she loved, one-by-one, to torture her. Then he would kill her. But now, she realized there was more to his plan. His cellmate, Vincent, had told her that her ex-husband not only wanted her dead; he wanted to destroy her life first – that he would get inside her head and use the information he'd received from Neil against her. And that was just what Ethan had done.

It would have been easy for her ex-husband to kill Brett when he'd murdered Cherie. But he didn't. He'd known about her fiancé's affair. He'd obviously wanted Ashley to discover the infidelity in the worst way possible. And by killing Brett's girlfriend, not only had he brought to light the information that would destroy Ashley's relationship, Cherie's death had also wounded Brett's heart in the process. A two for one.

Part of his plan now seemed crystal clear: Ethan wanted to make Ashley's loved ones suffer before he killed them.

Once Ashley's life had been completely shattered, he would kill her.

She glanced at the clock on the dashboard. 7:28 p.m. Kyle and Shane would be off from work, but it was Friday night. Both payday and the start of the weekend. They'd likely be out with their girlfriends or playing pool and drinking with the guys.

Her father's red Ford pickup popped into view as she neared the end of the drive. At least he was home. Ashley heard Ace's familiar baying as she swung out of her sedan. The hound ran up to greet her and she knelt down and scratched him on the head, thankful that her father had the dog to keep him company. And to alert him whenever someone came onto the property.

Leaving her carry-on suitcase in the car, she trudged toward the house with Ace at her side. She had mixed feelings about staying with her father. She knew Ethan already had her family in his crosshairs, but if her ex-husband found out she was here, it might accelerate his plan to harm them. There was no telling what he might do. She wouldn't put it past him to set the house on fire. But where else could she go? At this point, her father's home was her only choice.

The front door of the farmhouse squeaked open, and she watched Spencer step out onto the porch. Although it wasn't quite dark yet, he'd switched the porch light on. Ashley climbed the steps wondering whether she should tell him that her relationship with Brett was over.

"What happened, baby girl?" her father asked before she even hit the top step.

She realized she had bad news written all over her face. Her eyes were no doubt red and swollen from all the crying she'd done. She hugged her father. He still didn't look well, but to her relief, he looked better than he had when she'd seen him last. His eyes were clearer.

"I broke up with Brett," she told him. For now, she'd decided to withhold the gory details.

Spencer nodded. He didn't appear surprised, but he also didn't appear happy as she'd assumed he would. There was more concern in his eyes than *I-told-you-so*.

"Reckon it's for the best," he said, his voice kind.

Once again, she believed her father was right.

The faint hum of an engine rose to a crescendo behind her. Kyle's white pickup pulled into the driveway. Shane sat next to him on the passenger seat. Ashley was glad the whole family was here. She wanted to warn them that Ethan had taken another life.

Kyle hopped out of the pickup and strode up to the porch with Shane close behind. They were both still wearing their blue shop uniforms, their names emblazoned on their left shirt pockets. They must have been working on a special project that required overtime.

Her older brother took one look at her face and asked, “Somebody else die?”

Her father answered for her. “She done broke up with her beau.”

“Hallelujah,” Shane said, almost loud enough to be a shout.

“Don’t be glorying in your sister’s misery,” Spencer admonished her younger brother.

Ashley had expected her family to be happy that she and Brett were no longer getting married, so Shane’s reaction had little effect.

“It’s okay, Daddy,” she said. She mustered a weak smile and punched her younger brother in the arm.

Shane returned the smile and then pulled his sister into a hug.

“You deserve the best,” her younger brother said, “and he ain't it.”

Ashley looked at the faces of her father and brothers. For the first time in years, she felt the love radiating from all three of them at once. A knot formed in her throat. They were her family and she loved them back. With all of her heart.

“Y’all come inside now,” Spencer said. He seemed pleased to have his family assembled together as well.

They filed through the front door into the living room. Ashley curled up in the corner of the sofa. Shane plopped down next to her as her father settled into his recliner and Kyle sank into the armchair next to the window.

With everyone in their seat, Ashley took a deep breath. It was time to tell them about the latest murder.

“Ethan killed a woman in Briarwood last night,” she informed them.

“Who?” Kyle asked.

She wondered whether she should just tell them it was one of Brett’s co-workers, or if she should spill the ugly truth. But she knew her family, and they knew Ethan. The murder of a colleague wouldn’t make sense to them. They would know she was leaving out a key detail. The truth won out.

“A woman who worked at Brett’s office – they were having an affair.”

“That sorry SOB,” Shane said as he shot up from his seat, his fists clenched. “I’ll kick his ass.”

Ashley should have realized that when her brothers heard about the infidelity, they would want to find Brett and beat him to a pulp.

"No, Shane. That won't help anything," she said.

"I'll drive," Kyle chimed in as he rose from his chair, anger clear on his face.

"I said, no!" Ashley yelled as she jumped from her corner of the sofa. "Look, I know you just want to teach him a lesson, but this is not the way to go about it. Besides that, you'll never find him anyway. He's gone into hiding until they catch Ethan."

"Ole money bags probably done left the country," Shane said, fury in his eyes.

Ashley felt certain Brett was still in Tennessee, but she didn't want her brothers to know that. Her ex-fiancé had broken her heart and a part of her hated him for it. She'd wanted to slap him herself. But physical violence wouldn't solve anything. And Brett was already dealing with his own pain. He'd lost both Cherie and Ashley in one day.

"The police detective on the case recommended that we fly to an island in the Caribbean," she told them. Which was a true statement. Lansing had begged her to talk Brett into hopping on a plane.

Kyle looked at her and shook his head. "He comes back to town," her older brother said, "don't give him no warning. He needs setting straight."

Ashley knew Kyle meant what he was saying. If he ever saw Brett again, he'd make her ex-fiancé sorry he'd ever met her in the first place. She just hoped she could talk some sense into her brothers before that day arrived. For the sake of their little niece or nephew.

"Y'all settle your feathers," Spencer broke into the conversation. "You done got your cart before your horse. Right now, your sister needs protecting. She's gonna stay here. Even if it ain't what she wants."

The expression on her father's face let her know that his mind was made up. He wasn't going to let her leave as long as her ex-husband was free.

"Daddy, if I stay here in the house with you, Ethan will find me by sun-up," she said.

"You can stay in my trailer," Kyle volunteered. "I'll take the couch."

Ashley appreciated her brother's offer, but she had another idea in mind. An older single-wide trailer sat on the back corner of her father's one-hundred-and-fifty-acre property. Her cousin, Frank, had lived there for a while after his divorce. He'd only moved out a couple of years earlier. It should still be inhabitable.

"Do you still have Frank's trailer hotwired for electricity?" she asked her father.

"Yep," Spencer said, smiling. He was obviously pleased with her suggestion. "But there ain't no furniture. We'll have to tote you a bed over there."

Suspecting that the trailer had been cleaned out, she'd stopped by both a sporting goods store and a discount store in Briarwood and had picked up all the supplies she thought she might need.

"I've got an air mattress and a sleeping bag," she told them. "That's all I need for now."

It wouldn't be the most comfortable night she'd ever spent, but as long as her family was safe, she'd be happy sleeping on a rock.

"All right, then," her father said. "I reckon I'll be staying there with you. You don't need to be by yourself."

"I don't think that's a good idea, Daddy," Ashley said. "If Ethan realizes you're not in the main house, he'll know something's going on. He'll start looking for you and he might find the trailer. We have to pretend that everything here is normal."

"She's right," Kyle said. "Ethan's not stupid. He'd be sure to notice a change."

Spencer nodded, relenting, but Ashley could tell he wasn't happy with her spending the night alone in the mobile home.

"The driveway's done grown up back there," Shane said. "Too many bramble bushes to get Ashley's car through."

She hadn't thought about that. There was no way she could leave her sedan parked in her father's driveway, shining like a beacon for Ethan to see.

"There's room for her car in the work shed," Kyle said. "I'll padlock it and give her a key."

With her car out of sight, they should have all the angles covered. Ethan would likely search for her here – had probably already done so more than once – but she hoped he would assume she was still in Briarwood when he realized she wasn't in the main house or in Kyle's trailer.

Her cousin, Frank, hadn't moved onto the property until after her ex-husband had gone to prison. Ethan probably didn't even know the other trailer existed, and its location in the midst of a thick grove of cedars would make it hard to stumble upon. At least one problem seemed to be solved.

The next move in her ex-husband's plan worried her. She didn't think he'd try to murder Brett yet – he would let her ex-fiancé drown in his misery for a while. Instead, she was afraid that Ethan would target her brothers. He most likely wouldn't kill them right away; he would torment them first. He'd destroy their lives hoping they would blame Ashley.

She figured that her ex-husband wanted to force her loved ones to turn on her – to make them hate her – before he killed them.

When they were married, Ethan had drilled into her mind the fact that he was the only person who had ever truly loved her. That no one else would ever care for her the way he did. He'd told her that the love of her family had stemmed from obligation only and that it would fade fast. She believed he wanted to prove it.

A horrible thought struck her. If Ethan wanted to decimate her brothers' lives, he'd most likely start with their relationships. What if her ex-husband went after the women they were dating?

"I don't think I'm the only person Ethan wants to hurt," she told her brothers. "I'm afraid he might try to kill your girlfriends, like he did Brett's."

"He touches Janet, he's dead," Kyle said, his eyes narrowed.

"Same goes for Robin," Shane stated.

"Call and tell them to leave town until the police catch Ethan. Tell them not to wait – they need to go right now."

She hoped the women had family they could stay with, far away from Mettler Ridge.

"That ain't all we're gonna do," Kyle announced.

The expression on her older brother's face sent a shiver down Ashley's spine.

"Grab your rifle, little brother," he told Shane. "Tonight, we're going hunting."

CHAPTER THIRTY

Kyle’s words ignited a deep fear within Ashley’s bones as she stood next to him in their father’s living room. Indignation seemed to flow from every pore in his body. She knew exactly what he’d meant when he’d told Shane to grab a rifle. It wasn’t a forest animal her older brother planned to kill.

They would be hunting Ethan.

A wall of dread hit her. But it was more than just a feeling; it was like a premonition. A fear that somehow, this night would change her family forever.

“There’s no way I’m going to let the two of you go gunning for my ex-husband tonight,” she told her older brother, her voice firm.

Ashley appreciated her family’s desire to protect her – and she knew both of her brothers’ girlfriends needed to be kept safe – but she didn’t want Kyle and Shane going to unnecessary lengths that would put their own lives in danger.

“You can’t stop us,” Kyle replied, a defiant look on his face.

She knew she couldn’t physically prevent them from running off into the woods, but she could try to dissuade them.

“It would probably just be a waste of time anyway,” she said. “Ethan’s most likely back in Briarwood searching for me and Brett.”

“Nah, he’s here,” Shane stated in a matter-of-fact tone.

Ashley’s gaze jerked toward her younger brother. He seemed confident in his words. Did he know something that she didn’t?

“What makes you think Ethan’s in Mettler Ridge?” she asked.

“Jesse Crowder said he seen him this morning down by Laurel Creek,” Shane told her. “Jesse hollered at him, but Ethan took off.”

So their old neighbor and Ethan’s former drinking buddy had spotted her ex-husband once again. She wondered why Jesse hadn’t called her. She’d made it clear that she would pay for information on her ex-husband’s location. Maybe because he didn’t have anything concrete enough to sell. Or maybe he was working with Ethan and the sighting was false, reported to her brother to throw them off of her ex-husband’s real trail. The possibilities made her head spin. She didn’t know what to believe.

“If you want to look for Ethan, can’t you at least wait until morning?”

Although the timing of Ray’s death was questionable, so far, her ex-husband had committed all of his murders during the night. She didn’t want her brothers to be the next casualties. If they insisted on going, she’d talk them into waiting until daylight and she’d go with them.

“We best catch him off guard,” Kyle said. “He won’t be expecting us now. He’ll think we’re defending the fort.”

Her older brother’s reasoning made sense. You stood your ground and defended your home when it was the most vulnerable – during the hours of darkness. Still, their plan worried her.

“Where are you going to start the search – Laurel Creek?”

“Uh-uh.” Kyle shook his head. “He knows he was seen there. He’d done be cleared out by now. I’m figuring we sneak up on some of his kin. Spy out their places.”

“And what will you do if you find him?” she asked, afraid of the answer.

Kyle stared at her. “We’ll be letting him decide that.”

A shiver ran through her. The steely set of her older brother’s eyes told her that his decision had been made. He and Shane would hunt for her ex-husband tonight and there was nothing she could do to prevent it.

The odds leaned toward one or more of the three men not surviving the encounter. She had to make sure it was Ethan that ended up in the morgue and not Kyle or Shane. If she couldn’t change her brothers’ minds, she’d have to convince them to let her go along, to better their odds.

Her father had remained silent up until now.

“You boys watch your step,” Spencer said, finally rising from his recliner. “Ethan ain't got nothing left to lose.”

Ashley knew her father’s words were true. If her brothers cornered her ex-husband, he’d never surrender. He’d kill Kyle and Shane even if it meant he’d die in the process.

“We’ll be careful, Daddy,” Shane assured their father. “He ain't got nothing we can’t handle.”

She hoped her younger brother was right – that they could outsmart and outfight Ethan. Kyle had always been the brains and Shane – both bigger and stronger – had been the brawn of the duo. Together, they stood an even chance. But if they became separated, if either of them had to fight Ethan alone, she worried they would come up short. Just one more reason she couldn't let them search by themselves. Once her brothers were ready to leave, she'd announce that she was going with them. And she wouldn't take no for an answer.

Spencer nodded. "First, we best get your sister settled up at the trailer," he said.

The worry was apparent in her father's eyes. It was as though he'd calculated the odds and had come to the same conclusion as Ashley. But like her, he seemed to know his sons had made their decision and they wouldn't be swayed.

"Daddy, I think they need to call Janet and Robin first and ask them to leave town," Ashley said. She didn't want to wait any longer in warning the women. They needed to get out of Mettler Ridge as soon as possible.

Her brothers pulled out their phones. She grabbed her cell from her purse, opened her contacts, and tapped on Detective Lansing's name.

He answered on the second ring. "Lansing."

"Detective, it's Ashley Hope," she said into the phone. "I think I might know where Ethan plans to go next. I think he's targeting my brothers' girlfriends here in Mettler Ridge and I was hoping you could contact the sheriff and convince him to check it out."

"Definitely. Just give me their names and addresses."

"Okay, hold on a sec."

Ashley had Kyle write down the information. "Janet Porter lives on Turkey Creek Road and Robin Lynch lives on Pine Hill Road. We're not sure of the house numbers."

"That should be enough to find them. I'll call the sheriff now."

Ashley ended the call, hoping the police would be able to surprise Ethan and catch him on the way to one of the women's homes.

"We best get you to the trailer," her father said.

"All we need to do right now is pull my car into the shed. Everything else can wait until I get back," she told him.

"Get back? From where?"

"I'm going with Kyle and Shane."

Kyle shook his head. "Oh, hell no. Ain't no way you're coming with us. You'd just get hurt."

"I have a pistol," she reminded him. "I've been practicing my shooting and I've gotten pretty good. And you have to admit, three against one would make much better odds."

"Nah, you'd just slow us down."

"That's not true. You and Shane could use the backup – you know you could."

"Not gonna happen."

It was time to stand her ground. Ashley couldn't let them go without her. She was to blame for Ethan's rampage, and it was her responsibility to see that it ended. If her brothers went gunning for her ex-husband alone and something terrible happened, she'd never forgive herself.

"Okay, fine," she said. "If you won't let me go with you, then I'll go searching for Ethan tonight on my own. And you can't stop me."

Kyle looked at her as though he thought she was crazy, but she knew that if she could convince him that she would go out and hunt for Ethan alone, her brother would give in.

"Just let her come with us," Shane said. "You know how hardheaded she is. She don't need to be taking off by herself."

Kyle hesitated, raked his hand through his hair. "Alright. But you have to do everything I say," he told Ashley. "We have to stick tight together. You can't be wandering off."

"I realize how dangerous this is and that's the reason I want to be there to cover you and Shane. I won't get in the way, and I'll do whatever you tell me to."

Her older brother nodded, but she could tell he wasn't happy with the situation.

"Let's go change into camo," he told Shane.

Ashley watched Shane mount the stairs leading to his attic bedroom while Kyle plowed back through the front door, headed for his trailer.

"You sure you're ready for this?" her father asked, his face lined with worry.

"Yeah, Daddy. I have to be. I'm the one who brought all of you into this mess and I need to make sure Kyle and Shane come out of it alive. And I promise I won't do anything stupid – I'll be careful."

"You remind me of your mama. Once she set her mind on something, couldn't nobody change it."

She smiled. "I inherited my stubborn streak from *both* of my parents."

Ashley pulled her ID from her wallet and stuck it in the front pocket of her jeans – just in case something happened, and it was needed. When she dropped her purse back onto the sofa, it spilled open, and a bottle rolled onto the floor.

Prenatal vitamins.

The large block lettering on the label of the over-the-counter supplement left no doubt as to their purpose. Ashley locked eyes with Spencer. This was not how she'd wanted him to find out he was going to be a grandfather.

"I was going to tell you once everything settled down," she said, hoping he'd understand.

He nodded, a smile spreading across his face. He was obviously happy to receive the news.

"Does your beau know?" he asked.

"You're forgetting that he's not my boyfriend anymore," she said, her voice tinged with sadness.

But she was sure her father hadn't forgotten. She figured he was testing her. Trying to find out if there was a possibility of her and Brett getting back together.

"But, no," she continued. "I haven't told Brett yet."

"You still love him?"

She thought for a moment. A part of her would always love Brett, regardless of his infidelity. And he was her baby's father. That meant they'd be connected for life, even if he wanted nothing to do with the raising of their child. But in her heart, she knew their relationship could never be repaired.

"It's over between us, Daddy. I don't see any way we could ever be together again, no matter how much I care about him."

Her father stepped toward her and pulled her into a hug.

"You always got a home here," he said, his voice soft in her ear. "You and the baby."

Tears threatened her eyes. She blinked and pushed them back. She now knew her father's love for her was stronger than she'd ever realized.

She let go of Spencer, feeling blessed to have him for a father.

"I don't want to tell Kyle and Shane yet," she said. "After what happened the first time – with Ethan's baby – I want to wait until I'm further along."

If something happened and she lost the baby, it would be easier if Spencer was the only person she had to inform. Other than Brett. But she still wasn't sure when would be the right time to tell her ex-fiancé about the pregnancy.

"That's up to you, baby girl."

She knew she could count on her father to keep her secret.

Ashley heard footsteps on the stairs. She grabbed the vitamins from the floor and stuffed them back into her purse. Shane appeared in the living room just as she zipped it closed.

"You wearing that?" her younger brother asked her, obviously referring to the pastel pink T-shirt she'd picked up at the discount store. The light color wasn't the best choice for someone who wanted to blend in with the night.

"I guess it probably would be a good idea to change," she said.

She was about to head out to her car to get her suitcase when the front door pushed open. Kyle strode into the living room carrying his rifle and a long-sleeved camouflage shirt.

"I know this here shirt's too big for you, Ashley," he said. "But you need to put it on. You can roll the sleeves up."

"Thank you, Kyle." She appreciated his thoughtfulness.

Ashley slipped the camo shirt on over her T-shirt and fastened the buttons. The tail hung down almost to her knees. She hugged Spencer goodbye, praying it wouldn't be for the last time.

"Try not to worry about us, Daddy," she told him.

She looked at Kyle and Shane and counted herself lucky. She knew she could always depend on them. And she vowed to be there for her brothers in return. As long as she lived.

"I'm ready if you two are," she said.

Single file, with Ashley in the middle, the trio headed out through the front door and into the darkness of the night.

CHAPTER THIRTY ONE

Briars clawed at the legs of her jeans as Ashley sifted through the underbrush near the edge of the forest, Kyle out in front of her and Shane following close behind. In the clearing down the slope, the lights from Lonnie Barrett's farmhouse glowed like stars, small patches of gold in the shadowy darkness.

Ethan's cousin had a long history of run-ins with the local sheriff's department. The whole county knew Lonnie was involved in the operation of several illegal enterprises – including moonshining and chopping cars – but although he'd been arrested on more than one occasion, the local authorities had never been able to make the charges stick. Lonnie had always managed to wrangle himself out of trouble.

He was slippery, like Ethan.

Of all the Barrett family members in Laurel County, Lonnie was the best known for being able to find creative ways to outmaneuver law enforcement. He was an expert at hiding things. Like moonshine stills and stolen car parts.

And, if her older brother's instincts were correct, maybe a cousin who'd escaped from prison.

Kyle came to a halt in front of her. He knelt next to the base of an oak, tugged off his backpack, and pulled out a pair of binoculars. He glanced up at Ashley and Shane and then killed his flashlight. Both she and her younger brother followed suit.

Ethan had been spotted at Laurel Creek – south of Mettler Ridge's city limits – earlier that morning. If he'd been camping in the area, it stood to reason that he'd abandon his post and head to the other end of the county to avoid being caught. Lonnie's place sat outside the north-east boundaries of the town, on the edge of the county line. His sprawling acreage seemed like the perfect hiding spot.

Ashley watched as Kyle peered through the binoculars, her eyes adjusting to the sudden darkness. In the distance a screech owl called out. The haunting cry frayed her already jangled nerves.

Kyle stood and then handed Ashley his binoculars. She scanned the property. The silhouettes of two outbuildings and a large barn loomed before her. She shifted her focus to the windows of the farmhouse.

Most of the curtains on the back side of the house gaped open, but she didn't see any people inside. She held the binoculars out to Shane, but he shook his head, seeming eager to get on with their mission.

"You two ready?" Kyle asked them, his voice just above a whisper.

"Yep." Shane was quick to reply.

Ashley knew Shane had been itching to hunt for Ethan since the minute her ex-husband had escaped from prison. If given the chance, her younger brother would most likely have shot her ex years before. When they'd first found out what Ethan had done to Ashley – that he'd abused her and dumped her into a hole in the ground – Kyle, Shane, and their father had all three wanted to kill him. The only thing that had stopped them was the fact that Ethan was already in custody. They couldn't get to him as long as he was in the hands of law enforcement.

Now, Ethan was no longer protected.

Ashley realized that as an escapee, her brothers believed that Ethan was fair game. And she knew they were determined to make sure her ex-husband never hurt her again.

"Let's start with the barn," Kyle said.

Single file, with Ashley still in the middle, they crept from the cover of the trees into the soft light of the quarter moon. With her eyes now fully adjusted, Ashley could identify most of the objects around her. The trio scurried across the clearing, heading toward the barbed-wire fence that encircled the barn and pasture area.

The fence snagged the seat of Kyle's pants as he climbed over. He helped hold the top wire down while Ashley crossed into the pasture. Straight ahead, a small herd of Black Angus cattle huddled next to a pond. She followed Kyle as he veered right, looped around the pond, and snaked toward the large wooden structure, mindful of where she stepped.

According to her brothers, the sheriff's department had swarmed Lonnie's property searching for Ethan on the day he'd escaped from prison. Unless they received a tip that he was hiding in the area, the deputies wouldn't be likely to return. But in the off chance they did come back, it would be smarter for her ex-husband to bunk in the barn's hay loft rather than in the house.

With Shane not far behind, Ashley stuck close to Kyle as he skulked along the side of the barn. When they reached the front of the building, Kyle motioned to both her and their younger brother and then pulled the AR-15 from his shoulder. Ashley nodded and drew her pistol. After signaling to make sure she and Shane were ready, Kyle inched back the right sliding barn door. Leading with the barrel of his rifle, he slipped inside. Ashley followed.

Skilled at stalking the woods in search of wild game, her brothers were accustomed to moving in tandem, not making a sound. Keeping between them, Ashley matched their careful stride, mirroring their every step. Without the aid of the moonlight, she could only see a few feet in front of her. She wished they could switch on their flashlights, but knew they needed to make sure Ethan wasn't lurking in the shadows first.

Kyle stopped in front of her. He stood still as though he was listening for an indication that they weren't alone. Silence filled the barn. If Ethan was inside, he was either asleep or he was hiding, waiting to ambush them.

With Ashley at his heels, Kyle plunged further into the gloom. They edged between a tractor and a row of metal barrels probably used to store grain. Just ahead of them, she could make out the shape of the ladder leading to the loft. Kyle looked back over his shoulder at her and Shane and pointed upward. She saw her younger brother nod in return.

As they neared the ladder, she heard movement above them.

Ashley froze. And so did Kyle.

The hairs prickled on the back of her neck.

She looked at Shane. Her younger brother had obviously heard the noise too. If her ex-husband was awake in the loft and Kyle climbed up, it would be like committing suicide. As soon as his head popped up over the loft floor, Ethan would blow his brains out.

An idea struck Ashley. She held up her hand – a sign for Kyle to stop and wait. She'd noticed a shovel leaning next to the tractor. It just might be what they needed. She slinked back through the shadows, retracing their steps. After grabbing the shovel, she returned to the company of her brothers. She holstered her pistol, motioned with the shovel and then pointed upwards.

As she made a move toward the ladder, Kyle caught her and pulled her back. From his hand signals, it was clear he thought she intended to climb into the loft and there was no way he'd allow it. She pointed to herself and shook her head. Then she pointed at the shovel and then to the loft. This time, he seemed to understand.

Knowing Kyle and Shane would cover her, she crept toward the ladder. Gripping the shovel, she nodded to her brothers and then prepared to climb upward. When her foot touched the bottom rung, she heard the noise above her again. A strange rustling.

Holding her breath, she eased upward. When she neared the top of the ladder, she hooked her right arm through the rungs and braced herself for the gunshot blast she knew would come. The handle slick with sweat, she inched the blade of the shovel above the floor of the loft.

In the gloom of the barn, the rounded blade would look just like a man's head. Ethan wouldn't be able to tell the difference. Ashley's pulse quickened as she raised the shovel just high enough above the floor that it would still look human.

She waited for the blow, her muscles tingling. Nothing happened.

She lowered the shovel and then raised it a second time. Still nothing. She was about to climb back down the ladder when she heard the rustling again. She looked up.

The sound rushed toward her.

Ashley choked back a scream as a large dark ball hit her square in the face.

CHAPTER THIRTY TWO

The ball slammed into Ashley's face with the force of a rocket, almost knocking her from the loft ladder. The shovel slipped from her hand and clanked to the dirt floor below as she clung to the right-side rail. The dark mass ripped down her left arm, heading for the ground. It was no ball that had hit her.

The dark form had teeth and claws.

Ashley's left cheek stung from either a scratch or a bite; she wasn't sure which. She was thankful the camo shirt Kyle had loaned her was long-sleeved or her arm would have been shredded.

Kyle grabbed her legs from below, steadying Ashley's feet on the rungs.

"Barn rat," Shane whispered.

There was no need to be quiet now. The clatter of the shovel crashing to the ground would have alerted anyone hiding in the barn. But she didn't think Ethan was here. Her ex-husband wouldn't have missed the opportunity to blow someone's head off. Or rather, to shoot at what appeared to be a man's head.

"I'm going up," she told Kyle.

"Oh, no you ain't."

"It was just the rat we heard. Ethan's not up there – I'm sure of it."

"That don't matter none. There could be more rats. Or something worse. You let me go first."

Ashley moved aside and allowed her older brother to mount the ladder. When he was at the top, she saw a beam burst forth from his flashlight. She decided it was time to follow him.

Getting a firm grip on the side rails, she climbed up the ladder into the gloom of the loft. At the top, Kyle stood about a yard in front of her. He panned his flashlight across the floor. Stacks of hay bales materialized on their right. Hearing Shane's feet thump on the ladder rungs behind her, Ashley moved further into the loft.

She pulled her own flashlight from the pocket of her camo shirt and aimed the beam toward the far-left corner. Part of a hay bale lay propped against the wall, the twine holding it together had been cut.

The remainder of the hay had been scattered across the floor in the shape of a bed with a clump for a pillow.

Shane appeared beside her.

"Look at this," Ashley instructed her brothers, shining the light on the makeshift bed.

"Well, I'll be damned," Shane said.

Ethan had been there, but how long ago? He had to have arrived after the sheriff's deputies searched the farm, but when did he leave? Was he still staying here? Was he up at Lonnie's house right now? If so, he could surprise them at any moment.

She stepped closer toward the bed. The rotting remnants of a bunch of bananas lay strewn about the foot. Probably what the rat had been eating. Blackened by time and the heat in the barn, they seemed to have been decaying there for a couple of days. Which meant Ethan had most likely moved on before today. Or he was sleeping inside his cousin's house.

Shane echoed her thoughts. "He ain't staying here no more," her brother stated.

Ashley swept the flashlight up toward the head of the bed. The beam hit something else.

A brown hard-backed book.

Moving next to the hay pillow, she picked up the book. It was an old church hymnal, the cover battered, the spine cracked. A piece of twine stuck out from the top, probably marking a page. Ashley opened the book. The pages were yellowed with age. A shiver ran through her when she read the title of the song.

Send In The Reapers

She skimmed the lyrics:

Send in the reapers
to reap the souls of the living
harvest the world
send their souls to be judged

Is that what Ethan thought he was doing? Did he consider murder to be reaping souls? Ashley knew her ex-husband had shunned all things religious, had never believed in a higher power. Was he searching for a way to justify his killing of innocent people in his own twisted mind?

Ashley flipped to the front of the book. The copyright date was 1968. The inside cover of the hymnal bore a faded blue stamp.

Now she knew where Ethan might be hiding.

The stamp read: *Property of Still Waters Chapel.*

"Do the two of you remember that old, abandoned church up by Mettler Falls?" she asked Shane and Kyle.

Her older brother met her gaze. "You think Ethan's there?" Kyle asked.

"I'd be willing to bet a hundred dollars on it – maybe a thousand."

The old, abandoned building would provide a good shelter. And the myths about the church being haunted kept the locals away, so if Ethan chose to hide there, he likely wouldn't be found.

"Let's check the house before we leave," Kyle said. "Make sure he's not inside."

They climbed down from the loft and made their way out of the barn. Before heading up to Lonnie's house, they checked the two outbuildings on the property. One turned out to be a chicken coop and the other appeared to be a tool shed, padlocked from the outside.

Lights no longer glowed in the windows of Lonnie's home as they had earlier. Ashley guessed the occupants had turned in for the night. Following Kyle, she mounted the back porch and then peered through the window into the living room. The interior was dark. She realized that short of breaking in, there was no way to know whether or not Ethan slept in one of the upstairs bedrooms. At this point, that was a risk they didn't need to take. The church seemed like a much better hideout.

"I think we should head over to the chapel," she told her brothers.

The trio crossed the pasture and then headed back into the forest. They picked their way through the thick underbrush, moving south to the small clearing where they'd left the two four-wheelers that belonged to Kyle and Shane. Ashley climbed into the seat behind her older brother while Shane mounted his own. Still Waters Chapel stood to the south-west, only a few miles away.

The engine of Kyle's ATV roared to life, the vibration traveling through Ashley's legs. They cut through the woods to the gravel road that led to their destination. She stared at the back of her older brother's head and wondered whether they were doing the right thing. Ashley would give her life to keep her family safe – there was no question. But she worried about Kyle and Shane. Her bond with her brothers felt stronger than it had ever been. It would crush her if something bad happened to either one of them. She wished she could have thought of an excuse to force Kyle and Shane to stay home. But she knew there was nothing she could have said that would have deterred them from hunting for Ethan.

As they rounded a bend, the silhouette of the old, abandoned church popped into view. The building sat back several hundred feet from the gravel road. Tall weeds flourished in what had once been the parking area. Kyle drove past without slowing the four-wheeler. Ashley guessed what he was doing. They'd park somewhere down the road and walk back. If Ethan was in the church, they didn't want to scare him away.

After they'd traveled about a quarter of a mile, Kyle steered the ATV off the side of the gravel road, up the ditch, and into the woods. He parked next to a large hickory. Shane pulled his four-wheeler up beside them.

Kyle spoke to them in a hushed tone. "I broke in the church back when I was sixteen. On a dare. I went through a side door. Wonder if that's how Ethan's getting in."

Ashley shrugged. The old church had been the backdrop for many of the ghost stories she'd heard as a child, so she'd stayed far away. She didn't know the layout of the place, only that the front door and windows had been boarded up, most likely before she'd been born.

"It sounds logical to me," she told her brothers.

With a nod, Kyle pulled his rifle from his shoulder. Ashley reached for her pistol. They had to be ready in case Ethan was prowling the woods. They left the four-wheelers and trekked through the forest. When the church came into view, standing at an angle before them, Kyle motioned to Ashley and Shane. They both nodded, indicating they were ready to go.

Taking the lead, Kyle broke from the cover of the woods and slithered through the weeds toward the church. Ashley matched his pace, keeping only a few feet between them. The chapel's old wooden siding glowed silvery gray in the moonlight. Originally a pint-sized schoolhouse for the children living deep in the mountains, the structure didn't look like a normal church. The windows were sparse and the steeple that had been tacked onto the top of the building as an afterthought was narrow. They crept along the back wall with Shane close behind. The windows on the rear of the chapel were covered by boards, the same as the front. They kept going.

Rounding the corner, they reached the side door Kyle had broken into all those years before. It still yawned open, but just wide enough that an adult would have to enter sideways. Kyle squeezed through first. Ashley followed. She noticed her older brother had switched on his flashlight. She figured it was a good idea. Even though it was important for them to do everything they could to keep from being detected, they needed to see where they were stepping. The floorboards could be rotten and snakes or other wildlife could be nesting inside. Kyle kept the beam pointed straight at the floor instead of ahead of him.

The first doorway they came to was on their right. While Shane stood watch, Kyle and Ashley eased inside. She wasn't sure what the tiny room had been used for by the church's congregation, but now empty beer cans and bottles littered the floor. Teenagers today obviously didn't have the same fear of ghosts they'd had when she was growing up.

Leaving the drinking spot, they passed Shane and ventured forward. The next room had once been the sanctuary. Old wooden pews still lined the walls. Ethan could be lying on one of the seats, the tall backs hiding him from view.

With both Ashley and their younger brother covering him, and his rifle at the ready, Kyle inched down the middle aisle, shining his light across each pew. The seats were all empty except for the hymnals tucked into the wooden pockets that lined the back sides of the benches.

Together, the trio searched the remaining rooms of the church, but there was no sign of Ethan. It seemed he'd covered his tracks and moved on.

This time, Kyle followed Ashley and Shane, retracing their path through the chapel. Their younger brother squeezed back through the side door first.

As she slipped out into the moonlight, Ashley wondered where Ethan had gone. Maybe he was still back at Lonnie's house after all.

Shane stopped in front of them, and then turned around.

"You smell that?" he whispered.

A breeze had stirred up while they'd been inside the church. The gust carried a familiar scent. Burning wood.

Kyle stood still for a moment, as if he was judging the direction of the wind. "It's coming from over there," he told them.

He pointed toward the woods at the rear of the building, in the opposite direction from which they'd arrived. There were no houses or hunting cabins in that part of the forest. It had to be a campfire.

"Let's check it out," Shane said.

Kyle took the lead again, leaving Ashley and Shane to fall in line behind him. As they pushed through the thicket into the forest, the odor of burned wood grew stronger. They hiked toward the scent, finally coming to a clearing about twelve feet square.

An abandoned campfire smoldered in the center of the glade.

Kyle kicked at a charred tree branch. Embers glowed orange beneath the limb. The fire appeared to have been doused within the last hour.

"Look what I found," Shane said.

Ashley glanced at her brother. Her pulsed quickened when she saw the purple paper clasped between Shane's fingers.

A Buster's Grape Bubble Gum wrapper.

They'd found Ethan's campsite.

CHAPTER THIRTY THREE

Shane knelt in the small clearing beneath the halo of moonlight and twirled the purple gum wrapper between his thumb and index finger. It was one of many he'd found littering the ground at the edge of the forest. His sister's ex-husband was the only person he knew who chewed Buster's Grape Bubble Gum. He remembered the man had craved the syrupy sweet flavor like an addict. This had to be Ethan's campfire. And with the embers still glowing, he hadn't been gone long.

"I reckon he ain't far away," Shane whispered to Ashley and Kyle.

Their brother nodded, sweeping his flashlight across the area surrounding the fire.

Ashley kicked dust onto the embers. "I don't understand why the police couldn't find Ethan's camp. Didn't they search this part of the county?"

Kyle nodded again. "Yeah, they even brought out tracking dogs," he said. "But Ethan was probably holed up with some of his kin. I figure he's been moving from place to place. He ain't stood still long enough to get caught."

Shane agreed with Kyle. The cops had combed Laurel County from top to bottom and had come up empty. But now, they finally they had a good lead. He couldn't wait to get his hands on Ethan. The man deserved to die for what he'd done to Ashley. Never mind the murders he'd committed since he'd escaped from prison. Shane had never met a man more evil in all of his life. He couldn't understand the reasons his sister had fallen for the piece of lowlife scum. He figured it must be because of her pure heart. She always looked for the best in people. Ethan had tricked Ashley into believing he was a good person, and then he'd abused her.

Shane planned to make him pay for it.

He stood up, wondering if they should hide and wait for his sister's ex to return to the site. It might take hours, but he didn't mind. When the man returned, Shane would make his presence known. He hoped the lowlife would give him an excuse – not that he felt he really needed one – to put a bullet in the man's brain.

"Look here," Kyle said, excitement in his voice.

Their brother directed his flashlight toward the ground between two oak trees. Tracks from a four-wheeler cut through the underbrush to the south-east and then disappeared into the darkness of the forest.

"And here too." Kyle pointed the beam at another set of tracks leading south-west.

Both sets appeared fresh.

One set of tracks was obviously where Ethan had come into the clearing and the other where he'd gone out, but there was no way to tell which track led away from the campsite. He could have fled in either direction.

"Which way?" Shane asked, wondering which track his brother wanted to follow first.

Kyle hesitated as though he was thinking the matter through.

"Maybe we best split up," his brother finally said.

They didn't know how much of a lead Ethan had on them. He was riding a four-wheeler and they were on foot. If they hoped to catch up to him, they would have to act fast. It made sense for them to split up, but was that really a good idea?

He locked eyes with his older brother. He had an uneasy feeling that something bad might happen to Kyle or Ashley if they parted ways. Although he was younger, Shane was both bigger and stronger than Kyle. He felt he could handle Ethan alone. But could his brother? Even if Ashley went with Kyle, Shane feared the fugitive might get the drop on his brother – might take away his rifle. If it came down to hand-to-hand combat, Kyle wouldn't win. And Ashley would be left to face her ex's wrath.

"We should stick together," Shane said.

Kyle shook his head. "You're thinking he might best me," he stated. "But don't worry, he won't. I'm smarter than him."

Somehow his older brother had always been able to read his thoughts. A skill that amazed and sometimes irritated him.

"Yeah, but …" he let his voice trail off.

Of the two of them, Kyle usually proved to be the one who made the better decisions; however, Shane still wasn't convinced that splitting up was the right thing to do.

"We need to hurry, before he kills somebody else," his brother reminded him. "He could be after Daddy."

Kyle seemed determined. And Shane knew he was right. Ethan might be on his way to kill their father. He couldn't let that happen.

"Okay," he relented, hoping he wouldn't regret it. He and Kyle had always shared a tight bond. His older brother was a part of him. If he lost Kyle, it would be like losing his right arm. And if anything bad happened to Ashley … he couldn't even bear the thought of what it would do to him. He'd have to make sure his siblings stayed together. So they could protect each other.

He wanted to stack the odds in his brother's and sister's favor.

"Ashley goes with you," Shane told Kyle. "And I'll go this way." He chose the track that led south-west – toward the location of their father's home. He guessed Ethan might be searching the property again, looking for their sister.

Kyle nodded. "Alright." He pulled out his cell. "I've got two bars of service. Put your phone on vibrate. And if you find him – don't do nothing. Hide and call me."

"Okay."

Kyle looked at him. Touched him on the shoulder. Shane smiled and pulled his brother into a hug. Then he wrapped his arms around Ashley and kissed her cheek.

"Please be careful and watch your back," his sister said.

Kyle and Ashley disappeared into the shadows.

After switching his cell to silent mode, Shane plunged into the forest, following the ATV tracks. He kept his rifle poised for action. He hoped he'd picked the right path. That he would be the one to catch up with Ethan – not Kyle and Ashley. He wondered whether the trail would lead back home, where his father slept.

He knew his father was armed. And Kyle had booby-trapped both the front and back doors of the house. If anyone broke in, they'd be met by a shotgun blast.

But Shane still wasn't sure that splitting up had been the right decision. Even if Kyle was strong enough to protect himself, what if something happened and he and Ashley got separated? Could she protect herself?

His sister had practically raised him after their mother died. She'd always taken care of him, had put his needs first when they were growing up. And she was the smartest person he'd ever known – except when it came to men. She had a habit of letting her heart rule her brain. He'd been too young to prevent her from sneaking off to be with Ethan, but he'd tried to warn her about Brett.

From the moment he'd first laid eyes on Money Bags, he'd sensed the man was no good. At least now his sister had come to her senses and had broken off her engagement. He just wished she hadn't been hurt in the process. But if Shane had anything to say about it, no man would ever hurt Ashley again.

A few yards ahead, he noticed a break in the tree cover. As he'd been walking, he'd felt like the tracks had gradually shifted direction. When he reached the clearing, he looked up at the sky, noting the position of the moon. He realized he was now headed due south. He checked the compass app on his phone to make sure.

The tracks were no longer leading toward his father's house.

They were heading toward the home of Kyle's girlfriend, Janet.

Maybe Ashley had been right. Ethan could be stalking the brothers' girlfriends. Shane plowed ahead, hoping that Janet was no longer home. That she'd kept her promise to Kyle and had left town. At least he knew Robin was already on the road. She'd called him when she'd reached Chattanooga, on her way to Georgia.

Shane heard a noise up ahead of him on the right.

A thump.

He stood still, holding his breath. It could be a forest animal – or it could be Ethan.

After a moment, he crept forward.

Thump ... thump.

He dropped to one knee, aiming his rifle toward the sound.

Without warning, Shane was hit hard from behind, his AR-15 knocked from his hands. He scrambled on his stomach, trying to reach his rifle, but the man was on top of his back. A fist slammed into the side of his head.

Shane jerked his body backward, trying to fling the man off of him. As he flipped to his side, in the glow of the moonlight, he caught sight of his attacker's face.

Ethan.

His fist crashed into the jaw of his sister's ex. Blood sprayed Shane's chest, along with what he thought was a tooth.

Ethan fell backward and Shane lunged on top of him, pummeling his fist between his attacker's stomach and chest. Then he aimed for the man's nose. Shane planned to beat the face of his sister's ex to a bloody pulp. And he wouldn't stop until Ethan's brains were splattered across the ground.

Before he could strike the punch, out of the corner of his eye he saw a dark object flying toward him. He dodged to the right, but it was too late. Ethan had managed to grab the rifle. The butt of the weapon bashed against the side of Shane's head.

The blow reverberated through his skull. Stars exploded in front of Shane's eyes. He blinked. The world was spinning, and he couldn't focus his vision.

Ethan slung him to the side. Shane rolled onto his knees and tried to regain his balance, to get his feet under him. But Ethan moved fast. Shane looked up. He glimpsed the rock barreling toward him.

Pain sliced through Shane's neck and ran down his spine.

A black haze engulfed him.

CHAPTER THIRTY FOUR

Ashley crept behind Kyle, silent as a bobcat, following the ATV tracks through the dense forest. Her face still stung where the rat had scratched her and sweat coated her back beneath the camo shirt, but she refused to let the minor discomforts get to her. She was thankful she'd been able to convince Kyle and Shane to let her join them. If she'd stayed home, she'd be pacing the floor, terrified her brothers would never return.

She hoped Shane would be okay by himself. Kyle seemed to think he would. Her older brother had spent hours upon hours hunting with Shane, trekking through the woods, dodging wild hogs, snakes, and even bobcats. Kyle knew their younger brother's strengths and weaknesses. He would never have allowed them to split up if he thought harm would come to Shane. But concern still tugged at her heart. Refused to let go.

The tracks curved hard to the right. Up ahead she saw a break in the tree cover. Kyle stopped and turned around.

"I know where we're at," he whispered. "That's the road the church is on. We done hit a dead end."

Ashley thought it looked familiar.

"I guess we should turn around and try to catch up with Shane," she said.

"Let me text him. Tell him to wait for us."

She watched as Kyle pulled out his phone and tapped the screen. She was glad they'd be meeting back up with their brother and wondered how long it would take to reach him. She hoped they'd have better luck on the other trail. But Shane obviously hadn't found any clues yet or he would have already let them know.

Kyle slipped his phone into his pocket, and they set out again, heading back toward the clearing.

***

On the other side of Ethan's campsite, Ashley followed Kyle down the tracks Shane had taken earlier. Keeping her feet inside the depression created by one of the ATV's wheels, she recalled a map of the area in her mind. A knot of fear formed in her chest when she realized the four-wheeler had taken a south-west path.

"Are we walking toward Daddy's house?" she whispered to Kyle.

"We was. But the trail's shifting. We've been turning south."

Ashley was relieved to hear that Ethan hadn't been heading toward Spencer's property. She knew her father was well armed and that he was an expert marksman, but she didn't want her ex-husband to go anywhere near him.

She looked up and noticed a clearing ahead. She wondered whether Shane had chosen that spot to wait for them or whether he'd already passed though when Kyle sent the text. When they broke out of the cover of the tree line, her older brother stopped short.

Kyle jerked his arm back toward her, blocking her path.

He looked at Ashley and shook his head. She scanned the clearing before them and noticed something on the ground a few yards away. In the moonlight, it appeared to be some type of animal. She couldn't tell whether it was alive or dead. But from Kyle's reaction, he believed it wasn't friendly.

He motioned for her to stay put. She obeyed, watching as her brother slinked toward the black form, poised to fire his rifle. When he reached the animal, Kyle dropped to his knees.

"No," he moaned.

Fear shot through Ashley's heart. She ran toward Kyle. As she neared the dark form, it morphed into the shape of a human.

It was Shane.

Tears streamed down her face, and she heard a cry echo from her lips. She knelt next to Kyle, as she fought to keep shock from taking hold of her body. Blood covered Shane's head, neck, and the back of his shirt. He was unconscious.

Please don't let him be dead.

The premonition she'd had earlier popped into her mind. Why hadn't she listened to her instincts? She should have tried harder to stop the hunt. If Shane was dead, it was her fault.

"He's still got a pulse," Kyle told her. "But we can't move him. I think his neck might be broke."

Ashley pulled out her phone and dialed 9-1-1, putting the call on speaker.

"9-1-1. What's the location of your emergency?" the operator asked.

"We're in the woods near Still Waters Chapel."

"No," Kyle interrupted. "We're closer to Turkey Creek Road. They need to come that way. When we hear them coming, we'll run down and meet them at the road."

"Did you hear that?" Ashley asked the operator.

"Yes. What's the nature of your emergency?"

"My brother's been hurt really bad. He's unconscious and we think his neck might be broken. We need an ambulance."

"Is he breathing?"

"Yes."

"It's important that you don't try to move him. Just keep him warm and wait for the paramedics."

"The man who hurt my brother is an escaped convict. His name is Ethan Barrett. I don't know for sure, but I think he may still be in the area."

"The police will be notified as well."

Ashley ended the call, releasing the sob she'd been holding back. She ripped off her camouflage shirt and draped it over Shane. She looked at Kyle and saw tears glistening in his eyes as well. She couldn't remember ever seeing her brother cry before, not since he was a small child.

Kyle returned her gaze.

He grabbed her hand and held it tight while they waited for the wail of the emergency sirens.

CHAPTER THIRTY FIVE

Ashley veered into the parking lot of Cedar View Medical Center and squeezed her sedan between a pickup and an SUV. Earlier, as the paramedics were loading Shane into the ambulance, Kyle had told her to ride along with them to the hospital. But after seeing the expression on her older brother's face, she'd refused. They only had room for one person, and she could tell Kyle needed to be there with Shane. She understood the bond her brothers shared, and she couldn't deny them that time together. Just in case they were the last moments of her younger brother's life.

A swarm of patrol cars had arrived along with the EMTs. She heard one of the officers say the TBI was on their way as well. They planned to scour the area searching for Ethan.

"Go take care of Shane," she had told Kyle, pushing him into the ambulance. "I'll get an officer to drive me to Daddy's house and we'll meet you at the hospital."

Now, as she jumped out of her sedan, she could feel her pulse racing. She glanced at her father. It broke her heart to see the pain that was etched on his face. They'd made it to Cedar View in record time. Escorted by a sheriff's deputy, his siren blaring, she'd driven twenty miles over the speed limit the entire way.

Ashley's phone chimed. It was a text message from Kyle.

Meet me on the third floor.

Ashley and Spencer didn't wait for the deputy – still sitting in his patrol car – instead, they hurried across the parking lot. When the automatic doors of the hospital opened, they rushed through, bypassing the information desk.

Tears threatened Ashley's eyes as she climbed into the elevator. She blinked, willing them away, not wanting her father to see how worried she was. Spencer looked older in the harsh florescent lighting, his face more weatherworn. His mouth pressed into a thin line; he dropped his gaze to the floor. When they reached the third level, the elevator dinged, and the door slid open.

Ashley stood back, letting her father exit first. Kyle met them in the hallway. His eyes were red, his face shrouded in concern.

"Is Shane going to be okay?" she asked. Her voice sounded strange in her ears. Like a high-pitched squeal.

Kyle looked at her. Shook his head.

"They don't know yet," he said. "The doctor told me to wait up here. He's fixing to operate on Shane now."

She followed Kyle and Spencer toward the surgical waiting room, anxious to hear exactly what kind of damage Ethan had done to Shane. With all the blood covering her brother's head, she hadn't been able to guess. How extensive were his injuries? Would he make it through the night?

Nearing the door, her steps grew labored. It felt as though iron fingers were clamped around her lungs, making it difficult for her to breathe. Her mind was spinning. She knew that somewhere in the hospital, her little brother was under a surgeon's scalpel, fighting for his life.

And she was to blame.

Kyle led them to a row of green upholstered chairs just inside the door of the waiting area, though they all chose to remain standing. Like Ashley, she figured her father and brother were too tense to even think about taking a seat.

Her brother opened his mouth as if to speak, but no words came out. He cleared his throat.

"Ethan crushed Shane's neck. Probably with a rock," he finally told Ashley and Spencer in a hushed tone. "The doctor said something about fractures and stabilizing his spine. The operation is gonna take several hours."

A moan caught in Ashley's throat. She feared her older brother's next words – already knew what they would be.

Kyle continued, "The doctor told me he might not be able to walk anymore."

Her assumption had been correct. Shane might be paralyzed. Ethan could have killed her younger brother – could have crushed his skull instead. But he'd chosen the option which would cause Shane the most suffering. Her brother might have to live the rest of his life confined to a wheelchair, unable to move or even feel his arms and legs.

She looked at her father. All of the color had drained from his face.

"I'm so sorry," Ashley said, her eyes filling with tears. "All of this is my fault."

Spencer looked at her. “You hush, baby girl,” he said. “You ain't got nothing to do with it.”

“Yes, I do. If I had listened to you and stayed away from Ethan – if I had never married him – Shane wouldn’t be in surgery right now.”

“We all got a path to walk. This is Shane’s,” Spencer told her. He put his arm around Ashley. “You was just a slip of a girl when you hitched up with Ethan. You didn’t know no better. Even if you’d spurned him way back then, he might have still been gunning for our family. You know those car-chopping Barretts hate us for trying to make an honest dime at the shop. We don’t buy none of their stolen parts. We done been a burr under their saddle for years.”

Ashley appreciated her father’s words, but she knew they were clouded by his love for her. She was to blame. Pure and simple. Her actions had brought the wrath of Ethan down upon their heads.

“Daddy’s right,” Kyle said. “If anybody’s to blame, it’s me. Splitting up tonight was my idea. If I’d stayed with Shane, Ethan couldn’t have gotten him.”

Spencer shook his head. “You done what you thought was best, Kyle,” he said. “You ain't to blame neither. Can’t nobody see the future.”

Ashley certainly didn’t blame Kyle. The decision to split up had been a logical one, allowing them to cover as much ground in as little time as possible. They’d been racing the clock, wanting to catch Ethan before he killed again.

She looked down at the green and mauve geometric-patterned carpeting, wishing she could go back in time and make things right. A tear splashed onto the toe of her once-white sneaker. It formed a dark dot in the middle of the rusty-brown coating of dust from the forest. She felt her lungs tightening again. It was as if the walls were pressing in around her, the room growing smaller with each passing second. She had to get out of there – away from the people she’d forced so much pain upon.

“I’m going to walk around a little bit and get some air,” she said.

“We’ll come too,” Kyle offered.

“No – someone needs to stay and wait for the doctor. And I really just want to be alone for a little while, if that’s okay.” It was a statement, not a question. She couldn’t stay in the room any longer, regardless of whether or not her family agreed.

Spencer nodded. She could see in his eyes that he understood. “You take your time, baby girl,” he said.

The look Kyle shot Ashley said that he thought her being alone was a bad idea. She figured it was because he regretted letting Shane go off by himself.

"Send me a text if you hear from the doctor before I get back," she told her brother.

Ashley trotted toward the elevator. She couldn't get away from her family fast enough. But what she was really running from was her overwhelming guilt. She almost wished she'd never been born.

An image of George Bailey standing on the bridge in Bedford Falls popped into her mind. *It's a Wonderful Life* had been one of her favorite films growing up. She had to believe her life had a purpose – that she was here for a reason. Who else would have helped raise Shane after her mother died? But still, she was responsible for bringing suffering into the lives of the people she loved the most.

The elevator dinged as it settled on the third floor. The doors slid open, and she bolted inside, thankful that she was the only passenger. Her reflection mocked her from the interior side of the polished steel doors. She looked like a contestant from a survival-type game show. Her hair hung in tangles, a large red scratch ran down her cheek, and sweat had stained her pink T-shirt.

But it was the reflection of her eyes that startled her.

Ashley stepped closer to the door. Dark circles underlined the hollow eyes that stared back. She'd likened her pale appearance to a ghost when she'd found out Ethan had escaped from prison. Now she reminded herself more of a walking corpse. A shell that was left over after the soul had fled.

Her hand snapped to her belly. She thought about the precious life growing within her and her face began to change. A genuine smile lifted her lips. Light appeared in her wearied eyes. She carried the future inside her. A future that would not be marred by threats from her ex-husband. She'd make sure of it.

Ethan would not win.

Ashley refused to be broken. She was strong – stronger than she'd ever realized. And now it was time to channel that strength into finding her ex-husband and putting an end to his reign of terror once and for all.

The elevator jerked to a halt on the ground floor, and she strode into the lobby with purpose. Where had Ethan gone after he'd attacked Shane? He wouldn't return to his camp or go near the abandoned church. The risk of him being captured was too high.

She crossed the lobby and the automatic doors whooshed open before her. Ashley left behind the antiseptic hospital air and pushed into the humidity that blanketed the night. She turned right and headed down the sidewalk toward a wooden bench, bathed in the harsh artificial light of a streetlamp. She had to think like Ethan. Put herself in his shoes and figure out where he'd fled after his hiding spot was discovered.

She sank onto the bench. Would he run to the other side of Laurel County and make a new camp in the forest? He had a four-wheeler so he wouldn't be deterred by the rugged terrain. He obviously had access to a car as well since he'd been traveling back and forth between Briarwood and Mettler Ridge.

The teddy bear he'd left at her back door and the fake sighting at Quail Falls Campground had been clues linked to Ethan's past with Ashley. He'd wanted her to remember – to believe that she belonged to him. Now that he knew her relationship with Brett had imploded, had her ex-husband headed to another location that he thought would ignite a memory in her mind of their brief time together?

Ethan would likely choose a spot that he believed held a special meaning for them. Their spur-of-the-moment wedding had taken place at the courthouse here in Cedar View, but the building was located in the middle of the town's square. The perfect setting would combine both a treasured memory for her ex-husband and seclusion.

Only one location stood out in her mind: Laurel Bluff.

The hairs on the back of Ashley's neck leapt to attention. She felt eyes focused on her. The hospital lawn and parking lot were deserted. She saw the car belonging to the sheriff's deputy – the man who'd just been assigned the task of guarding her family – but it was empty. He was probably inside looking for her. There were no people anywhere in sight. However, she knew the sensation was real – not just her imagination playing tricks on her. She was being watched at this very moment.

By Ethan.

The impulse to draw her pistol raced through her body. Ashley fought back the urge. She couldn't let her ex-husband know she was armed. She had to fool him into believing he had the upper hand against her. That he had won. That was the only way he would let his guard down enough to be lured into a trap.

Ashley sprang from the bench and gazed up at the sky.

"I've been so stupid," she cried out as if speaking to the heavens, pleading for a higher power to help her. "No one could ever love me the way Ethan did."

She knew her ex-husband was watching, but was he listening? Would he believe the lies she proclaimed? Would he take the bait?

"I just want to feel close to him again," she shouted, hoping to appeal to his overinflated ego.

Keeping her eyes focused on the sky, Ashley forced a tone of longing into her voice.

"I have to go back to Laurel Bluff."

CHAPTER THIRTY SIX

Ashley glanced in her rearview mirror as she merged onto the main highway leading to Mettler Ridge. A pair of headlights danced in the distance behind her. She wondered if they belonged to Ethan's vehicle. She activated the cruise control and set the speed for three miles under the posted limit. Slow enough to allow her pursuer to catch up and hopefully pass her, but fast enough to prevent him from becoming suspicious.

She was certain that Ethan had been hiding in the shadows at the hospital, surveilling her every move. But did he believe the words she'd shouted to the heavens? Would he fall into her trap?

Her current plan entailed holding her ex-husband at gunpoint at Laurel Bluff until the authorities arrived. But if something happened and the plan failed, she wouldn't hesitate to shoot him. She knew he wouldn't think twice before murdering a member of her family. Of course, his actions had proven he preferred to make them suffer first.

The sign for Tucker Cave Road popped into view ahead of her car. The narrow road snaked through Tucker Holler and then connected to the road that climbed upward to the bluff. The shortcut would shave ten minutes off of Ashley's drive time. But instead of turning, she stuck to the main highway. She watched her rearview mirror as she passed the road. The headlights that had followed several car lengths behind since she'd left Cedar View veered to the right and then disappeared.

The vehicle had turned down the shortcut.

Deep in her soul, she knew the driver was Ethan.

He would arrive at the bluff ahead of her, just as she'd hoped. Her stomach knotted as she imagined their confrontation. Ethan would be armed as well – that was a certainty. She would be forced to lure him out into the open and trick him into dropping his weapon before she drew her pistol. In order to do so, she'd have to appear vulnerable. Weak. Eager to give in to all his demands.

Ashley slowed her sedan as she entered the city limits of Mettler Ridge. The town lay still and silent, as though holding its breath in anticipation. She turned south, winding her way up the side of the mountain toward Laurel Bluff. Over eight years had passed since she'd last traveled the road. Nothing seemed to have changed. The way was still lined with banks of limestone and cedar trees with a scant number of farmhouses and trailers peppered in.

When she reached the top of the mountain, the tree cover split apart on her left. Below her the lights of the small town of Mettler Ridge sparkled like gemstones. Ashley maneuvered her car off the road and onto the makeshift parking area of hard-packed dirt. The bluff was a popular make-out spot for the local teens.

The place where she and Ethan had first made love.

She remembered the night clearly, though not fondly. Thinking their love would last forever, she'd agreed to consummate their relationship in the bed of Ethan's truck under a blanket of stars. A week later they were married.

And that's when her nightmare had begun.

Taking a deep breath, Ashley pushed her sedan door open and slid out, scanning the bluff to the tree lines on her left and far right. Her heart thumped in her chest. She didn't see Ethan, but the weight of his eyes pressed against her once again.

He was here – watching from the darkness.

Beneath the light of the quarter moon, she ambled across the parking area toward a large flat rock that served as a bench for people who wished to enjoy the view from the overlook. She timed her steps, being careful not to move too fast. It was important for her to appear lost in thought, as though she was reminiscing about her days with Ethan.

Sweat coated her palms as she fought back the fear surging in her chest. Ashley knew the scene she was about to perform had to be award-winning. Convincing enough to impress the toughest critic.

Her baby's future – his or her very life – depended on it.

When she reached the rock, she halted and remained standing. She gazed out across the valley of twinkling lights. This was her stage. Her audience hidden in the shadows. It was time for the show to begin.

"I'm so sorry, Ethan," she shouted into the night. "I was wrong."

She glanced to her left and right pretending she was feeling her ex-husband's eyes on her for the first time.

"You're here, aren't you?" she yelled. "I can feel your soul next to mine. We'll always be connected – for all eternity."

She listened for movement around her. The harmony of tree frogs and crickets rang out in the night, but she could hear no other sounds.

"I never should have testified against you. I realize now that you would have come back for me – that you would have pulled me out of the pit. I know you were just trying to teach me a lesson."

The chorus of forest creatures continued around her, but there was no sign of her ex-husband.

"I wish I could go back in time and make things right. But we both know I can't. We can only go forward."

Her next words would be critical. They could mean the difference between her life and her death.

"I belong to you!" she cried out. "To you and only you – forever."

She breathed in deep, steeled herself for what would happen next.

"If you're here, Ethan, come out where I can see you. Come and claim your wife."

A split second after the words had boomed from her lips, Ashley caught sight of a dark form moving near the tree line on her left.

Terror struck her heart like a bolt of lightning.

Ethan slithered into the moonlight, a smile on his face.

CHAPTER THIRTY SEVEN

Ashley's muscles trembled and her knees threatened to fail her as Ethan sauntered into the moonlight on top of Laurel Bluff. Blood stained his camouflage shirt, his jaw appeared bruised, and his wicked grin was missing a tooth.

His cold eyes bored into her, igniting a fear in her soul that was stronger than any she'd ever felt. They were alone. Face-to-face. He could kill her now – throw her body over the cliff – and there would be no witnesses to force him to pay for his crime.

The plan had been to fool her ex-husband, to make him believe he had won his twisted game. To disarm him and hold him at gunpoint – shooting him if necessary. Then she'd call the police, keeping Ethan as her prisoner until they arrived. But now that he was here – with just a few feet separating them – she realized she may have been fooling herself. Did she possess the courage and wit to follow through? Was she cunning enough to defeat him?

Or, after all these years, was Ethan the one who was still in control?

A smile danced across his lips as he reached out and slid his fingers along the curve of her jaw. Her skin stung from his touch. She wanted to jerk backwards, seize her pistol, and fire round after round into his chest, not stopping until his lifeless body fell to the ground. But although he carried no visible weapons, like Ashley, he might have a firearm holstered in the waistband of his pants, hidden underneath his camouflage hunting shirt.

In a contest for the quickest draw, she would be sure to lose.

She'd have to wait for the right opportunity. Her timing had to be perfect. Otherwise, both she and her baby risked forfeiting their lives.

Fighting the impulse to flee, Ashley stood still, allowing Ethan to look her over. She couldn't flinch. She had to keep up the pretense that she was glad they'd been reunited. His eyes swept across her body from head to toe. She kept her arms pressed close to her sides, hoping he wouldn't notice the bulge of her pistol.

"Been a long time, girl," he said, lust heavy in his voice.

His tone soured her stomach. She resisted the urge to slap him, fixing a counterfeit smile on her face instead.

"I've missed you, Ethan," she lied, trying to inject a note of longing into her words.

He shook his head. "You ain't missed me none. You been shacked up in that fancy house with some rich man."

"It's over between me and Brett," she assured him. "We're not together anymore, but I bet you already know that."

Of course he knew it. The breakup had been a part of her ex-husband's plan – she was positive. Ashley knew he'd counted on her ending her relationship with Brett when she learned of the affair. One more loss to make her suffer through.

"Shane didn't give me no choice tonight," he said, watching her eyes. "I had to do it."

Pain ripped through her heart at the mention of her little brother, but she refused to let it show. She realized Ethan was testing her, trying to get a read on her true feelings.

"I remember all the times you tried to warn me about my family – told me that they didn't really love me," she said. "I know that if I let them stay in my life, they'd still try to keep you and me apart."

Ethan stared at her, as if he was wondering what to make of her words.

"But you've had family problems of your own now, haven't you? I know you pushed Ray off of the cliff near Quail Falls Campground."

He laughed. "Ray deserved to die. He was gonna double-cross me. Didn't want to help me no more after he found out what I did to the guard. So I put him out of my misery."

"What about Neil?"

"He done his own self in. Saved me the trouble."

Ashley had been right on both counts.

"Hand over your phone," Ethan ordered.

She didn't want to relinquish her cell. It could prove to be her lifeline. But if she refused, he would realize this was a trap. He'd kill her. She pulled the phone from her back pocket and placed it onto the palm of her ex-husband's outstretched hand.

Ethan slipped her cell into the side pocket of his camo pants. "That rich man weren't no good for you," he said.

She nodded, playing along. "I realize that now. No man could ever love me the way that you did."

She'd never allow another man to terrorize and control her like that again.

"Damn right." Ethan straightened his posture as though he was proud of the abusive way that he'd treated her during their marriage.

"You weren't born to be no city girl," he told her. He gestured toward the tree line. "You belong in these here mountains. Or some like 'um."

"I belong with you, Ethan," she cooed, looking directly into his eyes, trying her best to make sure he believed the lie.

She was having trouble reading him – couldn't tell whether she'd hit the mark. He refused to allow his reaction to her words to show on his face.

"You still belong *to* me," he stated, matter-of-factly. "Can't no Judge take away what's mine."

Ashley knew he was referring to the judge that had granted her divorce, based on the grounds that Ethan had been convicted of her attempted murder.

He pointed his index finger at her chest. "Everything I done since I broke out was for your own good. You needed teaching. It ain't right for a woman to go against her husband." He shook his head and braced his hands on his hips. "You should of knowed that."

"I promise you; I've learned my lesson now and I won't ever repeat my past mistakes."

This time she'd make sure Ethan never hurt another innocent person. She'd kill him first.

Ashley inched to her left, trying to get a better look at her ex-husband's side. Searching for the slightest protrusion – proof that his clothing concealed a weapon. Although she failed to spot a lump or bulge, she still wasn't convinced that he was unarmed.

"I ain't sure you're done learning yet."

His words prickled the hairs on the back of her neck. What did he mean? Had he already made the decision to kill her here and now? Or did he plan to kidnap her and kill her family first? She had to defuse the situation.

"I know that I'm to blame for everything that's happened. You don't need to do anything else to prove it."

Even though she'd been young and naïve, she'd married Ethan of her own free will. She'd brought him into the lives of her loved ones, and she'd carry the guilt of his crimes with her until the day she died.

A fire lit in his eyes. "It ain't a woman's place to call the law on her husband. The price got to be paid."

Panic began to rise in Ashley's chest. Her plan was falling apart. Rather than calming Ethan down, her words just seemed to kindle his anger. She had to shift the focus of their conversation.

"Come and sit down on the rock, Ethan," she said, stepping toward the slab often used as a bench, the remnants of a campfire in the hand-dug pit in front of it. "Instead of talking about the past, we can talk about our future together."

If she could entice him to sit down, she might be able to gain an advantage over him. It would be harder for him to draw his gun – if he had one. She could begin massaging his shoulders, get him to relax, and then shove her pistol into the back of his neck.

"You think I'm stupid?" Ethan laughed. "You don't want no future with me. You want me dead."

"Don't say that."

Ashley realized she was running out of time. She had to convince Ethan that she still loved him before he decided to kill her. "I want to get married again and have a home and a family."

The statement was true, but as Ethan had said, she didn't want him in her future. And he was right – she hoped he would be sentenced to death for his crimes.

"You want a life with me?" A wicked smile crossed his face. "Then prove it." He stepped toward her. "Right now."

A chill coursed through her, as though ice water had been injected into her veins. She feared what his expression implied. Would he try to rape her? She had to play along and pretend to be interested in him. Divert his attention so that she could draw her pistol.

"Have a seat on the rock," she said, forcing an alluring tone into her voice. "We can get comfortable and then I'll prove to you how I feel."

His cold steel-blue eyes raked across her again.

Ethan sidled toward the flat slab of limestone; his gaze fastened to her. Suspicion reeked from his pores. He eased down onto the end of the rock.

In an attempt to lessen his apprehension, Ashley had been standing in front of him, between the slab and the stone-rimmed fire pit. She inched to his side and settled her left hand on his shoulder. The feel of his body beneath her skin sickened her.

Hatred flooded her heart.

She kneaded her fingers into the muscles beneath the camouflage fabric of his shirt. Ethan tilted his head, keeping her under his watchful eye. She smiled down at him while her insides quaked. In a slow deliberate movement, she slid behind him, gripping his other shoulder with her right hand. She pressed her thumbs into the sinews of his back and continued to work his muscles.

"How does this feel," she asked, her voice just above a whisper.

"Mm."

She felt the tension escaping Ethan's body as he began to relax.

It was time to make her move.

She knew she only possessed this single chance to overtake him. One wrong step and both she and her unborn child could end up dead. Breathing in deep, she struck fast.

Ashley yanked her pistol from its holster.

At the same moment, Ethan jerked toward her as his iron fingers clamped around her left wrist. He flung her forward, spinning her body around. The weapon flew from her grasp.

She hit the ground hard, the wind knocked from her lungs.

Ethan jumped on top of her.

His evil laugh echoed in her ears.

CHAPTER THIRTY EIGHT

Ashley gasped for breath as Ethan lunged on top of her, his teeth shining like fangs. For an instant, both her mind and body felt paralyzed. Her diaphragm burned as though it was on fire. Her back had smacked the ground so hard that all the air had been forced from her lungs.

Ethan's cackle split the still night like the screech of a wild man.

"You think you can kill me?" he shouted.

Her chest heaved as she gulped in precious oxygen. When her thoughts began to clear, Ashley's first concern was for her child. She had to save her baby – prayed the little one hadn't been injured.

Ethan's cold blue eyes had turned dark – as black as his soul. "I can crack your skull like an egg," he warned her.

She knew his words were true. It would be even easier for him to crush her windpipe. She had to get him off of her. Squirming, she tried to buck her hips, but her ex-husband held her tight.

He pinned her shoulders to the ground. "You gonna be real sorry now."

Desperate to break his hold, she raked her left hand across the dirt, striking something solid. Her fingers curled around a stone that rimmed the edge of the fire pit.

Her ex-husband's face pressed closer, his smirking lips mere inches from her own. The sickly-sweet odor of his breath singed her nostrils.

"You ain't never felt no pain as bad as what I'm fixing to give you," he said.

Ashley slammed the stone into the side of Ethan's head. He cried out in agony as he toppled to her right. Blood streamed down his temple. She needed to get up onto her feet. To race to her car and lock herself inside. She scrambled backwards and wriggled her legs out from under his weight.

Before she could stand, Ethan caught her left ankle, his grip as strong as steel. She writhed and kicked, trying to break free. Her right heel crashed against her ex-husband's face. The bones in his nose snapped. He cried out again as more blood erupted from his face and ran down his chin.

Ashley jerked her leg from his grasp. This was her chance to flee – her only chance to survive. She jumped to her feet and flew toward the parking area.

Footsteps pounded the ground behind her. Ethan was stronger, stood taller, and possessed a longer stride. Panic surged through her heart as she realized he was gaining fast. She wouldn't make it to the car. His arms cinched around her waist, and she felt herself falling forward.

Ethan tackled her to the ground. She landed on her forearms. The force jarred her bones, her face inches from the dirt. The weight of his body bound her hips and legs. Ashley was trapped again. This time she feared she wouldn't be able to escape.

Pain shot through her scalp as Ethan yanked her hair, jerking her head back.

"I was gonna make you suffer a real long while," he told her. "Had plans to drag it out for weeks. You're still gonna die slow. But now, it's gonna be today."

Ashley heard a noise ahead of her – a low rumble. A pair of headlights flashed on. The sudden brightness stung her eyes. She realized a car had rolled into the parking area under the cover of darkness.

"Stop! Police!" a voice shouted. "Put your hands up!"

She recognized the voice. It was Detective Lansing. Relief fluttered just outside the edges of her grasp. A part of her was glad Lansing had arrived, but another part wondered whether the detective was prepared for what he'd walked into.

Ethan scooped her up off the ground, allowing her to stand. His right arm clamped around her neck like a vise. She struggled in his arms, but each move just tightened her ex-husband's grip.

"I'll break her neck!" Ethan yelled.

"You don't want to do that," Lansing told him.

"I ain't got nothing to lose. If I die, she's going with me."

Ashley wanted to shout out for Lansing to shoot, but she had no doubt that Ethan would follow through on his threat to break her neck. If he killed her, her baby would die as well.

"Let's talk about this," the detective said. "We can work something out,"

"Ain't but one deal I'll be making. Get in the light so I can see you."

Lansing stepped forward into the glow of the headlights. His weapon was aimed at Ethan. "I know you don't really want to hurt her."

"You don't know nothing 'bout me."

"I know that deep down, you love Ashley. Let her go."

She felt her ex-husband's body tense, his left arm tightened around her waist. She knew the detective was trying to negotiate, but his words seemed to make Ethan more determined to kill her.

"She got me locked up," her ex-husband said, hatred in his voice.

"Not because she wanted to," the detective said. "She was scared. She just did what her lawyer told her to do."

Ashley had wanted Ethan to be sentenced to prison for the rest of his life. She realized Lansing was looking for any excuse he could find to persuade her ex-husband to let her go.

"That don't matter none. Here's what we're gonna do. You're gonna toss your gun over this way. Real gentle like."

"Let her go first, and then I'll give you my weapon."

"Nah, it don't work that way," Ethan told him. "You're gonna give me your gun. You don't do what I say, I'm gonna break Ashley's neck. Then you can shoot me, and we'll be done."

The detective hesitated. "It doesn't have to end like that. There's a chance for you to make things right. I can talk to the judge and tell him that you cooperated. He'll go easier on you."

Her ex-husband had no plans to return to prison – Ashley was certain. She knew he'd rather die first. And he was determined that she die with him.

"You got five seconds. Then she's dead." Ethan started his countdown. "One … two …"

"Okay," Lansing said. "Just don't hurt her."

Bending his knees, the detective tossed his gun toward her ex-husband.

"You step back now," Ethan said.

Lansing obeyed, staying within the circle of light.

Ethan shoved her forward, but kept his arms fastened around her torso. He inched them both toward the gun.

As she hobbled in front of her ex-husband, Ashley's thoughts jumped to Shane. She imagined her brother lying in the operating room, fighting for his life, knowing that he may never walk again. Then she thought about Steve, who she'd found out was planning to be married later this summer. She remembered Ray. Although he'd helped Ethan, he'd regretted it in the end. And there was Dr. Fisher. He'd been so kind to her after she'd lost her daughter. Neil, who could have had a wonderful life ahead of him. And Cherie. The woman may not have even known that Brett was living with Ashley. And if she had, she still didn't deserve to die.

All of Ethan's victims had deserved to live. Unlike him.

Ashley knew this was the end for her as well. Once her ex-husband picked up Detective Lansing's weapon, he would kill her, her baby, and the detective. After that, he'd murder her father and brothers. She couldn't let that happen. She refused to let her ex-husband hurt another innocent soul.

Ashley swung her right leg as hard as she could. Her toe collided with the detective's pistol. The weapon flew across the ground into the darkness.

"Stupid bitch!" her ex-husband yelled in her ear as his arms dropped from her waist.

Ethan's fist slammed into her jaw.

Pain sliced through her face. Knocked sideways, Ashley tumbled to the ground.

A dark haze clouded her vision as a loud ringing echoed in her head. The sky, trees, and earth swirled around her. She couldn't tell which direction was up and which was down. The taste of acid flooded her mouth. She struggled to hang onto consciousness.

Closing her eyes, she forced herself to breathe in deep. Her jaw throbbed. She pressed her palms against the ground, trying to regain her sense of balance. The ringing in her ears began to fade – the noise replaced by the clack of blows.

Fists smashing bone.

Ashley opened her eyes. Ethan and Detective Lansing battled back and forth, volleying for position, both landing and then receiving punch after punch. Her ex-husband was stronger – a walking wall of muscle – but he'd already sustained a broken nose and a gash on his temple. Lansing was quicker, dodging Ethan's fists. But she knew the detective couldn't evade her ex-husband for much longer.

Pushing herself up, she tried to stand. The world began to spin before her eyes again. Ashley dropped to her knees and crawled toward the direction where she had kicked Lansing's gun. She had to find it.

Once outside the illumination of the detective's headlights, her eyesight dimmed. She stretched her hands forward, sweeping them across the ground, searching for the gun. If she didn't locate the weapon soon, she feared her ex-husband would kill Lansing.

A guttural moan rang out behind her.

She looked back over her shoulder. Ethan had Lansing pinned to the ground. His fists pummeled the detective's head. Her time was up. If she didn't find the gun fast, Lansing would die.

An image popped into her mind. She remembered seeing her own pistol lying between the fire pit and the edge of the bluff. Ashley pushed herself to her feet. With her balance still off, she half stumbled, half ran across the parking area toward the fire pit.

As she neared the limestone slab, her night vision returned. She spotted the black silhouette of her Smith & Wesson near the rim of the cliff. She prayed she'd have time to save Lansing. Footsteps boomed behind her. She knelt beside the gun and then glanced back.

Ethan barreled toward her.

As Ashley's fingers closed around the pistol, her ex-husband hit her from behind. Their bodies crashed to the ground at edge of the bluff, inches from tumbling over. She landed on her stomach with Ethan on top of her, her right hand pinned beneath her abdomen. To her left, the earth cut away, plunging into the valley below. One wrong move could send them both plummeting to their deaths.

He lifted his body just enough to roll her onto her back. She met his gaze for what she felt would be the last time. His soulless eyes appeared swollen. Blood caked his face. His lips parted in a wicked smile.

"Time for you to die, girl," her ex-husband spat out.

Ethan's fingers clamped around her throat.

She gasped as her source of air cut off. Digging the fingernails of her left hand into Ethan's forearm, she squirmed beneath the weight of his body. She wriggled her right hand up between them.

Her premonition flooded her memory, proving true once again. This night would change the lives of her family forever.

Ashley shoved the barrel of her pistol under Ethan's chin.

Her ex-husband's swollen eyes widened as the cold steel of the muzzle pressed against his skin. His gaze locked with hers. The startled expression spreading across his face screamed that he realized he'd just lost the game he'd always thought he would win.

His fingers cinched tighter around her throat, depriving her lungs of oxygen.

Time seemed to freeze as a hoard of memories rushed through Ashley's mind. The day she'd met Ethan. The day they'd eloped. The day he'd thrown her into the pit. The entwining of their lives had culminated in this singular moment.

Ashley closed her eyes and squeezed the trigger.

Ethan's head exploded.

CHAPTER THIRTY NINE

Blood and bone and brain matter splattered Ashley's face and hair. The blast from the gunshot struck her eardrums. A sound similar to a high-pitched siren blaring inside a tunnel filled her head. She coughed out bits of her ex-husband's flesh as she fought to catch her breath. The realization that she had inhaled skin and blood made her stomach churn.

Her lungs burned as though they'd been scorched by fire, and her jaw still ached, but she was alive. And though she'd suffered knocks and bruises, she believed with all her heart that her baby would survive as well. That her little one was healthy.

The weight of Ethan's body flattened her to the ground. She opened her eyes, but her vision was limited by the film of blood and tissue stuck to her eyelids. The remnants of her ex-husband. She'd killed him. But she'd had no choice. If she hadn't been able to get her pistol – if she'd lacked the strength to pull the trigger – both she and her child would be dead now.

Ethan's limp fingers were still coiled around her neck. Repulsed by his touch, she shoved his body upward. She wriggled her legs and torso out from beneath him, scooting away from the edge of the bluff. The corpse rolled off of her and tumbled over the side of the cliff.

Ethan's twisted game was over.

And she had won.

Her ex-husband would never be able to hurt her or her family again. Except for that fact, there was no sense of glory in her victory, only sadness. Grief for the innocent lives that had been taken and sorrow that her ex-husband had chosen a murderous path.

She thought about Shane – wondered whether he was still in surgery. Her heart ached for her younger brother. Would he be able to walk again? Or would he be bound to a wheelchair for the rest of his life?

Ashley scrubbed her face with the tail of her shirt. A metallic taste lingered on her tongue.

Ethan's blood.

As soon as she had wiped away the sticky film from her eyelids, enabling herself to see, she sprang to her feet and ran back to the parking area. Detective Lansing laid crumpled on the ground in front of his car.

Blood marred Lansing's face. His nose appeared broken, and his jaw was bruised and swollen. She checked for a pulse. He was alive, but unconscious. She needed to call for help, but her phone had sailed over the cliff in Ethan's pocket.

The door of the detective's sedan was unlocked. Ashley climbed inside and grabbed the microphone for the police radio.

"Hello, my name is Ashley Hope and I need help. A police detective has been injured. He's unconscious and needs an ambulance." She paused, her finger still pressing the talk button, feeling the weight of her next words. "And another man is dead. We're located at Laurel Bluff. Please hurry."

With her ears still ringing, she had to focus hard to understand the voice responding to her on the radio. But her call had been heard and help was on the way.

She rushed back to Lansing's side. Before leaving the hospital in Cedar View, she'd texted the detective telling him she was driving to the bluff and that she believed Ethan might also be headed there. Assuming Lansing would be asleep at four in the morning, she'd never expected him to show up. She'd just wanted him to know where she'd gone in case something went wrong. In case she never came back.

Briarwood was a two-hour drive from Mettler Ridge. How had the detective reached the bluff so fast?

Lansing began to stir. His eyes opened and she saw his mouth move, but his voice sounded muffled. She wasn't sure what he'd said. He winced as she helped him sit up.

"An ambulance will be here in just a few minutes," she told him.

He nodded, holding his ribs. "Did he get away?"

The detective's voice was faint compared to the buzzing in her ears, but she understood him. And she knew he was talking about her ex-husband.

"Ethan's dead," she said. "I shot him."

Reality hit her as she said the words out loud. She had taken a human life. Tears streamed down her face. Not because she mourned her ex-husband, but because she felt something had changed deep within her. Like she'd lost a sense of innocence. Ethan was a murderer. He'd deserved to die for his crimes. Although she was glad it had been at her hands rather than someone else's, she wished it had never happened at all.

Lansing met her gaze. She could see sympathy in his eyes.

"You had to," he told her. "He would have killed us both."

She knew the detective was right. If she had aimed her pistol at another part of Ethan's body, simply wounding him instead, he would have thrown her off the side of the bluff. Killing him was the only way to save the lives of her child and Detective Lansing.

"I'm really glad you got my text," she said. "If you hadn't shown up … I don't even want to think about what Ethan would have done to me."

"Something tells me you still would have come out on top."

She attempted a smile, but the action sent a wave of pain radiating through her jaw. "How did you get here so fast?"

"It was your tip about Janet Porter and Robin Lynch. The Laurel County sheriff offered to let me team up with him. To see what all we could find. We'd just wrapped up things at Robin's house. I was halfway back to Briarwood when your text came through."

Ashley was amazed at the detective's dedication. He'd gone out of his way to ensure the safety of her brothers' girlfriends.

"I can't believe you traveled two hours just to test a theory," she said.

"Yeah, but it was worth it. You were right."

A bolt of fear hit her. Had her ex-husband taken another life? She knew Robin was okay, because she'd visited Shane in the hospital, but Ashley hadn't seen Janet. Had Kyle kept her death a secret?

"Did Ethan …"

"Both women are fine," he assured her. "Thanks to you. They got out of town just in time."

She was relieved to hear that no harm had come to her brothers' girlfriends.

The detective continued, "We got to Janet's trailer first. Ethan had kicked in her back door. He ransacked the place. He also left something behind. A Buster's Grape Bubble Gum wrapper on her porch."

"What about Robin?"

"He broke a window to get into her house. Tossed her place too. Both women owe their lives to you."

Instead of taking credit, Ashley again felt a pang of guilt. If she hadn't married Ethan, the lives of Janet and Robin wouldn't have been in jeopardy in the first place. She was just thankful she'd figured out her ex-husband's plan before he could strike.

The detective looked at her, appreciation in his eyes. "You've got great instincts, Nancy Drew," he said, with what appeared to be an effort to smile in spite of his swollen jaw. "And you obviously know how to handle a weapon. You should think about joining the force."

Although she appreciated the compliment, Ashley couldn't even consider the idea right now. She needed time.

The wail of emergency sirens echoed across the mountain. Ashley looked toward the east, past the edge of the bluff. The first rays of morning light broke over the horizon. A new day had begun.

It would also mark the start of a new life for Ashley and her family. She realized the journey ahead would be long, and the road to recovery – especially for Shane – would be difficult. But she knew that together, they would make it. They would draw strength from each other. And she knew just how they would begin.

CHAPTER FORTY

TWO WEEKS LATER

The plastic dispenser squealed as Ashley rolled a length of packing tape onto the cardboard box, sealing it closed. The last of her things – a stack of winter sweaters and a pair of leather boots – were tucked inside. She took a final look around the master bedroom. It felt strange to be back in the house where she'd once dreamed of raising a family. A sense of sadness hung in the air, as if the walls had absorbed the pain she and Brett had endured.

Her ex-fiancé had purchased most of the furniture when they'd moved into their home on Marigold Court, including the bed, dresser, and other matching pieces. He'd sent her an email offering to divide the furnishings, but she'd declined. Everything Brett had bought, she wanted him to keep.

The only things remaining in the house that belonged to Ashley were memories.

And few of them were happy.

Kyle appeared in the doorway. He had a half smile plastered on his face. She knew her brother was glad she'd found out about Brett's affair before her wedding. But along with his desire to see her move on with her life, Kyle had also expressed his sympathy for her broken heart.

"This is the last box," she told him, hearing a note of melancholy in her voice.

He nodded. "Let me take it down to the truck."

She appreciated Kyle's help. Was thankful that her bonds with her family had been strengthened.

Every day for the last two weeks, Ashley had sat at Shane's bedside at Cedar View Medical Center. The road to his recovery would be a long one, but his doctor was optimistic. Her younger brother was strong and determined. With continued physical therapy, there was a chance that he would walk again.

After Shane's release from the hospital early that morning, she, Kyle, and two of their cousins had picked up a U-Haul truck to transport her meager belongings to the trailer on the rear portion of her father's property. The mobile home was old and small, and the air conditioning only worked half of the time, but it felt like a good place to start over. And there was a second bedroom she could decorate as a nursery.

She was especially grateful for the health of her baby. Her doctor had assured her that her pregnancy was advancing normally and that everything was fine. No harm had come to her child.

Ashley trudged down the stairs and headed for the kitchen. She stared at the white envelope that bore her name, lying on the island counter. It was a letter from Brett. She'd noticed the envelope when she'd first arrived at the house, but she hadn't wanted to open it. Not in front of Kyle and her cousins.

Brett had texted and emailed her several times, expressing his desire to repair their relationship. Although she'd read each message, she hadn't responded. She'd only texted him once – earlier in the week – to let him know she'd be picking up her things today and that she wouldn't be taking his furniture.

Expecting her ex-fiancé to be here when she arrived, she'd been surprised to find the house empty. She had planned to take this opportunity to tell him he would soon be a father. But the news would have to wait. The announcement needed to be made in person, not on the phone or in an email.

She wondered if Brett had finally accepted the fact that their relationship was over. If this was his goodbye. She picked up the envelope and tore open the flap.

Ashley,

I know that I've hurt you and I'm deeply sorry. My hope is that one day you will be able to forgive me. I still believe that we could have a wonderful life together.

I'm headed to Florida with my parents. Dad thought that a golf getaway would do me good. We'll be back in four weeks. I hope that when I return, we can meet up and talk.

I still love you, and I always will. Please consider giving me a second chance.

Brett

Tears welled in Ashley's eyes as she crumpled the letter and tossed it into the trash. There was no going back. Only forward. She turned around and saw Kyle standing between the open kitchen and family room. She wondered how long he'd been watching her. From the compassionate look in his eyes, it had been long enough for him to know she'd read Brett's message.

"We're ready to go," he told her.

She nodded. "I'll see you at home later."

As Kyle disappeared into the foyer, Ashley zipped open her purse. She removed the house key from her keyring and placed it onto the center of the kitchen island. It was official: this was no longer her home. In her heart, she wasn't sure it ever really had been.

Ashley left through the front door, locking it behind her. She waved at Kyle and watched the U-Haul pull out of the driveway before heading to her sedan. She glanced at the clock on her dashboard. 2:37 p.m. She had an appointment to keep.

***

Ashley sipped her herbal tea as she watched the traffic whir by through the window of the coffee shop. The crowd had thinned for the afternoon, and she'd had her choice of tables. The corner location combined a nice view with a fair amount of privacy.

Staring out at the clear day, the memory of her first time in the shop floated into her mind. A tinge of sadness hit her. She and Brett had discovered *Best Beans* the week they'd moved to Briarwood. When their relationship had still been on track. Before Cherie.

The old-fashioned bell on the entrance door dinged and she looked up to see Detective Lansing striding into the shop. He nodded at her and smiled before heading to the counter to place his order. She glanced at her phone perched on the table. Lansing had arrived early, but of course, she had as well.

"Hello, Detective," she said as he slipped into the chair opposite her. She noticed he still had faint bruising visible around his nose. Other than that, he looked no worse for wear from his fight with Ethan.

"Don't you think it's time you started calling me Daniel?" His blue eyes sparkled.

"Will you still call me Nancy Drew?"

He laughed. "The name fits. Ethan Barrett might still be on the run if you hadn't lured him to that bluff."

Surprised, Ashley stared at Lansing. She'd never confided that she'd tricked her ex-husband into following her to Laurel Bluff. She'd only told the detective that it was a location from their past. That she'd suspected Ethan would be heading there.

After taking statements from both the detective and Ashley, the police had determined Ethan's death to be a clear case of self-defense – which it was. If they'd suspected she had lured her ex-husband to the bluff, they may not have believed her. But Lansing had lived through the ordeal along with her. He was well aware she'd had no choice but to pull the trigger.

"How did you know?" she asked.

He smiled. "I didn't for sure. Not until just now. But it's what I would have done."

Getting Ethan to follow her to the bluff was the only thing Ashley could have done to save her family. But she still wished it had ended a different way – with her ex-husband in custody, on death row. The fact that she'd taken the life of another human being, no matter the circumstances, would haunt her for as long as she lived.

"We finally got word back from the M.E. on Neil Wilson," Lansing said. "The official ruling is suicide."

Ashley was glad she would no longer be considered a suspect in the death of Ethan's cousin.

"What about Ray?" she asked. "I know Ethan's confession to me is considered hearsay, but have they made a decision yet?"

The detective shook his head. "Not yet. Alabama HP hasn't found any definite evidence they can use that points to homicide."

The lack of clues didn't surprise her. When it had suited him, Ethan had been a master at hiding his tracks. It was only as his game neared the end that he'd become complacent, allowing himself to be caught on camera.

She glanced down at the table, catching sight of the paper shopping bag sitting on the floor next to her chair.

"I almost forgot about the reason I asked you to meet me here," she told him. She picked up the bag. "Your T-shirt and shorts – freshly laundered."

He accepted the bag of clothing he'd loaned her at Neil's house, placing it back on the floor beside him.

"And there's one more thing," she said. "I wanted to tell you that I'm taking your advice."

At the hospital when Shane was in surgery – when she'd had the fleeting wish that she'd never been born – Ashley had realized she was here on this earth for a reason. Now she felt certain she knew her life's purpose. There were thousands of Ethans in the world. And thousands of innocent people who needed protection from them.

Ashley was determined to make sure the victims received justice.

"I've made the decision to enroll in the police academy. I want to become a detective."

"It's a lot of work. You sure you're ready?"

She smiled. "I'm more than ready."

NOW AVAILABLE!

<u>LET ME OUT</u>
(An Ashley Hope Suspense Thriller—Book 2)

Ashley Hope is an average Southern woman, happily engaged—until dark secrets from her past tear her life apart. On track to join the state police's violent crimes division, Ashley is assigned to a case near her hometown: a female, 22 year-old meth addict has been found murdered. Can it be the work of a serial killer?

While Ashley embarks on hew new life, going through the police academy, hazed by fellow recruits, the state police summon her, as they realize they need to make a rare exception and enlist her help on a case immediately. The murdered victim has been found in the backwoods, in a small, rural town neighboring Ashley's own Grundy County. The locals are hostile to outsiders and police, and only Ashley stands a chance of getting through to its hardened folk.

At first glance, the victim seems like just another meth addict-turned prostitute, caught up in a routine drug murder.

But as Ashley digs deeper, she sees things that others do not, and suspects something far more sinister may be at play.

Ashley digs deeper, refusing to put the case to bed.

But if she digs too deep, Ashley, herself, may become the target.

A dark crime thriller full of mystery and suspense, the ASHLEY HOPE mystery series is rife with twists and jaw-dropping secrets as it unfolds into a riveting psychological thriller. Join this brilliant new female protagonist as she hunts down a serial killer, keeping you spellbound and turning pages late into the night. Fans of Rachel Caine, Teresa Driscoll and Robert Dugoni are sure to fall in love.

Book #3 in the series—LET ME LIVE—is also available.

Kate Bold

Debut author Kate Bold is author of the ALEXA CHASE SUSPENSE THRILLER series, comprising three books (and counting).

An avid reader and lifelong fan of the mystery and thriller genres, Kate loves to hear from you, so please feel free to visit www.kateboldauthor.com to learn more and stay in touch.

BOOKS BY KATE BOLD

ALEXA CHASE SUSPENSE THRILLER
THE KILLING GAME (Book #1)
THE KILLING TIDE (Book #2)
THE KILLING HOUR (Book #3)

www.ingramcontent.com/pod-product-compliance
Lightning Source LLC
Chambersburg PA
CBHW030618310726
48979CB00003B/771

* 9 7 8 1 0 9 4 3 9 2 9 0 5 *